GHOST WRITER

A Supernatural Suspense Mystery

ARJAY LEWIS

MIND
BENDER
PRESS

Content Edit: Libby Broadbent
Copy Edit: Kathleen Shamp

ISBN: 979-8989828142

Mindbender Press
474 South Main Street
Phillipsburg NJ 08865
www.mindbenderpress.com

Dedication

To Parke Godwin

Who still inspires my work

from the other side

"Now I know what a ghost is. Unfinished business, that's what." — *Salman Rushdie*

"True love is like ghosts, which everyone talks about and few have seen."— *Francois de La Rochefoucauld*

"Our feet are planted in the real world, but we dance with angels and ghosts."— *John Cameron Mitchell*

One

The Bequest

It was Franklin D. Roosevelt who said, "I think we consider too much the good luck of the early bird and not enough the bad luck of the early worm."

That day, I understood how that worm felt.

I've had plenty of bad days, but as I glared at Chandra — my second wife — across the court tables for our divorce proceedings, I felt it was just one more indignity piled on top of all the others.

I was hungover, and I couldn't even have a little of the hair of the dog, because they frown on you showing up in court with liquor on your breath.

Of course, this was the last step. Lawyers had parsed the details of our agreement as if it were of biblical origin. The lawyers investigated and deliberated over each sentence to find its true meaning.

Chandra's lawyer, the Shark, was there, smiling like she'd taken down Al Capone. My own ineffectual lawyer was there as well, a cordial enough man recommended by my publisher. On the first day of negotiations, the Shark had chewed him up and spat him out.

I bought a house ten years ago, restored it, and paid it off with my royalties and book advances, so I owned it free and clear.

Now after five years of marriage, my ex owned it free and clear.

The case was simple — it was the State of New Jersey. I possessed a penis; therefore, I must pay.

We had no children, so no child support. She accepted the house instead of alimony, accompanied by a large cash settlement, which dwindled my savings greatly.

I was currently living in a tiny cottage in a crowded neighborhood in Lake Hopatcong. One tiny bedroom, a bathroom with a shower stall, a minuscule living room, and a kitchen.

Not that I had much to put in it. All my good furniture stayed in the house that Chandra now owned.

Except my leather recliner. I had to have my recliner.

As she signed the divorce papers, Chandra looked up at me and winked.

I clenched my teeth so hard, it's a wonder I didn't crack a few of them. One more indignity.

I hated her, and at the same time, I desired her so badly it was surprising I didn't become aroused right there in the courtroom.

That was the thing with Chandra. She was bad for me. She was poison. All I had to do was see how she treated a waiter with her condescending attitude.

But, my God, the sex.

She was a fire I couldn't quench. I wanted her, and I wanted her badly. That was the one thing the divorce didn't change.

I drank to control my lust for her, especially as our marriage fell apart. She encouraged the drinking so that I would keep writing.

After all, you don't want to kill the golden goose, not until you receive a few more golden eggs.

Once the judge had approved the agreement, Chandra, me, and our lawyers stepped out into the hall to finish signing the paperwork

"You're off to your uncle's funeral," Chandra said as I finished signing. "Joe, give my best to the family. I always liked Rick. I'm sorry he died."

As a writer, I should have a great retort. Something worthy of Oscar Wilde, Mark Twain, or Dorothy Parker. But I wrote stories of spies, guys, and willing ladies. Lacking a comeback, I muttered, "Yeah, sure."

Brilliant! I missed my calling as a stand-up comedian.

She did like my Uncle Rick. He'd been beneficial to her, or at least to her plans. Richard Riley had been a renowned literary agent, and when I wrote stories as a child and teen, he encouraged me. We were a family of readers, and I was fortunate enough to grow up in the 80s and 90s when people still read books.

He helped me sell my short stories to magazines, and when I wrote my first novel, *A Man Called Soul*, he gave me excellent pointers and guided me to a content editor who brutally ripped the tale apart and had me rewrite it several times.

By the time of publishing, the book was so polished, it all but glowed.

Uncle Rick sold the book with a fair royalty for a new writer. I was thrilled, and taking my gains, I started the second book in what became a profitable series.

My lead character, Soul Mason, was a CIA agent helping to stop terrorists and evil plots. In the latter part of the 2000s, with terrorists as the bad guys, a brave, chisel-jawed CIA agent was just the sort of thing people wanted to read.

The second book in the series, *Body And Soul*, got me the money to buy my house, now the property of the ex-missus Riley.

She announced to me during our divorce negotiations that she would keep my last name. Since her maiden name was Crapanzano, I don't blame her. Riley is much easier to spell.

I left the Morris County Municipal Court a much poorer and bitter man, and my next port of call was Uncle Rick's funeral.

Chandra had been fond of Rick. She started working for him about six years ago as his assistant. I had dated no one seriously since my first marriage went bust before I sold my first novel.

That lasted only one short year. That must have been a long year for my ex, Elaine. I was a troublesome man to live with, struggling with my desire to write and my frustration at what I produced. I was an angry, sullen would-be writer.

There was no monetary settlement, and I remained in the New York City apartment we had shared.

Years later, once I was writing and sold some books, I got out of the city and bought the house. Six years ago, I showed up at Uncle Rick's office with a new book ready to go — and there was Chandra.

After six months of dating and the most mind-blowing sex I'd ever experienced, I proposed. We married a few months later and Chandra quit her job.

"I have to, Joe," she explained. "This way, I can help you with the next book. I'll fix your errors and help with the editing. I'll be your muse."

She was my muse alright, and I thought things were good, as we blissfully fornicated and she lubricated me with alcohol into a state of passivity.

But by the time I wrote *Soul To The Devil*, I realized my wife was living well beyond our means ,and I did not know where my money was going. She had taken over the finances so I could, as she put it, "focus on writing." Dummy that I am, at the time it seemed like a good idea.

It was about that time, six months ago, Uncle Rick informed me my book advances were going to be less.

The ebook revolution had gained momentum and was devastating the publishing industry. For years, the agents and publishers kept the riffraff at bay. But with the gatekeepers silenced, and the gates broken down, anyone could publish.

To the Stephen King's, the James Pattersons', and the Nora Roberts' this was no big deal. They were worth millions and their multi-million dollar advances, as well as the royalties, would keep rolling in. To a middle-of-the-list guy like me, it meant my income was going to go down.

I sobered up, figuratively and literally, and tried to figure out what happened to my money, which Chandra always referred to as "our money."

Which apparently meant "her money."

I moved out of my carefully restored house into a crummy little shack, hired a divorce lawyer and a forensic accountant, but they found little of the money. She siphoned it off slowly and cleverly, and boffed me into a state of unawares. Then she hired the Shark, who plucked my house and half my remaining savings.

The Shark argued I was still at the height of my productivity as a writer and would probably see much more money in the future. She said it was right to make a claim on future royalties as her client, "Was a vital part of the creation of Mr. Riley's very successful books."

Even my lame lawyer got that thrown out.

Of course, Chandra and the Shark knew something that my lawyer didn't. My latest book, tentatively titled *Lost Soul*, had netted me a small upfront advance, but I wouldn't get the rest until I delivered the book. In the past, I delivered a book or two after the requested deadline.

The due date for the latest book was two months away.

I had written exactly ten pages.

Chandra may have only been looking out for herself in our marriage, but she was correct: she was my muse. Her offerings of steady sex and booze kept me going, kept me working.

For the last few months, I'd done little writing.

All of this whirled through my mind as I arrived at the Stanley Funeral Home in a town called Clinton. It was a large, stately house, a Victorian converted for business use.

Uncle Rick's services were to be held in the largest room.

I arrived just as people were being called to sit down for the service. I saw my older cousins, Robert, Liam, and Ashley. Neither of my brothers came, which was fine by me. We had never been close, and they lived far away. Growing up, I was always closer to my cousins than my brothers. To the cousins, I was a fun visitor. To my brothers, I was the annoying baby of the family, and either a pain to deal with or someone to be bullied.

Walking in, I could see the open coffin at the front of the room. Uncle Rick looked as he did in life, a tall and lean man, around six foot-two with an excellent physique. His white hair gave him an air of maturity and wisdom. They had combed his hair neatly, and dressed him in one of his expensive suits; he looked ready to get up and take a meeting.

Uncle Rick was the last of that generation, as my parents died in a car accident when I was thirty-seven. Now, it was just me, my brothers, and my three cousins. That was all the family I had left.

But it wasn't like we all got together and hung out for the holidays.

I was still fighting a headache and wishing I had brought something with me to take a little nip, just to clear my head.

As I sat, a reverend spoke comforting words at the front of the room. From the gist of it, this eulogy could have been a prepared speech made from a template or thrown together by an AI program.

When he finished his opening tribute, he asked people to get up and talk about Rick.

Robert was the oldest son, so he rose and gave an excellent speech. I figured all those years working as a real estate salesman and investor gave him skills as a speaker.

When he finished, his younger brother Liam got up. Despite being in his late forties, Liam had yet to establish a solid foundation for his life. He was a chain smoker of cigarettes and pot, as well as imbibing in other substances, and squandered his nights away on alcohol and questionable company.

Not that I could judge, considering my ex-wife.

He constantly relied on others for money, with promises to pay them back that never came to fruition. I knew from experience, having given him about a thousand dollars by this point. I was smart enough to say it was a gift, because I knew there was no way in hell he'd ever pay me back.

Liam rambled his way through an unprepared speech, and all of us were thankful when he finished and sat.

My youngest cousin, Ashley, got up to speak, and to my surprise, she started reminiscing about summers in the Poconos in my uncle's rustic cabin. Growing up, all of us, my parents and brothers, my uncle Rick and aunt Betsy, and the cousins would all hang out for a couple of weeks there in the summer. Thinking back to all those people in the one cabin, I wondered how we all fit.

Whispering Pines.

That was the fanciful name Rick had given it.

Nestled in a national forest, the cabin stood out like a beacon among the towering trees. There were acres of woods and we had a dock on Sandy Rock Lake, large enough that we could swim and fish.

I recalled those times as she spoke. Memories of long-forgotten laughter and carefree summers flooded my mind, thoughts of sun-dappled days and warm nights.

From a young age, I looked forward to those annual trips to Uncle Rick's cabin.

It gave me a taste of life disconnected from the modern world. Back in the 90s, we didn't have screens and smart phones so we had to actually go outside and play, like kids are supposed to do.

All of us, brothers and cousins, slept in sleeping bags on the main room floor, while the adults had the two bedrooms.

I was the youngest of all my brothers and the cousins, and Ashley, like a little general, made sure the older boys included me in everything that was going on.

God, I adored her when we were kids, a mix of hero-worship and awe. She was six years older than me, with blonde hair and a powerful personality. We played games, roughhoused, and ran around those woods like little savages, all orchestrated by Ashley.

Then, as the sun dipped below the horizon, we would all gather around a crackling campfire. The adults shared stories as laughter echoed through the trees, and the scent of pine trees and freshly caught fish mingled with the aroma of wood smoke.

It was listening to these stories that made me want to be a writer, to tell stories to other people, and make them feel like I did on those nights.

My current life didn't have any of the peace or joy I felt when we stayed up in that cabin.

The service ending brought me back to awareness as everyone started getting ready to get into their cars and form a caravan to the burial site.

I just wanted to get a drink.

"Joey?"

I came around to see Ashley approach. She pulled me into a hug, the first hug I'd received from a woman in months.

"Hey, Ash," I said. "I'm so sorry."

She pulled back, and her short, chestnut-brown hair framed her face, her bright blue eyes wet. As usual, she dressed impeccably in a black pantsuit with a gray satin blouse. "At least it was quick. Not like Mom, slowly eaten away by the cancer. This was a shock, but it was almost easier."

I nodded sagely. What could I say? Is there ever a good way to die?

"Are you coming to the burial?" she asked.

"No, I've got other things," I said, avoiding the question as best as I could. "I divorced Chandra this morning."

Ashley's expression changed, and the tears were gone. "That bitch," she murmured. This was a stretch for my cousin, as she never used coarse language about anyone. "She took you for everything, didn't she?"

I lifted my shoulders in an attempt at a shrug. "She got the house."

Ashley shook her head, and I saw the fury in her eyes. My protective older cousin. She'd fought my battles as a child and looked like she would happily do it again. "I warned you about her. Didn't I tell you to get a prenup?"

I hung my head. "Please Ash. Today's been rough enough."

She put her hand under my face and lifted my chin. "All right, Joey. But don't be a stranger."

I nodded and forced a grin.

Other guests pulled her away, and a hand slapped me on the back. "Hey Joey."

My oldest cousin, Robert, pulled me into a bear hug. He was about fifty at that point, stocky with his dark hair showing traces of grey at the temples. He pulled back and looked at me. "You holding up alright, Joey? You look terrible."

"I divorced Chandra today," I said with a sigh.

"Ding-dong, the witch is dead," he murmured.

That got a grin. "Heard from her? I understand she called my brothers."

Robert shook his head. "She probably was looking for people to take her side. No, I was lucky enough not to be on her call list. How did you make out?"

"I got screwed, lost the house. My lawyer said if we went before a judge, I'd get screwed even worse. Her lawyer would portray me as a rich writer who was bad with money—"

He frowned. "I thought Chandra handled the money?"

"My first mistake. They'd make me look like a drunk kept solvent by my loving spouse, who deserved everything I owned because of my spendthrift ways." I shook my head.

Robert smiled his real estate agent smile. "I think we can help you take your mind off the situation. Come to the wake."

"Will there be food and booze?"

"An Irish wake?" He easily slipped into a fake brogue. "What else would ye have, Joey, me boy?" He dropped it and glanced around the room. "It'll be tonight at the Shamrock's Embrace Irish Pub right here in Clinton."

"Could they give it a more cliché name?" I asked.

"I would have gone with the Leprechaun's Asshole, but that's me," Robert grinned. "Look, I'm staying at the Holiday Inn right on the outskirts of town. I've got two beds if you want to crash."

I nodded. "That would be good. I need a release."

Matt glanced over at the door. "Looks like the convoy for the burial site is getting ready. I'll see you tonight."

I waved at my other cousin Liam as he headed for the door. Most of the people were strangers to me, and I tried to decide whether I should start drinking now or wait until the evening.

Maybe it was time to make a change and fight my impulses.

A voice said, "Are you Joseph Riley?"

I faced a man about six feet tall with a lean build, neatly trimmed salt and pepper hair, and a meticulously groomed beard. He wore a suit that looked like it cost more than my last book advance.

"Not if you have a subpoena," I said. I meant it as a joke, but with the way my day was going, it could have happened.

The man made a facial expression that suggested a smile but was far too practiced and fake. "I'm Benjamin Clarke, with Bayson and Clarke."

He didn't offer a hand to shake, and neither did I.

"I'm representing Richard Riley's estate," he said in a clipped tone. "I take it you received our notice about the probate and release of the will?"

I tried to appear wise. "I've been in the middle of a divorce, so my mail might not get to me," I explained. That wasn't the truth. I hadn't been looking at my damn mail. I'd been on a bender that had started about a week before. "What does that have to do with me?"

"There is a bequest for you in the will," he said, handing me a business card with a local address.

I stared at the card in my hand. "A bequest to me?" I repeated.

He seemed nonplussed by my response. "Yes. We are meeting after the burial, as we need all the heirs to sign releases. Could you be at my office at 5 PM today?"

"Sure," I said, and glanced at my watch. It was two-thirty, and where did I have to go?

"I'll see you then," he said with that rigid smile, and followed the group out to their cars.

I stood staring at the card in my hand, my mind racing.

What could Uncle Rick have left me?

Two

—❦—

You Get What You Need

I was the first to arrive at the lawyer's office at 4:30. I used the time between the service and the meeting to visit my cousin's cafe, Brew Haven, in the heart of Clinton.

Ashley created this about five years ago, converting a charming, historic building, once the town's general store. It had a rustic charm, with exposed brick walls and large windows. She'd transformed the space with local artwork, handmade pottery, and whimsical decorations.

I didn't know when Ashley had become an expert with coffee, but it showed in the latte prepared by the barista on duty. My beverage was fantastic, dark and hot, yet not overpowering. A perfect blend, and it was the first thing that helped ease my headache.

I sat and had coffee and a freshly baked scone as I puzzled over what Uncle Rick had left me. He knew about my divorce from

Chandra, and that she was bleeding me dry. I know it troubled him, as she had been his employee when I met her.

Perhaps he left me a tidy sum to tide me over the next months until I could finish the book.

Or to tide me over if I couldn't finish the book.

He didn't know I'd only written ten pages of *Lost Soul*.

I would not let my agent know I had writer's block, even if he was my uncle.

I sat there sipping coffee, forty years old, divorced twice and unable to work. Yeah, my life was just peachy. I envied Uncle Rick. Maybe I should take up golf and try for a massive coronary.

Uncle Rick had looked a lot happier in that coffin than I felt.

By 4:45, all three of my cousins had arrived. While Ashley talked with a secretary, I sat with Robert and Liam. Robert was still in one of his 'power' business suits, black for the funeral, with a strong black tie.

Liam looked like an unmade bed. He wore a baggy and rumpled black suit, his shoulders hunched from a lifetime of slouching. His hair, an unkempt mess of dark brown curls, fell haphazardly over his forehead, obscuring his narrow brown eyes. His appearance was further worsened by his scruffy facial hair, which he unsuccessfully attempted to grow into a beard. A perpetual smoker, he smelled of tobacco from several feet away.

At 5:00 precisely, a junior secretary escorted us to Mr. Clarke's office. We went into an empty room, and the four of us chatted about the funeral.

Mr. Clarke came into the office with a sheaf of papers. "Please remain seated."

I wondered what I was doing there at all.

Mr. Clarke went through a bunch of legalese and how he was the executor of Richard Riley's estate, et cetera, and he would supply each of us a copy of the will. He also expected us to sign individual releases in order to receive our inheritances.

"Now, I am sure you've all seen on television where the lawyer dramatically reads a will," Clarke explained. "That's not accurate. I have a copy for each of you, and I have only asked you all to be here in case there is some confusion about the bequests, or in case a conflict may arise."

"What would Dad have in the will that would cause a conflict?" Ashley asked.

"Actually, it is the bequest to Joseph Riley that may concern his other heirs," Clarke said, and all eyes went to me.

"I have no idea what this is about," I muttered.

"Why don't you all read the will, and we can discuss it," Clarke said.

The entire will was only a few pages, and most of it seemed straightforward. He was leaving his investments to be split equally among the three children and created a trust for Robert's two kids for college and beyond. The family home in Clinton was to go to Ashley as she lived in the town. There were several charitable donations, and specific monies designated for longtime secretaries and staff people who worked in his office.

Then I reached a paragraph that read: "I leave my cabin in the Poconos, named Whispering Pines, to my nephew, Joseph Riley. It always brought him great joy when he visited there, and I believe he could use more joy in his life."

I sat there stunned. I spent most of the funeral service lost in thought about the cabin. Oddly, this made a shiver run up my spine.

I met Mr. Clarke's eyes. "Uncle Rick left me his cabin in the Poconos?"

"Yes," Clarke said, and glanced at the others. "I was not entirely sure this would be agreeable to your relatives."

"I think Joey would love it there," Robert said.

"I don't know," I said. "Ashley, you always went hunting with Uncle Rick."

"Damn straight," Ashley said proudly. "He taught me to shoot. But I'm too busy with the restaurant to go on a retreat."

Liam nodded. "Yeah, I just hope you'll invite us once you've fixed the place up."

"Fixed up?" I asked with concern. "Is it in disrepair?"

"No one's stayed up there in, like, a decade," Liam pointed out.

"But Dad kept the place up," Robert said. "He had a property management company watch over the place."

I frowned. "A property management company?"

Robert nodded. "Yeah, some place called Pocono Pines Property Care. They sent out a caretaker every few months to check the place out. They hired workmen to do repairs and made sure the pipes didn't freeze."

"Are you three okay with me inheriting it?" I asked, still unsure.

They looked at each other and nodded, and I saw Mr. Clarke relax.

"Very well. If all of you sign your releases, we can move the will to probate first thing Monday."

And yet, a part of me felt uneasy. Wasn't a lonely cabin in the woods the beginning scene of every horror movie?

At the Shamrock's Embrace Irish Pub, it was quite a party for Uncle Rick. In true Irish tradition, my cousins wanted a grand farewell at his wake. Friends and family from near and far gathered together, sharing stories, laughter, and tears. A live band played traditional Irish music, filling the room with a sense of warmth and belonging. Guinness and whiskey flowed freely as those gathered raised their glasses to toast the life and legacy of Richard Riley.

I was still in shock. The idea of losing one house and gaining another on the same day was enough to make any man dizzy. At least I could finally have a drink, but so far I'd stuck to the beer.

I was savoring my second pint of what they call a 'black and tan', a blend of Guinness stout and Bass pale ale, watching the crowd of revelers and the band. Observing people was something I always did as a kid. I think it was part of what made me an excellent writer. I spent so much time watching people, scrutinizing how they acted, how they talked, until I had an ear for dialogue and a sense of how people behaved and how to describe it.

Finally, Liam came over. He was already two sheets to the wind, much drunker than I was.

"I heard you dumped the bitch today," he said in lieu of a greeting.

"That's true." I said.

"Good on you," he said, and attempted to focus. Then, out of the blue, he said, "Your mom hated Chandra. Told my mom all about it."

I looked at him, shocked. "This is a fine time to tell me that."

He shrugged. "When was a good time? We all knew how you two were in the early days. To you, she was the one. There was no talking you down."

I shook my head. "My mom liked everyone."

"Except Chandra," Liam said. "She wouldn't say anything to you because she hated interfering mothers."

The band broke into an old Irish tune, The Wild Rover.

"You know, I always wanted to play Irish music," Liam said. "Of course, I'd have to learn to play an instrument first."

He wandered off to get closer to the band.

Ashley approached with her own half-finished pint of black and tan sloshing around in her glass.

"I thought you'd be ordering champagne," Ashley shouted in my ear to be heard over the music. "Lose a viper and gain a house."

"It's all overwhelming," I said.

"Are you going to move out of that tiny house in Lake Hopatcong you told me about?"

"That dump," I chuckled. "It's so small, I have to step outside to change my mind."

"When you put the key in the door, do you break the window?" Ashley said with a grin.

"Yes, and all the mice are hunchbacked," I said, hoping this would end the jokes.

"So you're really going to go live in Whispering Pines?" she said. "Out in the middle of nowhere?"

"I think I am," I yelled back. "I have only a card table, two folding chairs, and my recliner. If I can get them in the back of my truck, I can do it."

I was driving an older Ford F150. When I moved out of my former house, I single-handedly manipulated the recliner into the truck bed and hoped I could repeat the process.

"All the old furniture is still at the cabin, beds and everything," she said, and appeared troubled. "But I don't know about living there. The last time I went there, the place had a weird vibe."

I leaned close so she could hear me. "When was that?"

She shook her head. "I dunno. I haven't stayed up there since I was in my twenties. But I've gone up a few times recently to check the place for Dad." She shuddered, as if the memory was unpleasant, and looked at me blearily. "I'm worried about you. There's nothing for miles around."

"Writers like solitude," I said. "Besides, there are towns within driving distance, and even a mall or two."

"You're alone on ten acres and the lake," she said. "I don't know. I think I would find it creepy. Are you switching away from heroic secret agents and taking a stab at horror?"

"Taking a stab at horror?" I repeated and shook my head. "You're a regular comedienne."

"Just be careful if you go, little cousin. There are bears out there, you know."

I knew. As kids, we saw them all the time. They were mostly brown bears and more scared of humans than we were of them.

But you had to be careful if there were cubs. Protecting a cub could cause a mother bear to charge.

Another guest pulled her away, and I lifted my beer in salute as she went.

Robert walked over to me. "Hey, Joey."

"Robert, are you sure you're okay with me getting the cabin?" I asked, still talking loudly over the music. "The last thing I want is to cause friction in the family."

"Who else could he leave it to?" Robert said, answering my question with a question. "I have a vacation house — on the Jersey shore, thank you, and Ash never wants to be far from her restaurant. Dad could've left it to Liam, but I don't think that would work out well. Liam barely gets by now. How would he do out in the woods without us to borrow money from?"

"He got a pretty good inheritance from Rick's will."

"It'll be gone in six months, if that long. He'll put it in one of his schemes he thinks will make him rich. Trust me, he'll flush it all away." He stepped closer so that he could lower his voice. "But look, if you don't want to be saddled with an old place like that, I could see what the market will take. Believe me, I could get you a good price for the place."

I frowned, confused about the direction he was going.

"I mean, none of us have been up there since we were kids," he went on. "All those memories we have of the place, we're just fooling ourselves. It wasn't much then, so it won't be much now."

"I'd like to try," I said. "Maybe fix it up. I'm not completely broke."

"From what I heard over the years, the locals avoid the place."

"Avoid it? Why?"

He glanced around to see if anyone else was nearby. "The rumor is that it's haunted."

"Haunted?" I repeated as I felt a shiver run up my back. "What do you mean?"

Robert shrugged. "Strange noises, flashing lights, people seeing shapes in the windows. A couple of neighbors heard screams in the night and called the police. They thought someone had broken in."

"Did someone break in?"

"Maybe, who knows? But the police found nothing, and they called the caretaker who comes around to check the place. Get this, the guy tells the cops he won't go in there at night and tells them where the spare key is."

I thought of the cabin nestled deep within the heart of the woods, the same place where I spent multiple summers and created countless memories. That it was now tainted with such a strange reputation was completely foreign to me.

Several people pulled Robert away, and I headed to the bar to switch my drink to whiskey. I felt I needed it now.

I sat alone in the dimly lit corner of the pub as music played and people chatted. I found my fingers tapping restlessly against the rim of my glass. The amber liquid swirled inside, mirroring my own tumultuous thoughts. People thought ghosts haunted my uncle's cabin, which was now mine.

Of course, any place that stands empty develops a reputation. But why wouldn't the caretaker show up at night?

And what if a restless spirit wandered around the place, longing for solace? Wasn't that what I wanted to do? Return to something I enjoyed in my childhood and bring some peace after my ruined marriage? Plus, maybe the place would inspire me. If I could get to work, I should be able to knock out a rough draft in two months. Hell, that was less than a thousand words a day.

I have a skeptical nature and have always scoffed at tales of the supernatural. But tonight, with the idea of living on my own deep in the woods and Uncle Rick in his grave, I found I fought to dismiss the chill I felt.

After all, I was a rational being, not some frightened child hiding from monsters.

Wasn't I?

Three

Moving Day

The next two weeks were a whirlwind of activity. I got in touch with Pocono Pines Property Care, which oversaw the upkeep of the cabin. Uncle Rick took care of the property taxes and escrow for their services, though they suggested I have the place cleaned (for a fee), activate the electricity, and get a supply of propane.

Since it was June, I didn't have to worry about frozen pipes, but coming into a clean house would save me one chore.

I did all the paperwork and linked my bank account to their escrow. It made me nervous moving the money around, as my savings were my sole source of capital these days.

Liam was kind enough to come by when I called him, and he helped me load my recliner into the back of my truck. We packed my other items, like clothes, chairs, and the card table. I was lucky, as I'd picked a sunny day. Moving in the rain is the worst.

"You sure you can handle this once you get there?" Liam asked, a lit cigarette dangling from the corner of his mouth.

"Yeah," I assured him. "Down is easier than up. I moved here by myself when I left Chandra."

He shrugged, and the ash on his cigarette fell to the ground. "I could ride up with you, help get you settled."

"I've wasted enough of your time," I said, and pulled out my wallet to grab a twenty.

"Hey, I don't want you to think I helped just to hit you up for cash," Liam said, but his narrow eyes stayed focused on the bill.

"No, please, buy yourself lunch on me," I said and slipped it into his hand. "You were a help, and I appreciate it."

He stowed the bill in his back pocket.

"Hey, once the summer is here, can I come up and visit? It would be nice to fish in the lake again." His eyes brightened with a memory. "Remember that trout I caught back in the 90s? It took all four of us to get it out of the lake."

"As I recall, it was you and Robert who got it out."

"You helped, and so did Ash," he said and smiled, showing his discolored teeth. "It must have been a foot-and-a-half."

"More like eleven inches," I corrected.

"It was our dinner that night, remember? I was, like, proud that I caught dinner," Liam said, smiling.

"I have plenty of room, but give me a few weeks to get acclimated," I said. "I have to get used to the place before I can have company."

"Yeah, sure," he said, disappointed.

"What are you going to do now that you're a man of means?" I asked.

"I dunno," he said as he threw down his cigarette, pulled another from a mostly empty pack, and lit it. His eyes went to his ten-year-old Toyota. "Get a new car, I guess. I got some deals I think will pay off once I get them going."

That was Liam, always working on a deal. Unlike Robert, who built himself an impressive real estate portfolio, Liam's deals always ended in disaster.

"Thanks again, Liam," I said, getting into my truck. "I want to get there while it's still daylight."

The drive was about an hour, and I felt pretty good. The small home I'd been living in had grown claustrophobic.

I made my way through New Jersey, mostly traveling up Route 206 and through Stokes State Park. The day was bright and clear, a blend of sunshine with a gentle breeze filling the air.

My route took me from New Jersey to Pennsylvania across the bridge at Dingman's Ferry. It is the last privately owned toll bridge on the Delaware River and one of the few remaining in the United States.

I rumbled over the wooden floor planks held in place with anchor plates and collar nails, and gave the female toll collector my two one-dollar bills.

"Have a nice day," she said with a smile, and I smiled back.

I navigated the winding roads, my mind wandering to the memories of our childish adventures as kids: fishing by the lake's edge, hiking through the lush trails, and the simple joy of watching the sunset paint the sky in hues of orange and red.

They seemed like fantastic adventures to my young self, and now, they ignited a longing within me to experience them again.

Yet, as I ventured deeper into the woods, an unsettling silence enveloped me. It was as if the vibrant chatter of birds and rustling leaves had parsed out a hidden tension. Shadows stretched longer beneath the trees, and the sunlight seemed to flicker hesitantly, as if the day itself tried to warn me about what lay ahead. A distant rustle caught my attention, and for a moment, the feeling that I was being watched sent a chill down my spine, contrasting with the deceptive warmth of the afternoon.

To banish the unsettling sensations creeping over me, I headed directly to the Weiss supermarket in a nearby strip mall. This mall conveniently had a 'Fine Wines & Good Spirits' state store as well.

I went to the supermarket first, got a good amount of canned food, pre-made bags of salad, and the bachelor's primary food source — ground hamburger. I took one other item when I moved out on Chandra, a one-cup coffeemaker, and I stocked up on K-cups.

The grocery bill was large, but I was now prepared with food.

My next stop was the liquor store, and I stocked up on cheap wines I enjoyed, and two massive bottles — one of vodka and one of scotch. Not the expensive stuff these days, but good enough.

Finally, I pulled off the paved roads and onto a rugged dirt road that led to the cabin. I was thankful for the GPS on my phone, as it had been so long since I'd been there; I was sure I could never find it.

Sunlight filtered through the canopy of trees, casting dappled shadows on the gravel roadway. The familiarity of this childhood stomping ground washed over me, and I felt a smile on my face as the worrisome feelings I experienced earlier dissipated.

I pulled into the driveway and made my way up the hill. The cabin came into view leisurely, like an aging stripper who removes her clothing slowly to make you wait for the last revelation.

I pulled up next to the log building. I thought it would look smaller since I was a kid, but after living in the tiny Lake Hopatcong house, it seemed huge.

I arrived at my sanctuary.

As I entered the cabin, the air was thick with a heavy silence. I cautiously stepped inside the cabin that had stood unused for so long. How long? I didn't know, but the air seemed to whisper stories of the past. The wooden floors creaked with each step I took, as if welcoming me back after the long absence. Memories filled my mind, and I couldn't help but feel a sense of nostalgia wash over me.

It surprised me it was much colder inside, as if it held the temperatures from the previous winter and not the current summer.

I gazed around the room. According to what Uncle Rick told us those nights around the campfire, the cabin was originally built in the late 1930s by a local craftsman. He was a skilled carpenter with a passion for nature and sought to create a retreat. With his own two hands, he painstakingly constructed the cabin from locally sourced timber, meticulously choosing every piece of wood and expertly fitting them together.

The main room of the cabin was undoubtedly its centerpiece, as it boasted a stone fireplace. On chilly nights, my parents, Rick, and Betsy built a fire that heated the entire place. A large, inviting couch sat in front of the fireplace — perfect for curling up with a good book. Against the wall and under a window was a desk, where both my father and Uncle Rick worked when we were up here.

Since the main room was an open-plan design, it seamlessly blended into the dining area and kitchen. The dining table, made from sturdy oak, was where we gathered for meals, sharing stories of our adventures in the woods during the day. The kitchen, equipped with modern appliances while maintaining a rustic feel, witnessed the creation of countless meals over the years.

Past the kitchen stood a tucked-away bathroom, which featured a clawfoot bathtub that also acted as a shower. The old-fashioned fixtures suited the cabin's history while offering modern convenience. The back door, just past the bathroom, opened up to a private deck with a view of Sandy Rock Lake in the distance.

There were two bedrooms at opposite ends of the cabin.

Walking from room to room, I saw the place was neat as a pin. The team of cleaners Pocono Pines Property Care sent to scrub the cabin had done a fine job.

So what was bothering me? Why was I still nervous? A shiver crept up my spine, accompanied by an unsettling feeling that I was an intruder in a space where I had no right to be.

I saw wood piled up next to the empty fireplace and decided I would get a fire going that night. All of us used to sit watching the fire in the evenings, but now those nights felt so far away — so distant.

I hesitated for a moment, thinking the memories held within these walls were what I was sensing.

Uncle Rick adorned the walls with photographs, capturing moments of the group of us from years back. Yet, looking at the photos, I felt disconnected from the people within them.

I looked at a group photo, my parents younger than I was now. There was also my aunt and uncle and all of us kids — all six of us. Ashley stood with her arms folded, the little general.

I went along the wall, looking at the different photos. There was one of Robert, Liam, and Ashley down at the dock on the lake, all long legs and goofy grins. One was of my two brothers and me, roughhousing as usual. There was one of Ashley and my uncle showing her how to hold his rifle, and one of my dad and I with a bow and arrow.

I pulled the curtain away from the picture window and gazed out at the breathtaking view. In the corner of my eye, I saw the old outhouse, still standing, unashamed, a dozen feet from the house. That came in handy, with ten people staying here and only one indoor bathroom.

The cabin was on flat land — solid rock on a hill, and the small green lawn fell away to dense forest. It all stretched before me.

I was truly here, and completely alone.

Would this change of scenery help? Maybe awaken my spirit so I could finish my current book?

"Brace yourself, Joe," I muttered under my breath.

With a renewed sense of purpose, I focused on the tasks to be done. The first thing I did was bring in my groceries to get them stowed in the various cabinets and refrigerator. The cleaners had done well with that too, and I opened the refrigerator and found it cool and spotless.

With the help of a step-stool, I soon explored all the cabinets, locating dishes and cookware and stowing my purchased items.

The chill in the air was getting to me, so I used some paper bags for kindling, loaded wood in the fireplace, and got a fire going.

I struggled to get the recliner into the house, as the door was almost not wide enough to allow it passage. In the end, I did it, fighting the chair the entire time. I placed it with a view of both the fireplace and the window that overlooked the property.

As the sun was setting. I brought my clothes and belongings into the master bedroom, which boasted a queen-size bed and antique furnishings. The cleaners had made the bed up with fresh linens, ready for use.

I found only one key for all the inside doors, which were fitted with mortise locks - those boxy old things built into the doors and use a large doorknob. The key was inside the bedroom, on the dresser next to the door. This made sense, as when we came up here as kids, the adults probably locked the doors at night when they wanted to fool around.

That bedroom was colder than the rest of the house. That was unexpected, as it was June and the temperature outside being warm enough. But this cabin was cold, and being the furthest from the fireplace, this room was the coldest of all.

I didn't recall that in the summers of my youth the rooms had this chill. It was as if the air possessed a heaviness, a weight to it.

My eyes fell on an old knitted afghan blanket folded up at the foot of the bed, and I knew it well. That would help fight off the chill.

Next to the bed was a small end table with an old clock radio designed with an illuminated dial. It had to be from the 70s. Whoever had cleaned the house set it for the right time, the two hands in silhouette against the green circle in the middle.

I wondered how many times my uncle and aunt had covered themselves with that afghan and looked at that clock during the times we stayed here?

Who needed a ghost? Everything I saw haunted my memories. Had I really felt so disconnected as a child, or was it the adult looking back at the childish memories in a new light?

I opened a large rustic set of drawers and filled it with clothing, hanging what I could in a pair of small closets in the room. After checking the truck to make sure everything was in the house, I added some wood to the fire. Pouring myself a scotch, I sat on the recliner with my laptop and opened the file for my latest Soul Mason novel, *Lost Soul.*

I was wise enough to print my rough plot outline, which broke the book into chapters with a brief rundown of what I wanted to happen.

Reading my first few pages, I tried to reconnect to what I wrote before. I brought my hands to the keyboard, ready to continue, my eyes fixed on the barren white screen that taunted me with its emptiness.

I had nothing.

The amber glow of the crackling fire in the background cast eerie shadows upon the walls, enhancing the stillness of the room. I reread the pages again.

The problem was writer's block. It was a relentless specter that shadowed my every step, ensnaring me in the oppressive prison of my own tortured imagination, not allowing me to move on.

After sitting there for twenty minutes, I got up to make dinner. I decided I was trying too hard, and mundane tasks would help.

I opened a can of beans, threw them into a pot, and started them cooking on the electric stove.

I had purchased fresh garlic and onions, which I fried up with cut up hotdogs and added to the beans. I put a salad together in a large bowl, opened a bottle of chardonnay, and sipped wine as I cooked.

I was pushing myself too soon. I just got here and needed a night off, a chance to wind down.

It wasn't like there were a lot of distractions. There was no Wi-Fi up here, and I would have to use my phone as a hotspot when I wanted to send an email or do research. But wasn't that the point? Eliminate distractions, get my head in the book and stay there.

But as I ate, I realized my head wasn't in the book at all. In fact, it was the last place my head wanted to be.

I switched back to the Scotch. If I were going to get some sleep, I would need some heavier medication.

The fire crackling away finally warmed the room, and there was a sharp, resinous quality dancing on the air.

I looked out the picture window at the gathering shadows.

I found my eyes going to the desk right next to it. Its surface bore the marks of ink and pen scratches. Faded ornate carvings embellished the edges and corners. The wood's natural grain was visible, adding depth to the overall appearance. Decorative handles or discolored brass knobs adorned each drawer. I recalled that the drawers only pulled out so far, as there was a catch that stopped them.

On top of the desk was a gooseneck lamp, bent at a ninety-degree angle, sitting on a heavy base.

I switched on the light and remembered writing a story at this very desk. I could picture the younger me, sitting in that chair, writing by hand, using lined notebook paper.

I stepped away from the side of the desk next to the window and caught sight of a tan object on the other side. It was a case, not as large as a briefcase, but too large and bulky for a laptop. I picked it up, pleased to find the cleaners had wiped any dust off it.

I laid it down in the center of the desk, and working the catches, I opened the oversized top, which folded back completely.

There, in front of me on the desk, was a blue and white typewriter.

I ran my hand over it and marveled at the old machine. It was a portable manual typewriter that worked without a plug or any electricity at all.

I thought about whether it was here when I was a kid, but no memories surfaced. Stuck where it was next to the desk, it could have been there for years, but I never noticed it, too wrapped up in the self-focus of being a child.

The bright blue and sleek white paint job on it made me feel a warm glow inside as I stared at it.

The story I wrote over thirty years ago was only about a page long. I told the story of a brave boy named Joey, who confronts a bear in the woods and scares it away. My mom and dad did the parent thing, and praised my one-page tale — I was maybe eight or nine. Uncle Rick looked it over, nodded and said, "Keep writing, Joey. Keep writing."

I would have loved to have typed it.

I leaned close and looked at the ribbon under the radiance of the overhead light. The cloth had long since dried out. Even closed in its case, it had been years since anyone had used it — maybe opened it at all.

On a whim, I went through the desk drawers and was shocked to find two white boxes labeled 'Typewriter Ribbons'.

I continued through the drawers and found a wrapped ream of typing paper. Hefting it out of the drawer, I noted it was actually about one-third empty, maybe only 300 or 350 sheets. As I looked in the wrapper, I saw the edges of the uppermost papers had yellowed. But as I went down lower, the only discoloration was at the very edge.

Under the paper was a sturdy cardboard box labelled "Carbon Transfer Paper". I set the paper next to the typewriter and pulled out the box. Once I lifted the lid, I saw the filmy tissue sheets inside and pulled out one. This made a carbon copy of a manuscript, an essential thing for a writer in days gone by. If you sent out an original manuscript and it got lost in the mail, not having a carbon was a disaster.

I frowned as I put the carbon paper back in its box. Someone collected all the things you needed to write in the days when computers were not available, or perhaps because they preferred a manual machine. But who? I was the only writer in the family.

And this didn't explain what I found: extra high-quality ribbons? Carbon paper? A ream of paper? These were the tools of the writer, and specifically, of a novelist from any time period from the 1960s onward. That was before laptops were affordable to most consumers and powerful enough to be a useful tool.

I'd written all of my books on a laptop, although it had been different machines over the last twenty years.

I looked over at my closed MacBook sitting on the table where I ate my dinner. I certainly wasn't getting anywhere with it.

I took a sip of the scotch and opened the removable top panel on the Olympia, exposing the type-basket and the type-bars.

I opened the plastic wrap on a set of unused spools and painstakingly threaded the ribbon into the machine. It took me a while, and ink marked my hands, but I got it hooked into all the different wires and holders so it would move freely.

I stared at the typewriter.

What was I doing? This was crazy.

Yet, I felt myself pulled back to the machine. I carefully went over the various levers and put the top back on the floor where I'd found it.

I grabbed two sheets of paper, stuck a carbon between them, and rolled the paper into the machine until I was a third of the way down.

Once it was in place, I typed:

LOST SOUL

A Novel

Joe Riley

I retrieved my outline from the computer bag. With that, I started the story from the beginning. I could have just gone and looked up what I'd already written on my laptop, but I worked from memory.

It wasn't as if I'd written all that much.

As I typed, I felt the story pulling at me. There is magic in being a writer when the writing works. You shift from being someone attempting to tell a story to becoming the vehicle the story pushes itself through. I can't explain it, but that is the essence. The story itself wants to be written.

That night, after months of failure and self-doubt, I knew the story was calling me, asking to be written.

This was to be the most challenging book for my hero, Soul Mason. He lost his best friend and fellow agent in the previous book, and Soul needed to find himself and renew the meaning of his life. To fit with the times, the Department Of Justice had become a politically charged bureaucracy more interested in politics than in protecting America. Could Soul, in all good conscience, stay with an organization that no longer sought foreign terrorists, but was pursuing its own citizens with charges of domestic terrorism?

I had to find the reasons for Soul to keep fighting the good fight and a mission he could throw himself into.

Feeling battle-worn from my divorce, and angry about the turns my life had taken, I easily wrote of the mixed emotions Soul felt. The fact that my main character had taken time off and spent his nights drinking hadn't made his options any clearer, and I could certainly tell that story.

To make sure I understood the drunken nights thoroughly, I refilled my scotch. I stopped and added wood to the fire now and then, keeping the room warm.

I drank, and I typed, lost in the world of my imagination, telling the tale of the despair Soul felt.

Finally, I pulled the tenth page, split the typed pages from the well-used carbon. I put each one face down on the pile for the manuscript and the pile for the carbon copies.

The last thing I did was to put a fresh pair of papers with a new carbon into the machine and shut off the light over the desk.

It was an incredibly odd feeling not having to hit a switch to turn the typewriter off, as I would have to do with my laptop. In a way, it felt wrong, but in another way, completely right. My next page was all set to start tomorrow.

Maybe I could get the book done on time, or close to the deadline.

Getting up from the chair, the room revolved a bit. I had wine and three good-sized Scotches. But I felt happy and productive, though bleary. I put the metal screen in front of the fireplace so that no burning embers could escape. Though at this point, the fire was little more than collapsed wood and bright coals.

It shocked me how cold the bedroom had become, even though I had left the door to the main room open. I went through my nightstand drawers and located a pair of winter pajamas. I had been planning to sleep in my T-shirt and boxers, but I was shivering.

I got into bed, pulling the heavy afghan up to my neck. It took a few minutes, but the bed warmed up from my body heat.

I went to turn out the lamp on the bedside table when something caught my eye. It was metal and connected to one of the exposed beams in the ceiling.

I stood on the bed to inspect it.

It appeared to be the silver wheel of an old pulley, but I couldn't figure out what it was for here in a bedroom. I followed the direction of the wheel, and on the wall, a little above waist level, was a cleat.

Probably someone put it there for one of those chairs made of rattan that people hang from the ceiling. Another thought ran through my mind. Did Uncle Rick and Aunt Betsy have one of those swings that allows all sorts of unusual sexual activity?

This put Uncle Rick and Aunt Betsy in a new light.

But looking at the position of the pulley, I decided that was probably not the case, and with the mystery unsolved, I lay down and pulled the afghan up to my neck, and with a glance at the illuminated dial of the clock, I soon fell asleep.

I heard a noise at about two AM, one that made me lift my head and listen.

Stumbling up, I made my way into the main room and found that the light over the desk was on. I'd apparently neglected to turn it off when I went to bed.

I went to the bathroom and used the facilities, then quickly shut the light off, stubbing my toe as I walked through the dark to return to my bedroom.

I cursed as I sat on the bed and rubbed my sore big toe.

I thought I heard something again, but peeking out into the main room, all was silent. I returned to bed and slipped into unconsciousness again. And yet I thought I saw something, a dim light coming from the front room.

As if someone switched on the light over the desk.

Four

<hr>

Extra Pages

I woke the next day with a hangover, but I'd had practice with that. A quick cup of coffee with just a touch of vodka was a great way to start the day!

By the time I had my second cup, with no liquor, I was feeling better and put some bread in the toaster. It was the same one we used when I was a kid, all shiny chrome with black handles.

The cabin was much warmer today. I felt hot in my flannel pajamas, and as the bread browned, I threw on some clothes: jeans and a light, long sleeve shirt. I always wear long pants and long sleeves when I go into the woods. My sensitivity to poison ivy made it a necessity. I would shower later in the day. If it got colder, I might have to bring in more wood, or I could even go into town.

Maybe if I made a list…

I glanced over at the typewriter on the desk—

And froze.

The light over the desk was on.

My heart raced, and I approached the desk slowly, warily.

I recalled getting up and turning off the light in the middle of the night. With the sunlight filling the room, I didn't notice that the light was on, but it was.

I switched it off and looked down at the typewriter, where I received a second shock. In my mind, I had a clear recollection of putting a pair of pages with the carbon in it before I went to bed. I know because I was concerned that leaving the papers there overnight might leave them with a permanent curl.

But the typewriter was empty, and the lightly used carbon lay on top of the box of carbon paper.

My two neat piles were on either side of the machine: one pile the original pages and the other for the carbon copy.

But both stacks seemed a little higher.

I left the pages facedown with my most recent typed page on top. I carefully turned it over. Along the top, it read:

Joe Riley   Lost Soul   15

I stood there, a mix of strange feelings washed over me as if I were not in my own body.

"I stopped at ten pages," I said aloud, my voice startling me.

I looked around the room, my eyes moving to every corner. Returning my attention to the pages, I tried to recall writing them.

I picked up the carbon pile; I carried them to the safety of the dining room table, where I could contemplate the machine from a distance from the corner of my eye.

I grabbed a pen so I could make minor corrections in the margins as I read my work. The first pages were exactly what I recalled writing. The opening scene, Soul, at a bar, almost gets into a fight, but backs down. Throughout the confrontation, he hears the voice of his deceased CIA agent and friend Brent Masters warning him to back off, or Soul might surely kill the man. The man taunts Soul as he walks out, not knowing how close he'd come to Soul breaking his neck.

Soul gets back to his apartment, continues drinking while talking to his old friend, who is only there in his mind. He finally passes out on the floor.

That was what I remembered writing, and it worked. It set up Soul's despair and the fact that he was barely in control of himself.

Page eleven started a new chapter.

A pounding on his door awakened Soul. Still fully dressed, he opens it to a striking woman, who walks in like she owns the place.

Her long, chestnut brown hair cascaded down in loose waves, which framed a face possessing intelligent features. Her captivating hazel eyes held a mysterious glint that drew him in, while her full, sensual lips emphasized her natural confidence.

"I'm Miranda Blackwood, FBI. I hope I'm not interrupting. Your name came up."

I frowned. Her description was fairly poetic for me, and the opening line could use some work — but who was this Miranda Blackwood? I had no recollection of this character, in my character list or notes.

I flipped open my laptop, scrolling through all my pre-book planning for *Lost Soul*. I listed all of my major characters and descriptions. This included Nikolai Romanov, the brilliant hacker who looked to find salvation by using the nuclear codes of both the USA and the Russian Federation to bring about World War Three.

But an FBI agent working with Soul?

So far, I followed the Bond concept: guns, guys, and a bevy of willing ladies who found Soul irresistible. Although the storylines had traces of misogyny and stereotypes, it kept Soul free to find a romance with each new book.

What I read both pleased and surprised me. Soul made a suggestive remark that she shut down. This earned his respect, and he took Miranda seriously.

As the pages unfolded, I found this woman was every bit Soul's equal, and a person who would demand he give his best.

At the end of page fifteen, I wanted to read more. It was captivating, and though it wasn't the direction I planned for Soul, it could work, and it could work very well.

Sometimes a character in a book does that. They don't just step out of your mind and say "hello." They stomp their way onto the page and demand your attention. It not only changes the direction of the book, but I saw how this woman could change the direction of every Soul Mason book I would ever write.

I went over the five new pages again. It was my writing style; the use of certain verbs and phrases suggested my technique. But there was also an unfamiliar voice, a strong voice, and it was coming out of Miranda Blackwood.

When I awoke at two-thirty and used the bathroom, I must have gone back to the typewriter and written the extra pages — maybe in a fugue. I went back to bed and simply forgot, which explains why I felt so tired this morning. My walking about in the wee hours interrupted my sleep.

But these new pages left me fired up.

I got myself another cup of coffee, slipped a fresh pair of sheets into the typewriter, and started typing.

It was past one in the afternoon when I hit page 25 and pulled the pages from the machine. I was tired but exhilarated. This had been a splendid morning, and the story advanced perfectly.

Miranda was such a strong character that I got pulled in by the power of her personality. She got Soul to pull himself together and pack for a mission that would take them not only to Europe, but into the Russian Federation itself.

Soul rose to her demands, got himself cleaned and shaved and ready to move out, contacting his superiors and informing them he was working with the FBI.

For some comic relief, I threw in a bureaucrat who was not pleased by Soul accepting a mission without going through channels, but Miranda quickly set the annoying little man straight.

At first, I was worried this was an awful choice. I mean, people loved the Soul Mason series as it was, with Soul being the guy in charge, the one who made the tough decisions, who got the job done.

Now, he was almost like a secondary character in his own book.

I was ravenous, so I made some oatmeal — the Irish kind, steel cut, not rolled into flakes. It's the kind you have to cook for about an hour. I threw in some raisins and dried fruit, and had more toast as it cooked.

I stood near the stove because I was cold again.

According to the thermometer outside the kitchen window, it was 75.

I wondered how high the thermometer would go if I brought it inside. Why did the cabin get colder as the day grew hotter?

I grabbed a cardigan.

If the cabin was this cold in the summer, what would it be like in the winter?

I didn't know whether they had hooked up the propane. I would ask the folks at Pocono Pines Property Care about getting me the instructions for the heater. If it were always this cold, I would have to do something other than rely on fires in the fireplace, even though they warmed the place.

I ate my oatmeal, which helped warm me up. After I finished it, I got more wood from the stacked woodpile out back to be ready to light a fire that night.

When I went outside, the difference was amazing. I was immediately too hot in my cardigan, so I took it off. I left it in the cabin and got more wood, and with each trip back and forth with an armful of wood, the difference between the warm outdoors and the cold inside puzzled me.

I decided to take a walk in the woods, and even better, a swim off the dock in the lake.

After all, it was mine now.

I grabbed a towel and headed out, and locked the cabin using the spare key we kept out back. An odd habit, after all, who would show up out here? But if you lived in Manhattan for ten years like I had, you always locked your doors.

I glanced over at the outhouse standing on the corner of the property. Faded paint of multiple colors covered the little shack. One summer, my cousins and brothers decided it was too plain, so we brought with us all the different paints we used on projects over the years, and the kids went crazy painting it.

And crazy we got.

Not only did we do multiple colors, often in more than one place, we ended up painting the grass, the nearby rocks, and each other. It was a colossal mess, but we all had a good time.

Afterwards, we all swam down in the lake to clean paint out of our hair and off our bodies.

I stared at the faded colors and marveled at the fact that our painting party had occurred about thirty years ago.

The air was warm as I went down the gentle slope into the woods toward the lake. I stopped to look in one of the dirty windows of the old work shed. It was a building the size of a garage with faded clapboard walls and a pair of double doors with two high windows. I went back into the cabin and got the ring of keys from a kitchen drawer. Soon, I opened the padlock that secured the outbuilding.

I pushed open the creaky door and stepped into the dimly lit shed. Light filtered in through the dirty windows, and dust motes danced in the air. A prickling sensation crawled up the back of my neck. The musty atmosphere hung heavily around me. I glanced around at the old, dusty tools lining the shelves, feeling a curious unease settle in the pit of my stomach.

Why did I feel like this? It was just an old shed.

I found a gas can and a gasoline-powered lawnmower. That was good. I would need it to mow the small lawn around the cabin.

I almost ran into a large object covered with an old tarpaulin. I carefully pulled the cloth to the side, exposing the hull of Uncle Rick's old aluminum rowboat. It was about eight feet long, from bow to stern. He'd stored it upside down, lifted off the ground on a pair of wooden sawhorses. I remembered as kids; it took all the kids and our fathers to get it down to the lake and into the water. If I wanted to use it, I would need help to get it to the dock.

I always remembered Uncle Rick covering the boat with a nice canvas cover, but what was on it now was old, frayed, and worn. Then again, it could have been the same tarp and had aged since I was a kid.

There was a wheelbarrow next to it, with a small ball of twine lying in the steel tray. I touched one handle and froze.

I had an inexplicable feeling someone was watching me.

My hand was on the wheelbarrow, yet the weight and reality of it seemed little comfort. I glanced around the dark room. It felt like a presence was hiding in the shadows and observing my every move.

I sucked in another deep breath, dismissing the idea. This had to be paranoia, as I was here alone. I replaced the cover of the old boat and stepped away.

I walked over to a workbench. As a kid, I once helped my dad build a birdhouse on that bench.

The only object on the workbench now was a hank of heavy white clothesline wrapped tightly. Someone had badly cut the end of the rope, making it resemble the decaying tendrils of a forgotten nightmare. I reached for it, and stopped, as once again, fear gripped my heart.

I stared at the rope. A surge of pure terror coursed through my veins. I felt that if I touched it, someone would die.

I backed away, stumbling as I went, and fell against the double doors of the shed, causing them to rattle. I got outside and slammed the doors behind me. My hands were shaking as I closed the hasp and put the padlock back on.

Suddenly I didn't want to go see the lake. I just wanted to get back into the cabin and hide under the covers of my bed, completely exhausted.

I forced myself on, but now the welcoming woods seemed foreboding. As I walked, an eerie unease settled all around me. I thought I should hear all kinds of forest noises: birds, animals rustling in the underbrush, squirrels scampering in the trees.

But no, it was silent, except for the warm breeze that did little to free me of the chill from the cabin.

The sunlight, which had been a source of comfort, went behind a cloud, and the shadows appeared to grow longer, casting eerie shapes and dancing patterns across the forest floor. Brittle leaves rustled under my sneakers, as if the very trees were whispering an ominous secret.

The path, once so familiar, seemed treacherous. Instead of easily leading me to the lake, it seemed to weave deeper into a twisted labyrinth. And beyond the thicket? The lake, where more forgotten memories awaited.

What was wrong with me? I loved these woods as a kid and always felt safe here. Now, I understood the reason behind the locals' belief that the place was haunted.

I pushed on, going up the short hill overlooking the lake.

As I went to the top, the land seemed to open up before me, and the sun came out shining brightly over the lush scene. It was a beautiful lake of clear water, without a ripple, and its surface reflected the beauty of the surrounding trees and the sky overhead.

The gentle breeze caressed my face, and I smelled honeysuckle and woodland scents, evoking a sense of nostalgia.

In the distance, I caught sight of the other cabins nestled around the shoreline of the lake. Each cabin stood at a respectful distance from the others, ensuring a sense of privacy and solitude. Some cabins sported their own docks, gracefully extending into the calm waters. The surrounding trees framed these structures and created a picturesque scene.

What had I been so scared of?

I walked down the hill, gazing at the tranquil water and the old wooden floating dock that pushed out into the water. It was still there and in one piece.

I peeled off my long-sleeve shirt and pants and stepped onto the dock, but the old wood bent and almost gave way underfoot, and I hopped back to safety. The wood was rotting in places, and I had to be sure not to step in the wrong spot.

Just what I needed, another expense.

Luckily, the wood around the ladder on the side of the dock was fine, and I used the ladder to lower myself into the lake. Since it was June, the water was still chilly.

I did the breaststroke for a few minutes, then flipped over and floated on my back. As I did, I saw a flash of light from one house looking out upon the lake. When I focused on it, it was gone. I floated for about ten minutes and then, chilled by the cool water, I swam to the ladder, pulled myself up, and used a towel to dry off.

I put the shirt on and stepped into the trees for cover as I removed my wet underwear and put back on my pants. Wrapping the wet garment in the towel, I started my way back to the house. My muscles felt loose and invigorated after the swim.

I would have to see about getting the boat to the dock, getting out on the lake to do some fishing. Rick's fishing equipment must still be here, probably somewhere in the shed.

Thinking back on my terror in the shed, I couldn't figure out why I didn't just turn on the light. The shed had electricity, and there was a light switch somewhere.

I reminded myself it was the first day, and I was still jumpy from the funeral and my divorce

That was all it was. It couldn't be anything else

Five

Things That Go
Bump In The Night

I spent the afternoon taking a nap.

The walk and swim were just the right amount of exercise, and I slept deeply in my boxers and T-shirt, but needed the afghan pulled up over me to stay warm enough.

I finally got up at about five thirty and stuck a frozen meal in the oven for dinner. That gave me a chance to shower, and I dressed in a flannel shirt and jeans because the cabin had grown cold again.

I built another fire and pulled another bottle of wine, but decided to have only one glass. The Scotch was more effective, and probably cheaper when you got right down to it.

Over dinner, with the fire warming the cabin, I reviewed the pages I wrote in the morning, making minor corrections. I didn't feel the need to write more. After all, I had done ten new pages.

Instead, I opened my laptop and used my phone as a hotspot to get my email, which was incredibly slow. I opened the Pocono Pines Property Care website. The company offered numerous cabins that were rentals and other services, such as cleaning and caretaking.

I emailed them for the instructions on how to operate the heater and hook up the propane tank.

I also went over my finances — I would have to make a budget. If I were going to make it work here, I would need better internet and maybe a satellite television hookup. In the meantime, I would have to find a location in town where I could use Wi-Fi and look into the cost of all these things.

I noticed an email from the Meredith Thompson Literary Agency, which gave me pause. Thompson was a name I knew. She represented critically acclaimed authors well-known on the bestseller lists.

I opened the email:

> *Dear Mr. Riley;*
>
> *Your publisher has asked me to represent you for your*
> *current work,* Lost Soul.

That seemed odd. We had signed that deal months ago. Why were they involving her at this point? I read on:

> *Some of your books missed the agreed deadline in the*
> *past, so they wanted to make sure someone was watching*
> *out for their interests and your own.*

The publisher wanted someone to babysit me.

> *Because of the unfortunate loss of your representative and relative, Richard Riley, I am sure you need representation. I would like to arrange a meeting with you in the next few weeks to discuss the possibility of our working together.*

This wasn't bad. A powerhouse agent like Meredith Thompson might get me better deals, and possibly convince my current publisher to put more advertising dollars behind my books.

> *Would it be possible to send me some of the current manuscript? I am aware it is due in seven weeks, and it would reassure the publisher to know that we will deliver the book on time.*
>
> *I wait to hear from you,*
>
> *Meredith Thompson*

Here was the downside. An agent like Meredith Thompson wouldn't make excuses for me and let it slide. Uncle Rick covered my ass with the last two books being late, but if I was going to work with Thompson, I would have to have my act together.

Then again, I had twenty-five pages. If I could get a few more days, maybe I could get it up to fifty.

I sent her a quick email response.

> *Dear Ms. Thompson;*
>
> *I would love to discuss an arrangement with you at your convenience, and I will be happy to send you some pages. However, I am currently living in a cabin in the Poconos, and using a typewriter. I will need to arrange a scanner to send you the work. Please give me a few days.*
>
> *J. Riley*

That should cover me, but I did not know where I could even get a scanner. Something else I would have to look into.

The email left me excited but concerned. I thought about working on the book, but just poured myself a scotch instead. I could probably go to an office supply store somewhere and buy a scanner. It would be the easiest thing to do.

As I prepared to shut down the laptop, I received an email from the property management company, telling me the caretaker would be by tomorrow morning to instruct me on the use of the heating system.

That was good. A real live person to walk me through the process would prevent me from blowing up the place.

Unsure of what to do with myself, I walked over to the cabinet next to the desk, what my parents would have called a hutch back in the day. It had drawers in the bottom half and bookshelves in the upper. The shelves contained books brought up here years earlier.

There were several Stephen King novels, but with the strange things going on, I passed. Instead, I grabbed a copy of the first Harry Potter book. Since I was born in the 80s, I had just become a teenager when the first one came out, and I had waited with bated breath for each book.

I put the screen in front of the fire and went to my bedroom to put on my pajamas. Once again, the bedroom was the coldest place in the house. I found the slippers I wore last winter at the Lake Hopatcong place.

Though concerned with my finances, I decided I might have to get one of those propane heaters put into the wall of this room.

I went back out to the main room and loaded the typewriter with paper and a carbon. I figured if I had gone sleepwalking and written such a prominent character, it could be my good luck charm. This was like baseball players who won't wash their socks or basketball players who wear the same shoes in a winning season.

It was superstition, but it also couldn't hurt. And maybe I would wander in the night and write.

I went to my bedroom, leaving the door open, pulled my feet out of the slippers, and got under the covers to read. Glancing up, I saw the pulley on the beam over my head, and noticed it seemed to gleam in the lamplight.

I focused on reading, but I didn't last long.

I soon found the words drifting in front of my eyes, and I slipped away in sleep.

There was a sound.

It wasn't an unpleasant sound, more like a background noise I slowly noticed. It was a steady rhythm and familiar, and oddly comforting. Still not quite awake, I looked over at the clock.

A childish refrain ran through my head — if the big hand is at the six and the little hand is at the two—

This roused my tired mind a bit.

What was so significant about two-thirty in the morning?

I also noticed something else unusual about the clock radio. Covering the dial were tiny white angular shapes at odd angles.

I was ready to ignore the noise and go back to sleep when there was a small bell and a ratcheting sound that made me realize what I was hearing.

Typing.

What I was hearing was the clicking of keys and the bell of the carriage return.

I sat up in bed, trying to make sure what I heard wasn't a dream. Blinking groggily, I exhaled a pent-up breath, which came out as a misty cloud.

The air all around me was beyond cold; it was frigid.

I looked at the illuminated dial of the clock again and realized what was distorting the numbers — ice crystals.

It was impossible. It was June, not January. I was indoors and ice formed on a clock? Impossible!

Yet, the sound of the typing continued: tick-tack-tackety-tack-ding-zzzzz.

My feet touched the floor, but it was so cold I had to pull my feet up and gasp. My breath came out in a cloud, and I carefully reached around on the floor for my slippers.

All the while, I heard the typing.

I reached to the floor and pulled my fingers back. The floor was so frigid; I felt a stab of pain.

With numb fingers, I found my slippers and pulled them into the bed with me. I knew what was happening. In *Body And Soul*, hypothermia almost took Soul Mason down. Writing that section of the book, I did extensive research.

My fingers had gone numb from the cold, but how could this happen inside a house? In June?

The numbing air bit at my exposed skin, infusing me with its icy grip. I pulled the slippers onto my feet and attempted to get up again. I left the afghan on the bed and stood. The cold air circulated around me. My hands and feet ached with cold. I stumbled to one of my closets and grabbed the doorknob, which made my hand pull away. It was so cold it felt like I'd burned my flesh as I pulled the door open. I grabbed my heavy bathrobe and threw it on, pulling the terrycloth close to my body.

Tick-tack-tackety-tack-ding-zzzzz.

I stumbled, shivering, to the door of the bedroom. Why had I closed it? I didn't remember doing it. My numb fingers were having trouble feeling the knob, and I couldn't get it to turn. I put my head against the door and heard the typing as it went on and on.

Finally, I got a good enough grip and pulled the door open, stumbling out into the large main room of the cabin.

Silence.

There was some light from the illuminated clock on the stove. The light on the desk was off, and all I saw of the typewriter was a dark silhouette.

This room was much warmer, and embers still glowed from my fire. I walked over to the fireplace to let the remaining warmth wash over me. My breath was no longer visible, and my shivering faded.

I wanted to go over to the typewriter, examine it to see if the paper I had placed there was still in it.

And to see if there was typing on it.

Yet I felt frightened about doing this.

The typewriter sat on the desk, beckoning me closer, as if daring me to unravel the mystery. I gritted my teeth and stepped toward it, my hand going to the light switch on the gooseneck lamp.

The light fired on brightly, and I had to shield my eyes. I staggered back, trying to clear my vision. Leaning forward, with my hands on the desk, I stared at the typewriter.

There was a blank page rolled under the carriage with a carbon paper and a second page. I grabbed the paper and yanked it from the typewriter. It came out with a 'grrrr' sound, as if the machine was protesting my mistreatment.

Both pages were blank, though the second page had marks from the rollers that left black streaks from the carbon paper.

I put the blank papers down, and my hand went to my aching head. I carefully reinserted the pages and rolled it into place to begin work the next day. Was I wrong? Had I only imagined it, dreamed it?

I didn't dream about the cold. I rushed back into the bedroom. There were no ice crystals on the clock, and my breath didn't mist. It was a little chillier than the main room, and certainly colder than it should be, but within the realms of the mountains in the summer.

I lumbered back into the main room, the bulb from the gooseneck lamp lighting up the desk, forming a spotlight around the typewriter.

I shook my head. It must have been a dream, yet such a vivid one. I rubbed my hands together, grateful they were finally warming up.

I walked back to the desk and noticed the two piles of manuscript, apparently undisturbed by everything that had happened. Since I had finished at page twenty-five, I picked up the face-down uppermost page and glanced at the top.

It read:

Joe Riley   **Lost Soul**   **31**

The paper fell from my hand, and I backed away from the machine. It was impossible! I had finished on page twenty-five. I knew I had.

Just like the previous evening, extra pages were there, this time six instead of five.

I wanted to throw on my clothes, jump in my car, middle of the night or not, and get the hell out of there. Find a hotel, motel, or even a goddamn homeless shelter, but I needed to go somewhere, anywhere, and get away from this madness.

But where would I go? This was now my only home.

I picked the page up from the floor and holding it away from myself like something alien and diseased, returned it to its pile.

I went into the bedroom and pulled the afghan off the bed. Returning to the main room, I rotated my recliner to face the desk and pulled the afghan over me. I was going to watch that typewriter all night if I had to, but I would see how this happened.

Reclining in the chair, staring at the light, I watched the typewriter carefully, my arms crossed. I would see it reveal its magic if it were the last thing I ever did.

I woke with a start.

Sunlight poured in through the window next to the desk and directly onto my face, making me stir.

I felt a blistering hangover, worse than the one the previous day. That was strange as well, considering I drank less the previous night.

In my sleep, I had pulled the afghan off, as I was perfectly warm. In fact, I was sweaty in my heavy flannel pajamas.

I rose to start a cup of coffee. As it brewed, I relieved myself in the bathroom, and went through the cabinet to see if there was any pain medication. If I did my trick with the vodka in the coffee, I felt I would throw up.

There were ancient bandaids, a sliding cardboard box of Q-Tips — I hadn't seen them packaged like that in thirty years. But I found a bottle of aspirin and, throwing some in my mouth, followed it with a glass of water. Then a second glass.

I grabbed my mug of coffee and sat at the dining room table, still keeping a wary eye on the typewriter. In the light of a cloudless summer day, everything I'd experienced the previous night had the fleeting sense of a dream, nothing more.

If so, it was a hell of a dream.

Leaving my coffee, I went to the desk and grabbed the carbon pile, bringing it back to the table with me, along with my red pen. I reread page 25, the work I remembered doing, and with my jaw clenched so tight it hurt, went on to the next page.

It matched what I had been writing, and my new character, Miranda Blackwood, was getting everything moving. She and Soul were getting to know each other's shorthand and understand one another.

There was an amazing undercurrent of raw sexuality subtly woven into what I read.

Soul was not known for subtlety. He was blunt, sometimes recklessly so, accustomed to confronting challenges head-on without hesitation or remorse. But Miranda was different; she inspired a cautious respect in him, urging him toward an unfamiliar self-control. Their partnership mattered more than he'd expected, grounding him in ways no one else had ever managed.

With what my outline held in store — Soul pitted directly against the monstrous Nikolai Romanov — he would need every shred of focus, every ounce of discipline he'd painstakingly cultivated over the years. The fate awaiting him was darker than he'd ever known, his skills and resolve strained to their limits. If Soul hesitated, if the fragile threads of his control unraveled, everything he cared about would shatter like fragile glass under Romanov's relentless cruelty.

I finished page 31 and put the entire pile of papers back on my desk.

In a way, I felt like the cobbler in the story where he goes to sleep at night and elves come and make shoes for him.

I wondered what I would have to give my benefactor for the extra pages.

I shook my head. The pages were in my writing style. I must be having some kind of fugue, or I typed more pages than I remembered.

Chronic drinkers experience blackouts, right?

That had to be the explanation... didn't it?

A Mystery at the Cabin

The next morning, a knock at the door pulled me from my thoughts. I was still in my pajamas but went to answer it.

I opened the door to a man in a T-shirt and overalls with a short beard and hair long on the sides, but balding on top. He smiled with a crooked grin.

"Mr. Riley?" he asked, with a voice suggesting too many long nights and too many cigarettes.

"I'm Joe Riley," I said.

He held out his hand and flashed his lopsided grin again. "Dan Stevens. I'm with Pocono Pines Property Care."

"I figured." I shook his hand. "Come in. Please excuse me for not being dressed. I had a rough night."

"Trouble sleeping?" he said as he stepped inside.

"Something like that."

He nodded as if he were knowledgeable about my situation. "A lot of the city people say that. It's just too quiet for them, and it takes 'em a few days to get used to the sounds of the forest."

I wished that was my only problem.

"Chilly in here," Dan said, looking around. "This cabin has always been colder than the other homes around here."

"Really?"

"Yeah, I've been watching the houses up here for the company for about fifteen years." He led me over to the propane heater hanging on the wall. "I always came to this cabin early in the fall. My guess is being near the lake and all makes it cooler. Sorry to hear about your uncle. He was a fine man."

"Thank you. It was a bit of a shock to all of us."

"It's a pity he didn't come up here much in the last few years. I heard his wife passed away."

"Yes, my Aunt Betsy. It was cancer."

He nodded knowingly once again. "That'll take the heart out of a man, losing his wife. But we maintained the place, and I was up here 'bout every month to make sure there weren't any squirrels or squatters takin' up residence."

"I'm sure my uncle appreciated that."

He looked at the heating unit. "I'll walk you through how this thing works, then show you how to turn on the propane tank and we can give it a go, alright?"

"Sure."

It was pretty straightforward. The dial in the center had three positions: OFF, PILOT and ON. He set it to OFF.

"Now, if you smell gas when it's off, stop right away," he explained. "That means you have a leak."

I nodded, thinking perhaps I should take notes.

"You turn the knob on the control valve to PILOT and push it in all the way and hold it in. That lights the pilot. Hold it 'bout a minute, then let it go and the control knob will pop back out. The pilot should remain lit. If it goes out, start over. Then you turn the knob to ON and let the thermostat take over from there."

It all seemed easy enough; even a writer could do it.

"Let me take you out back and show you the tank," he said.

"Out back?" I repeated. "Isn't the tank just under the house?"

This made him laugh, and it was a hearty laugh. I also felt he wasn't laughing at me for my lack of knowledge, but because he liked to laugh.

"I'll explain when I take you out back," he said jovially. "Why don't you throw on some clothes?"

Once dressed, he led me outside through the back door off the kitchen. It was much warmer outdoors, and it felt good to have the sun on my face. We walked to the side of the house, past the old outhouse, where a large tank sat about a dozen yards away.

It was a large metal thing, and at first it surprised me I hadn't noticed it, but it was on the one side of the house that didn't have a window.

"Why's it so far from the house?" I asked.

He chuckled. "Safety. Propane can explode."

He lifted a circular dome on top of the tank, exposing a large valve and a red device connected to a hose that went down into the ground. He twisted the handle on the valve.

"That's the shut-off valve, and I opened it, so the gas will flow," he explained. "Got that?"

"What's the red thing?" I asked.

"Pressure regulator. The propane in the tank is about a hundred psi. That thing lowers it to ten." He closed the dome, so it covered the valve and the regulator and walked me to the cabin, where I saw a copper pipe coming out of the ground and into a round device on the wall of the cabin.

"That's your second-stage regulator. That drops the pressure to about one psi." He pointed at a yellow knob next to the regulator. "That's another shut-off valve."

"Seems like the heater has a lot of safety features," I said.

Dan's face twisted into his grin again. "Yes, but a propane heater is a good choice."

"The bedroom I've been using seems to be the coldest room in the house. Would it be possible to add a propane heater there as well?"

He shrugged and glanced back at the tank. "You've got enough of a supply. We could get a plumber out here and run a gas line to that room. Show me which one?"

I took him back inside and showed him my bedroom.

He pointed at the wall at the end of the room. "That's the same wall your current heater is on. It would be real easy to split the line. It would warm this room very well."

"How much would something like that cost?" I asked.

"I'd have to talk to the company," he said. "I'd say a couple of grand."

I nodded, feeling the twist on my finances yet again. But if the cabin was this cold during the warm summer months, I had to make a plan for the winter. I didn't want to end up sleeping in the main room just to stay warm.

We discussed some of the other things the house needed, and he made several friendly suggestions of suppliers for internet access and a satellite TV plan. I grabbed a sheet of paper and took notes.

He got the heater going and took a cord that hung loose from the heater and plugged it into a nearby outlet on the wall. "That's your thermostat. It needs electricity, but the heater will run without it if the power goes out."

"Does that happen often?" I asked.

"Around here? All the time, especially in the winter. You get a snowstorm, a few tree branches fall, and the electric goes out for the entire area."

As we talked, the heater vented hot air, warming the cabin quickly.

I made both of us a cup of coffee, and we sat at the table. I leaned back in my chair and asked the question I'd been waiting to ask.

"Tell me, has anything weird ever happened here?"

He looked at me blankly. "I don't know what you mean."

I shrugged and tried to be nonchalant. "Some people in the area say this place is haunted."

He forced a smile, but I could tell he was faking it. "What do you mean?"

"Strange lights, strange sounds. I was told that a neighbor had called the police once."

He sipped his coffee. "People imagine a lot of things."

I gazed at him over my mug. "I heard that when the police came to investigate, the caretaker wouldn't come to the cabin at night."

It was clear from the long breath he let out, he felt caught and knew it. "I make it a habit not to go to the properties at night."

"Nothing more?"

"Look, if the company thought I wasn't doing my job, I could get fired—"

"It's nothing like that," I said. "It's just since I got here, strange things have been happening. I'm trying to understand it."

"Like what?" he demanded.

"The cold rooms in summer, for one," I said. "And some other things. Did anything happen here I should know about?"

He sighed and stared at the liquid in his cup. "I've heard stories from the old caretaker, Ben Connelly, when he was showing me the cabins the company oversees. But any of those stories were from before my time."

"Any insights would be helpful," I said.

He nodded. "According to Old Ben, a woman staying at this cabin went missing — must be about twenty years ago."

"A woman? Staying here? Alone?" I asked, surprised.

"Yes, Ben said she was a friend of your cousins, or as he put it, the 'young Riley kids'. According to what he told me, the four of them all came up in September, just about the end of the season. After a week, your cousins went back to their lives, and the woman stayed here alone."

"Why did they do that?" I asked.

"I don't know. Ben said she stayed in the cabin to work on a book and felt this was the place to do it."

The typewriter in the corner caught my eye. This explained my supply of paper, carbon paper, and ribbons. There had indeed been someone here who used those tools. But twenty years ago?

"What happened?" I asked.

His shoulders lifted in a shrug. "No one knows. The way Ben tells it, he came by once during the winter to check her heater, and the next time he came by, she was just gone. No sign of her anywhere."

"What about a car?" I said. "Maybe she just got her book done and left."

"Don't know. Like I said, it was before I was here."

"Is there any way I could talk to this Ben Connelly?"

He looked up at the ceiling as he thought. "Sure, I guess. He still lives in the area, must be in his late eighties by now, because he was an older guy when he gave me the property tour."

I wrote my cell phone number on a corner of the sheet of typing paper where I had written my notes. Carefully, I ripped it free and handed it to Dan. "If you could let me know where he is, I'd love to talk to him."

He took the slip of paper. "I'll ask Ben and make sure he don't mind. But if he's willing to talk to you, he'll call you."

"It might be better if you didn't tell Pocono Pines Property Care about my request."

I received another of his odd grins. "I don't want to tell them." He looked at me and grew serious. "My concern is, why is this important to you?"

Why was it so important? Yes, finding the typing paper, ribbons, and carbon had been a surprise, and those appearing pages were downright spooky. Why did I feel the need to learn more?

"Just idle curiosity," I said.

I didn't believe that at all, and I didn't think caretaker Dan Stevens did either.

Dan left soon after, and I glanced at the typed pages in the two piles on my desk. I needed to find somewhere to scan them or purchase a scanner. Then get what I had to Meredith Thompson.

And one more important errand.

I drove the forty-five minutes to East Stroudsburg, where I bought a scanner from an office supply store.

I also got another ream of typing paper and another box of carbon paper.

So much for my budget!

I was seeing the disadvantages of living out in the woods. There was food nearby, and booze, but I would have to get everything from Amazon unless I wanted to drive all over Hell and creation.

I went north on my return journey and into the town of Milford, Pennsylvania. Milford is a kind of throwback to a simpler time, with a real main street and a lot of businesses that formerly were homes. But there are also gas stations, pharmacies, and the Pike County Library. The building is a newer construction with an old-fashioned look to it, but the inside of the building is state-of-the-art.

I went to the reference desk. There sat an attractive woman with brown hair pulled back into a ponytail, which accentuated her oval-shaped face. She wore glasses with a heavy frame, and from the look of them, the lenses were powerful.

"Excuse me, do you have copies of the Pocono Record on microfilm?"

As a kid, when I was first writing my stories, I would often bicycle to my local library and look at old headlines on microfilm that would inspire what I wanted to write.

She met my eyes. Her glasses made her eyes larger — brown eyes. When I approached, I thought she was in her early twenties. But looking at her closer, I realized she was near thirty.

And very attractive.

She smiled. "Microfilm? Sir, has it been a while since you've been in a library?"

I was sure I flushed red as a beet — I felt like a kid. She had a point. I had used the internet for twenty years, as even in the Lake Hopatcong place there had been Wi-Fi.

"Yeah, I-I guess."

She rose to her feet, standing at about five foot eight with great posture and a slender and graceful figure. She lowered her voice. "Sorry, I didn't mean to embarrass you."

"No harm done," I said, trying to recover. Why do women intimidate me so much?

"We don't carry microfilm. In fact, most libraries don't anymore," she explained. "You can look up old newspapers online. But I should warn you, most of those sites are subscription-based."

"Ah!" I said, attempting to sound intelligent, but I had a feeling that ship had sailed. "That's a problem for me as well. I just relocated here, and I live out in the woods. No internet except my phone, and that's pretty unreliable."

"Fortunately, the library has computers you can use." She led me to a nearby computer and punched in some codes. "I would suggest you do a search based on your criteria first, and see what comes up. If you need to use the Lexis Nexus, the library has an account."

I nodded, and she gestured to the chair. I could pretty well handle it from here, but I desperately wanted to keep her nearby to talk to her. "Thank you so much."

Smooth Joe, real smooth. You're a regular Casanova.

With another of her dazzling smiles, she headed back to her desk. She wore a classic outfit, with a tailored blouse and slim-fitting trousers. It seemed perfect for working in a library.

I put my criteria in the computer search engine: missing author, female, 2000-2005, dingmans ferry, pa.

Several articles from newspapers and other online sites popped up.

I opened the first, which was The Pocono Record.

Police Blotter: Missing Author

Police are seeking information on the whereabouts of best-selling author Rebecca Hawthorne, who was staying with friends in a cabin on Five Miles Meadow Road in Dingmans Ferry.

Ms. Hawthorne (30) is the author of several books, most notably "Whispers Of Moonlight" and the critically acclaimed "Shadows Of Deception" which reached number five in the New York Times best-seller list in 1999.

She was on a writing retreat to finish her newest book, when a friend, Liam Riley reported her missing. Police and her husband are offering a reward for any information—

The article went on, but I was too busy staring at my cousin's name. Liam reported her missing? Did he have anything to do with any of this? He'd mentioned nothing about it.

Then again, it was twenty years ago. I was a struggling writer working as a waiter in Manhattan, too wrapped up in my head to be aware of anything besides myself.

I did an online search for Rebecca Hawthorne.

An author photo appeared. It was probably the one used on the back of her books.

I saw an attractive woman who possessed a certain elegance enhanced by her refined features and smooth, fair complexion. She had straight brown hair that fell to her shoulders and swept away from her face. Slightly arched eyebrows framed a pair of piercing green-brown hazel eyes, resulting in an inquisitive expression. Her face kept an air of youthfulness, but the lines around her eyes hinted at a life that carried its own share of burdens.

I clicked through to Amazon, entered her name, and found the two books mentioned in the article. They were still on sale and had thousands of reviews, giving her work a 4.9 rating.

I wish my books did so well.

I considered downloading the book, but I was in a library!

I wanted to see if they had either book. After all, it had been twenty years, and they were probably out of circulation. If I asked about them, it would give me a chance to talk to the reference librarian again.

She was finishing up with a young man of about twelve. He was chubby, had striking red hair, and looked at her as if he wanted to bow down and kiss her feet.

"Okay, Julius," she said. "Will that get you on the right track for your report?"

He nodded, and spoke with a voice in the cracking phase, not totally a baritone, and still slipping into an alto. "Yes, thanks, Miss Anderson."

He walked away completely smitten, and 'Miss Anderson' regarded me. "Did you find what you were looking for?"

"Perhaps. Do you have any books by Rebecca Hawthorne?"

She seemed surprised by my request, but smiled. "You like Rebecca Hawthorne?"

"I don't know. I've read nothing by her," I said. "Do you know her work?"

Miss Anderson sighed. "I must have read *Whispers Of Moonlight* a hundred times when I was a teenager. Let me check to see if either of her books is on loan or here in the library."

She leaned forward to type on the computer, her graceful form creating a tantalizing silhouette. I felt the urge to stare, lost in the allure of her elevated curves. With a deliberate effort, I averted my gaze from the enchanting outline of her hips.

"Yes, we have both *Whispers Of Moonlight* and *Shadows Of Deception*. Would you like me to get them for you?"

"Yes, thank you, um, Miss Anderson." I saw my chance. "I'm Joe, Joe Riley."

This made her smile. "Like the author?"

I let out a breath that made a sound but not any words in response.

Her eyes grew wide. "Wait! You're him!"

"I'm afraid so," I mumbled.

She stared at my face. "I thought you looked familiar." She pulled open a drawer on her desk and yanked out a hardcover copy of *Body And Soul*. She held up the book with the cover facing me, comparing my picture on the back to the actual person in front of her.

"They photoshopped my author photo, and I was younger—"

"Shut the front door," she muttered, lowering the book and looking at me open-mouthed. "I thought you lived in New York."

"I did. Now I live in Dingman's Ferry," I said. "Are you enjoying the book? You're not my usual demographic."

She smiled again. "Loving it. And I like all kinds of genres, and action adventure is great fun. I don't know why I only discovered this — um — your series recently."

"I'm working on the next book right now."

"That's so exciting," she gushed.

"You know my full name — what's yours?" I asked.

"Emily Anderson," she said and put out her hand, which I shook, and we smiled foolishly at each other.

She had brilliant eyes, magnified as they were behind her thick lenses.

She jumped as if realizing she'd forgotten something. "Oh, yes! Let me get you those books."

She rushed away, and I stood there watching her go. We had switched roles, from me being intimidated by her to her being intimidated by me.

I hadn't looked at women for the last few months, between the divorce and my spending most of my time drunk. I had been hanging out in some pretty seedy places that didn't cater to smart, attractive women like this one.

After Chandra, I saw my desire as an enemy. It had been my desire for Chandra that had allowed me to be manipulated and used.

But now—my desire returned, and it was like a revelation. I was probably turning red again.

She came back a moment later with the pair of books in her hand. They were both a bit worn, but hardcovers.

"I don't have a library card."

"Oh, right? Of course you don't, you just moved in." She reached into her desk and pulled out a preprinted index card. "Here, fill this out. We'll mail you the card."

"That probably means I can't take out the books?"

"Normally," she said. "I took them out under my name."

I smiled. "That's great." I felt tongue-tied, but I would have to get back into the game at some point, unless I wanted to die bitter and alone. "I'd — um — like to repay you. Could I take you out to dinner — uh — sometime?"

I sounded worse than young Julius! Was I always this bad at talking to women, or was I merely out of practice?

"I'd like that," she said, and handed me a slip of paper with her name and phone number. "Today's Wednesday. I'm not busy on Friday."

"That's great! I'll call you, and maybe you can choose where to eat. I don't know what's good out here."

"I can help with that," she said with one last dazzling smile.

I walked away, feeling a little like young Julius as I went.

Seven

The Woman In The Chair

When I got back to the cabin, I went directly to the typewriter.

Miss Anderson filled me with both dread and excitement. I wanted to imbue these feelings into the scene I was writing for Soul.

He was flying to Europe with Miranda, and he was feeling — and fighting — his own attraction to the captivating woman. I kept his inner conflict going on the flight as he battled his desire to focus on the mission against his wish to focus on Miranda.

This was new for my character. The women in the other Soul Mason novels were easily replaceable and secondary to the story. But Soul, losing his mission partner, Brett, made him vulnerable in ways I never saw coming.

It was 9:00 when I finished my tenth page, which brought my count up to a respectable forty-one pages, and Miranda and Soul had arrived in the Czech Republic. I would have to go to the library tomorrow and use Google Maps to walk around Prague with them, to get a feel for what they would see.

It was another chance to visit the captivating Miss Anderson, as well.

Thinking about Rebecca Hawthorne, I pulled out my phone, intending to call my cousin Liam.

I stopped myself. What would I ask him?

Hey cuz, you reported a missing woman about twenty years ago. What's that about?

And I thought Soul Mason wasn't subtle.

In the end, I poured a scotch and started one of Ms. Hawthorne's books. Maybe that would give me some insight into her.

I mean, she couldn't be here anymore, right? She went missing twenty years ago.

I opened *Whispers Of Moonlight*, expecting it to be the typical fare of the romantic/suspense genre. The story was about two people who meet over a mystery, attracted to each other, but from different places. After much to-do, they finally solve the mystery and find love with each other.

It was a successful formula and used to death by writers everywhere.

When I started reading, I realized I was wrong — amazingly wrong.

I found fully developed characters that quickly involved me and a captivating, genuine mystery.

And the language.

Hawthorne was a woman who used words powerfully and simply. Her style at first reminded me of Ernest Hemingway, a brilliant writer who used words like knives to stab his stories home. Hemingway was a genius, even drunk off his ass.

I saw why she'd climbed the best-seller lists, and if she hadn't gone missing, she would have stayed there for years to come.

As I continued to read, I saw things that were familiar.

Writers leave fingerprints in their work. Some of these are bad habits our editors beat out of us.

But there are still signs of a writer's technique the editor can't hide or avoid. Phrases or style, every author has a unique voice.

In *Whispers Of Moonlight*, I was seeing familiar phrases. This led me to thumb through some of the typed pages from my pile.

The extra pages that appeared each morning had a style that reflected Ms. Hawthorne. No, it was different. It was as if Rebecca Hawthorne wrote the pages, emulating my style, with little peeks of her own talent sneaking through.

I wondered why the extra pages had so much range to them. It was as if a best-selling author at the height of their powers was collaborating with me, and easily, maybe effortlessly, mimicking my style.

By now it was after eleven, and I had indulged in a couple more scotches. My eyes grew heavy, but I went to the desk and inserted my nightly pair of pages into the carriage of the machine.

I contemplated sleeping in the recliner, but my neck was sore from that attempt the previous night. I put my slippers and my robe next to my bed, easily within reach.

At first, I lay in bed in my pajamas, listening intently for any sound — specifically the sound of typing.

But after the scotches, I was soon fast asleep.

I was having a lovely dream, outside on a pair of skis. I saw a resort below from a steep mountain. The icy breeze stung my cheeks and my breath blew out in a mist. I wasn't a skier, yet I seemed comfortable on this high mountain, as if I had done it a thousand times.

I pushed myself forward and started down the mountain, the stiff wind against my exposed face. As I flew down, the skis made a strange sound: tick-tack-tackety-tack-ding-zzzzz.

This brought me fully awake, and I realized my face was indeed cold. I looked over at the clock-radio, which read two-thirty once again.

Ice crystals coated the circular dial, and my breath came out as a fog. Silently, I reached over and pulled my slippers over. The slippers were still chilly to my touch, and I sat up in bed to slip them on. Shivering, I stood and pulled on the robe, still attempting silence and clenching my jaw so my teeth wouldn't chatter.

A sense of unease crept up my spine as I slowly made my way toward the main room, and to me it sounded like each footfall echoed.

At the door, the knob was so wintry it sent a shock of pain into my hand. Damn it, I would have to go to bed with winter gloves on. I spun the knob and opened the door.

The light was on at the desk and a woman sat in the chair, her back to me.

I was so shocked; it took everything I had not to cry out.

She was typing.

Not just typing, but typing effortlessly, her fingers gliding over the keys. Words materialized on the page, as if woven from the essence of her being.

That was when I became aware she was naked.

The gooseneck lamp was behind her, lighting the desk, and leaving her body in silhouette. Her long legs draped either side of the chair, her bare back, and the straight brown hair that touched her shoulders—

All at once, she stopped.

I stood where I was, unsure what to do. I was too frightened to speak, and too entranced to run.

She spun around and looked into my eyes.

It was Rebecca Hawthorne. A totally naked Rebecca Hawthorne.

She rose to her feet, locking her mesmerizing green-brown gaze onto mine, as if casting a spell. The fullness of her curves was enticing, and the sight of her pert nipples added a thrilling edge. My eyes wandered down to her wide hips as she shifted from foot to foot, each movement a tantalizing invitation.

She emanated a raw sexuality, and despite the cold, I was totally and completely aroused.

Chandra had easily seduced me, but staring at the naked woman before me, she seemed to possess knowledge beyond that of any courtesan. I knew without a doubt if I made love to her, I would forget all thoughts of Chandra.

Her eyes went to the bulge in my pajamas, then returned to mine as a smile played on her lips.

Suddenly I could see the desk lamp and the typewriter behind her — no, through her.

Her glorious naked body faded away, and as she disappeared, she blew me a kiss.

All the while, those amazing eyes remained focused on mine.

Then they were gone as well.

I released a pent-up breath. It came out as mist.

I was alone, and still in possession of a massive hard-on. I pulled the robe tightly around me, ignoring my excited state, and approached the desk.

In the typewriter was a half-finished page.

Page fifty.

I took a step back, trying to understand what I saw and why it affected me so viscerally.

With trembling hands, I poured a scotch with no ice, as I needed the fiery liquid to warm myself.

The room was warming up as the heater came on.

I stood there dumbly, staring at my typewriter.

Or was it now our typewriter?

I had seen a ghost. An actual freakin' ghost.

I gulped down the rest of the Scotch. I had to do something, anything, to understand, to make sense of this evening.

I used my phone as a hotspot and got online with my laptop. Since it was the middle of the night, there seemed to be little interference and I had a powerful signal for once. It loaded pages slowly, but I started a full web search on Rebecca Hawthorne.

I wanted to know more about her, not the stuff the police issued when she vanished, or her publisher put out to sell books.

I found an article in some online blog titled:

Five Female Writers As Fascinating As Their Fiction

The article featured Virginia Woolf, Mary Shelley and others, including Rebecca Hawthorne. The article was a collection of rumors about each woman, some proven, written in an evocative style.

Rebecca Hawthorne was born in Connecticut in the 1970s. She was an exceptionally intelligent child who excelled in both poetry and art. She married at nineteen and was plagued by mental illness during her early twenties, suffering terrible postpartum depression after her daughter's birth.

Claiming she could only write in solitude, she produced her two novels while living away from her husband and daughter. Claiming this was necessary, she said it was because of her habits, such as writing in the middle of the night and preferring to write while naked. In an interview, they quoted her as saying, "When I write, I want to be totally free of everything: responsibilities, a normal life, and even my clothes."

She disappeared in 2004 while in the Pocono mountains on a writing retreat. Some say she wanted no more of her old life, assumed a new identity, and lives in hiding to this day.

I knew the last part wasn't true. Whatever happened to Rebecca happened here, in this cabin.

And I had just seen her ghost to prove it.

I looked up a few more things and tried to track down her husband or her daughter, but I had little luck.

Finally, exhaustion washing over me, I sat in the recliner and leaned it back. Wrapped in my bathrobe, I closed my eyes.

I am sure I fell asleep and was dreaming. I was standing in the cabin's main room, looking at the typewriter on the desk.

A pair of hands came up from behind and wrapped around me.

"I can feel you," a woman's voice said, deep and throaty in my ear. "I haven't been able to feel anything for a long time."

Long, red fingernails rubbed my chest. I felt her breasts against my back.

I swallowed and croaked, "Rebecca?"

I felt her chuckle, which sounded like purring, against my back. "You know me?"

"I know of you. I would like to find out what happened."

She nibbled my ear. "I'm not sure myself. Maybe you can help me remember."

My phone pulled me out of the dream. I came awake, lying on my recliner, my heart going like a triphammer and, once again, completely aroused.

It felt like I closed my eyes only moments before, but there was sunlight pouring in the window.

I staggered to my phone. "H-Hello."

"Mr. Riley?" The voice had a thick New England accent, New Hampshire or Maine.

"This is Joe Riley. Who's this?"

"This he-yuh is Ben Connelly. Dan told me you wanted to talk to me about something that happened back in aught-four."

I had a crashing headache making me feel my head was splitting open, but tried to stay focused. "Yes, sir. Could I meet with you?"

"I have the time. But I gotta tell you, I'm not one to go spreading tales about any of the folks I was a caretaker for."

"It's okay, sir," I said, rubbing my forehead. "I'm Rick — uh — Richard Riley's nephew. I only want to know about a guest who went missing."

There was a long silence on the other end of the phone. "The writer lady."

"Yes sir. Trust me, I will keep anything you tell me in the strictest confidence."

"We'll see about that, young fellah. Let me give you my address…"

I quickly jotted down his information, and he said I should come by at noon.

"I have to warn you, Mr. Joe Riley, you might not like everything I have to say."

With that, he ended the call.

My head was spinning from my adventure in the night, my odd dream, and his even stranger warning,

I started the coffeemaker as I wondered if I was going to get any answers today.

Or if I even knew the right questions to ask.

Eight

Researching Rebecca

The address he gave me was a thirty-minute drive away in Hawley, Pennsylvania.

I pulled off the main road and onto a side street, and finally a dirt road before I pulled into the driveway at a cabin in the woods.

Such was life in the Pocono Mountains.

As I reached his cabin, he was sitting outside on the porch. He was a weathered, yet dignified, older man. Although he was in a chair and sat with shoulders hunched, I figured standing up, he'd be around six feet tall. His thinning hair was a distinguished shade of gray with streaks of white. He dressed in a denim shirt and pants with work boots, and his clothing had spots of paint and stains on them. He raised a hand to acknowledge my arrival.

I pulled up next to a ramshackle pickup truck that looked like it survived a war — barely. The back of the tailgate had the word 'INTERNATIONAL' and from the rounded corners and overall design, I guessed someone built it in the 1940s or 50s.

I walked up to the porch and Connelly rose, meeting me eye to eye. He possessed a kind face, lined with wrinkles that bore witness to a life well-lived.

"Thank you for seeing me, Mr. Connelly," I said, offering my hand.

"Ay-yuh," he responded. "Wish it could be about better business, I'll tell yuh."

He looked me over from head to foot and gestured to a chair. As I sat, he returned to the rocker he'd been in when I pulled up.

I glanced at the door of the house. "Is there a Mrs. Connelly, sir?"

"There used to be. I was married to her for right near fifty years. She passed away, 'bout five years back."

"I'm sorry," I said.

"We had a good life, a good marriage. No children, I'm afraid we weren't lucky in that department, so we just accepted it as the Lord's will." He looked at me. "But don't feel bad for me, young man. The problem with gettin' old is you lose people, more 'n more."

I nodded, not sure what to say.

"Why are you interested in that lady writer?" He went on. "No one's asked me about her for damn near twenty years."

"I inherited the cabin from my uncle just recently, and the history interests me. I mean, I'm going to live there."

"You planning to stay he-yuh year round?" he asked with a lifted eyebrow.

"Yes, sir."

"Better get yourself a good snow shovel," he said. "As I recall, Mr. Riley was only a summer guest."

I decided I should get to the reason I came. "What can you tell me about Rebecca Hawthorne?"

"I was they-yuh at the cabin the day she arrived. She rode up with young Mr. Robert and your cousins," he said.

"Liam and Ashley," I said. "All three of them were there?"

"Ah-yuh, and having a high time, let me tell yuh," he said. "It was about three or four in the afternoon, and I was certain they'd been drinkin' already. The younger boy was almost falling down. Mr. Robert, he hid it well enough, but I saw the flush in his cheeks. So the three of them help her move a couple suitcases into the cabin, and they're laughing and carrying on."

"What was your impression of Ms. Hawthorne?"

"She was a looker, I'll tell yuh. She was older than your cousins, 'bout thirty at the time, be my guess. But a man looking at her might think about givin' up anything to be with her. She was like a force of nature, and your cousin Liam stared at her like he was dying o' thirst and she was the last bottle of water on earth. Made you feel sorry for the fellah."

"Did he seem attracted to her?" I asked.

"Smitten would be the word I would use, and that Ms. Hawthorne — she played him like a fiddle."

"So they all stayed there at the cabin with Rebecca?"

"Best as I know. Word out at the time was they were playing music late into the night, and there were rumors they went swimming in the lake."

"That's no big deal. All of us swam in the lake as kids."

"Well, they weren't kids, and it was the night of the full moon. Now, I'm not one to spread rumors, but one of my clients had me up fixing' her water heater that week. She lived in the cabin across the lake. She told me that the four of them were swimming at night without nothing on."

From the little I read online about Rebecca, such actions didn't surprise me. But Robert, Liam, and Ash? I couldn't picture it.

"She saw them at night?"

"Mrs. Kinney — that was the lady's name — she was a bit of a busybody. She always had a pair of binoculars near the window that opened out on the lake. I imagine she got herself an eyeful that night. Claimed the men and women just lay out on the old dock with towels and nothing else."

I still couldn't imagine my cousins acting that way. But the thought of Rebecca, standing naked in my front room, continued to linger in my mind.

"So after 'bout a week, the others all go back to town, leavin' the writer lady up there, and things stayed pretty quiet into the fall. Your cousins were visitin' her on the weekends. Sometimes it was Mr. Robert. Sometimes it was Ms. Ashley. Mostly it was the younger cousin, Mr. Liam. That got people's mouths flapping, I'll tell ya. The word was that Ms. Hawthorne was a married lady with a husband and a daughter."

A husband and a daughter. That was what I read in the article online. I wondered if I could track them down.

"One day she calls the company, and back then, we were called Pocono Property Maintenance. So they get a call from the writer lady saying her heat went out. This was in early October, and I knew what it was. It was an old propane heat-uh back then, not the fancy thing Dan Stevens said you got now. It ran off a pair of propane tanks the size of helium tanks. I figured the tank she was using had run out, and it was time to switch tanks. Well, that was a full day for me, and I didn't get up there until late, eight or nine at night. But I got a flashlight, and I figured I could handle it."

He sat back in his chair, lost in the memory. "I knock on the door and the lady opens it, wearing a bathrobe wrapped around herself and a fire going in the fireplace. She looks at me, glad to see me, like we're old friends. She brings me in and points at the heater, and does this little pouting thing that would make any man drag himself over glass to make her happy."

He rocked, as if the recollection so affected him, he needed to move. "I get the tanks switched over, go back inside and get it going. She claps her hands and laughs like it was the funniest thing she ever saw and pours me a drink. We sit and talk for a minute, and she looks at me like I was the most interesting fellah she ever met. It was pretty cle-yuh she was a few drinks ahead of me. She leaned forward and her robe opens enough for me to see her goods."

He stopped rocking and planted his feet on the ground, his eyes locked with mine. "Lemme tell ya, young man. I was sixty-five back then. The missus and I were going through a rough patch, as married folk sometimes do. I had been faithful to my wife for over thirty years. But for a moment, and it was a long moment, I wanted that writer lady like I'd never wanted a woman before in my life. And sixty-five or not, I was ready, I'll tell yuh."

"So what happened?"

"I finished my drink real fast and headed for the door. The writer lady says I should stay; we'll have some fun. But I got outta there like the devil was chasing me, and I'm not sure he wasn't."

Having confronted Rebecca's spirit the previous night, I understood perfectly.

"So a week goes by, and young Mr. Liam shows up at the management office. I know it was late October because I was putting up the Halloween decorations. This was about a week after I fixed her heater and she offered me that drink."

"What did he want?"

"He comes around and calls up to me on a ladder, asks if I've seen Ms. Hawthorne. I tells him I fixed her propane heater a week earlier, and he leaves. Next thing I know, the police come around wantin' to talk to me."

"Talk to you?" I repeated. "Why you?"

"Seems like I might have been the last person to see Miss Hawthorne before she disappeared."

I frowned. "Were you a suspect?"

This made him smile. "In what? She was gone, her luggage with her, and no one knew anything. I told the police about fixing her heater and having a drink, didn't mention that I thought she made a pass at me. Then again, maybe she was just trying to get a rise out of an old man for shits and giggles."

"And that was the last of it?"

"Some reportahs came around and asked a few questions, and I just told them the whitewashed story I told the police." He paused for a moment. "You're actually the only fellah I ever told that she made a pass."

"I'm sure you thought it would only cause trouble."

"It would've caused hell with my missus if she ever found out. But my wife's gone to her reward, and I guess Ms. Hawthorne did, too. So there ain't no harm talking about it at this point."

"I appreciate everything you told me. It really helps give me a clearer understanding of the woman."

"All right then, Mr Joe Riley. You want to tell me why you're so interested? I know you're a writer. The missus bought one of your books."

I felt my face grow red at this. "Really?"

"Ah-yuh. She said it was a good read. But I got to ask yuh, why're you bringin' it up now? It's long over, and they-yuh ain't no good to pick at an old scab."

For a moment I almost said, "Because her ghost is haunting me, and I need to find out why."

But I didn't. I thanked him for his time and headed out.

Driving back, I stopped at a place called the Carini Brick Oven. It offered artisanal coffee, and I got an eggplant parmigiana sandwich that was excellent. I was ravenous, as I had not eaten that morning, except for the cup of coffee.

I thought about my next move.

Using my phone and the Wi-Fi at the restaurant, I took the time to contact a local satellite internet service. I went through all the information and filled out the form — difficult on my phone. Once done, I saw it would be days before someone came to hook it all up.

I wanted to go back to the Milford library, do some research for my novel, and get the feel of the places I was writing about in my book. I also had to send my current pages to the waiting agent, and read those eight-and-a-half pages my ghostly companion added to my manuscript.

Why on earth did I want to play detective with a disappearance that was twenty years old?

Because I had a ghost in my living room.

I still wanted to call Liam, ask him about it, and a better idea occurred to me. I could call Ashley, get her take on all of it. She visited Rebecca with Robert and Liam, and maybe she noticed things that could give me some insights.

Knowing how busy her cafe was, I decided to wait until the evening.

So, I drove to the Pike County Library in Milford, and was glad I'd thrown my laptop in the car. Instead of using the library computer, I would get on the library's Wi-Fi and download anything I wanted to review.

As I went in, Emily looked up from the reference desk and smiled.

"Can't keep you away," she said.

I held up my laptop bag. "I have no internet, but the staff here is friendly and helpful."

She pulled a preprinted slip of paper off her desk and handed it to me. It had the name of the server and the passcode.

I nodded. "That speeds things up."

"How do you like Rebecca Hawthorne?"

I was tongue-tied.

She looked disheartened. "You didn't have time to read her books yet?"

I breathed out heavily, realizing she was talking about the books I'd borrowed. "Actually, I started *Whispers Of Moonlight*. It's good, superb. It surprised me."

"I love her stuff. Her use of language, the plot twists," she said, her eyes grew wide. "Oh! I don't know how far you are in the book. I'd better not give anything away."

Her expression when she said this was the cutest thing I'd ever seen a lady do.

"So tomorrow night is still good?" I asked.

"Sure. How do you feel about having dinner here in Milford?"

"What do you like?"

"Well, if you want a really nice dinner, there's the Waterside Inn. But if it's a budget thing, there's—"

"No, that sounds fine. Let's hammer out the details before I leave today, okay?"

She smiled again. "You know where to find me."

That went better than our first meeting. I was a little more relaxed. I wandered around until I found a semi-comfortable chair and booted up my laptop. After spending some time researching Prague for my novel, I brought up a new search for Rebecca.

This time, I downloaded the news stories about her disappearance. It helped give me dates I might need to know.

I did a web search for Rebecca Hawthorne's husband, but I still couldn't find any information. I would have to read over the downloaded articles when I got back to the cabin.

I shut down my laptop and went to talk to Emily, who was at the reference desk, working on her computer. "I have to get back to my place and get some work done."

She frowned. "You can't work here?"

"To be honest, I'm writing my latest book on a typewriter."

"Really?" she said. "I like the computer because I'm a terrible typist."

"Hard to believe."

"No, it's true. I'm one of those people who look down at my fingers instead of the page when I type. I get all the letters, but they're usually in the wrong order."

"Tomorrow. Should I pick you up?"

She sat up straighter in the chair. "I hope you don't think I'm controlling—"

I felt my jaw tighten at this. That was one of Chandra's lines, right before she told me what to do.

"But can you pick me up and drop me off?" she said and handed me a small sticky note. "This is my address. I would also like you to make the reservation."

She handed me a second note with the Waterside Inn and the phone number.

"I'm happy to do it," I said.

"Good! I like the gentleman to make arrangements, but since you're new to the area, I felt I should help a little."

"And I'm hardly a gentleman," I said and heard how that sounded. I quickly added. "After all, I'm a writer."

This made her chuckle, and I felt I'd saved the moment. First dates are the worst, because you never know how you're supposed to act. But I liked Emily and looked forward to going out to dinner with her.

"See you tomorrow around six," I said.

"Six is good," she said.

"If anything comes up, I have your number."

"Okay," she replied and went back to her computer.

I headed out before I said anything stupid, or had I done that already? It had been years since I'd dated, and I was never good at it. It's probably how Chandra came in and took over my life — I let her. Letting her dominate me and tell me what to do made life easier. Meanwhile, I wrote books, lost in the worlds of my imagination.

I drove home, gathering my courage to face the extra pages typed last night. Once there, I made some coffee and glared at the scotch, wanting a drink in the worst way.

It shocked me when at six, a van pulled into my driveway, with a ladder on its roof and the sides emblazoned with StellarNet. I walked out as a man in overalls came out of the driver's side of the vehicle.

"Are you Joe Riley?" he asked, looking at his clipboard. "I have you down for an install."

"Glad to hear it."

"Yeah, I got everything in the van: satellite dish, mounting hardware, coaxial cables, and a satellite modem that's also your Wi-Fi router."

"That sounds great. Do you need any help?"

"Nah, I do this all the time," he said, then glanced at the van. "If you could help me with the ladder, though. I usually have a second guy with me, but he called in sick. That's why I'm still working this late in the day."

I helped him get the ladder down. We went around to the back of the house, and together we put it up.

"Yeah, this is good," he said, as he made sure the ladder was stable. "You've got a clear line of sight to the southern sky. You should get a good signal."

"Glad to hear it. It's been rough without an internet connection."

"Up here in the mountains, the satellite's the only way to go," he said. "Do you mind helping with the ladder when I'm done?"

"No problem," I said, and went back into the cabin.

I heard him up on the roof, mounting the brackets to hold the dish, as I brought in wood from the nearby woodpile. For some weird reason, I didn't want to work on the pages with another person there.

Soon he had the dish up and connected wires from it to a handheld device about the size of an iPad. He called down to me. "You got great alignment."

I paused with my load of wood. "That's good."

A few minutes later, I saw a long drill poke through under the eaves, and a coaxial cable shoved in through the wall. He quickly came inside, connected it to the modem, and put it on top of a bookcase, out of sight. I helped him carry the ladder back to his van. He handed me my paperwork and drove away.

Finally alone, I went through the pages.

Once again, the writing was clear, concise, and pushed the plot forward easily and neatly. It was still my style, but with those little nuances that made me think of Rebecca's book.

I made dinner and drank only one glass of wine. I wanted a scotch; I stuck to wine for the part I had to do next.

I phoned Ashley.

"Finally, I get a night off, and my favorite cousin calls," she said as she answered.

"Hey Ash. How's Brew Haven?"

"My manager, Kate, is a gem, and I even get nights off. I might have to have a social life."

"That's good," I said, and tried to think of how to bring up the situation. "Um… Ash… can I ask you about something?"

"Sure, what's up?"

"It's about Rebecca Hawthorne."

Silence on the other end of the phone.

"Hello?" I said.

"Sorry, that just came out of the blue. What are you asking about?"

"Back in the day, didn't you, Liam, and Robert, hang out with her?"

"Joey, that was, like, twenty years ago," she said instead of an answer.

"That's what everyone keeps telling me. It's just I was talking to some locals—"

"Fucking busybodies!" Ash snapped, which surprised me. "That's the reason I haven't been back to that cabin all these years. That old biddy, Mrs. Kinney, was always watching us with those damn binoculars."

"I heard you might've gone skinny dipping," I said.

"Damn straight," she said with a hint of pride. "That was Rebecca's idea. She said if the bitch was going to spy on us, she'd give her something to look at. All four of us went down to the dock without a stitch of clothing."

She suddenly burst out laughing.

"Can you tell me anything about Rebecca? How did you meet her?"

"Why are you bringing this up, Joey? What's going on?"

Not much, Ash—she's just working with me on my book and stirring up some intense feelings of desire.

I didn't say what I was thinking.

"I'm curious. She disappeared, and I read Liam reported her missing." I let that sink in. "Were Rebecca and Liam an item?"

This made her laugh again. "An item? No, I don't think they were an item. Liam followed her around like a puppy, and would have done anything she asked. He adored her, worshipped her. But Rebecca wasn't looking for any kind of connection. She just wanted to use the cabin to write a book."

"But the—"

"Look, if you want to know how we met her, talk to Bobby. He introduced her to us."

"Robert did?"

"Right. If anyone was involved with her, it would be him. I have to go."

Abruptly, she ended the call.

I sat there staring at the phone. Robert was having an affair with Rebecca? He wasn't married back then, so it was possible.

But why was Ashley so annoyed I brought it up?

Nine

A Visit In The Night

It was later than I liked to work, but I went back to the book.

It was one of the weirdest things in my life to start on a half-finished page someone else typed. But even stranger, it felt completely natural to start there.

In only a few minutes, in my mind, I was in Prague with Soul and Miranda and their team. They were desperately on the trail of the one hacker who could get past the security of the US and Russia, as they dealt with setbacks and complications.

An informer sent them to a location (a building I saw during my visit to the library using Google Maps) where they could catch the madman. Instead, waiting for them was an execution squad. With speed and cleverness, Soul and Miranda took out the bad guys and captured one to get information. Unfortunately, they lost a member of their team.

Gun battles and describing them were my forte, and I created a tapestry of the battle in a captivating narrative, including the smell of gunpowder, the flash of weapons, and the stink of sweat as Soul and Miranda fought.

I had ten pages done before I knew it.

It was past eleven, and I was all in. I changed into my pajamas, put on socks, and brought the afghan out to the main room.

I put the paper into the typewriter like I did every night and shut out all the lights. The moon bathed the main room in a soft glow streaming in through the window. I could see the desk and typewriter in silhouette and could make out the stone fireplace.

Since it was seasonably warm, I felt silly lying with the afghan on me, but I wanted to keep it on my lap in case I needed it.

I was craving more alcohol and felt restless; the afghan was making me sweat. I pondered getting up and having one little Scotch. That would be enough to calm me down, help me sleep.

While arguing with myself, I fell asleep. When I next opened my eyes, the room looked totally different. The clock on the electric stove read 2:30 in the green digital display.

Typewriter keys tapped a staccato rhythm like bones cracking.

I raised my head and gasped.

Bathed in the dim light, a figure spun around in the desk chair and faced me.

Rebecca Hawthorne… naked once again.

She smiled. "Did I wake you?" She rose and took a step toward me, a hungry look in her eyes.

Her lips moved, but I didn't hear her voice. I felt the words in my mind.

Her eyes were on the empty couch, and not on me, as if she was speaking to someone I couldn't see.

I spoke. "You can't be here."

She didn't answer me, but said, "Since you're awake, I need some inspiration."

I got up with the blanket wrapped around me, aware of how cold the room was, and went to the sofa to intercept her gaze. Those amazing eyes, green in the middle, surrounded by brown.

She continued to stare at the couch, but I was now in her line of vision. She kept speaking. "If you don't want to, then go back to sleep. I've just hit a rough patch and I need to work it out, and you know it helps me."

She reached out a hand and brushed my face.

I felt it. Her touch was icy and yet warm on my cheek at the same time.

Her eyes were now on me, aware of me, aware of my presence.

"That's nice, isn't it?" she leaned close, pressing her naked breasts against me. They also felt cool through the flannel of my pajama top.

"This is impossible," I croaked in an unfamiliar voice.

She pushed gently, and I fell back onto the couch.

"Let me take charge." She stood over me with a smile still on her face.

She climbed on top of me, and I could feel the weight of her, the same as a woman of flesh and blood. She put her lips to mine. They were cold, but her tongue snaked into my mouth, and it was warm and alive.

This instantly aroused me, and her soft laugh hummed through the kiss.

She pulled back, and a chilly hand reached into my pajama bottoms. The coolness of her hand made me groan, but it also made me harder.

"Yes, this is what I need," she said. "Just a little inspiration."

The entire situation was impossible — but I didn't want it to stop.

She slid down and took me into her mouth.

It was unlike anything I'd ever felt before. The chill of her lips, but the heat of her mouth — the pleasure drove a primal moan from my throat.

"How are you able to do this?" I groaned.

She lifted her head, her lips glistening in the lamplight. "I want more." She gazed down at my hard-on with hunger burning in her eyes. "I want it all."

With a look of intense concentration, she straddled me, lowering herself onto me with aching deliberation.

I gasped, penetrating her so slowly, it was blissful agony. She threw her head back and moaned. Her breath fogged, as if joining with me had transformed her into solid flesh, warm and alive.

I reached up to caress her breasts as moans of pleasure escaped from deep in her throat. All I wanted was to touch, feel, and become one with her.

Shifting, she drove her hips against mine, plunging me deeply into the center of her. Rational thought became impossible. She thrust herself against me, slippery and aching. The contrast of her cool breasts and her fiery center almost sent me over the edge. I fought for control as her body seemed to grow warmer, her rhythm increasing, her pace speeding up.

She was becoming more real, her breasts turning a dusky pink as I massaged them. Her cheeks flushed as she frowned in concentration, pushing against me, reaching for her climax.

Her speed increased, becoming almost frantic, like the dance of a whirling dervish. She thrust her hips against mine so hard it was almost painful.

All I could do was thrash under her, moaning and crying out in both pleasure and pain. We filled the air with the musk of sex, and I knew I could not hold back much longer.

She stopped moving abruptly, her eyes opened wide, her mouth fell open with a cry, and her pelvis vibrated. Actually vibrated on top of me.

Her body pulsed against mine, her body flushed and solid, her head thrown back in rapture.

The power of my orgasm was so strong, I blacked out, losing all sense of the world.

When I opened my eyes after what had only felt like a moment or two, daylight was pouring in the window. I was naked and exposed.

It had all been a dream, nothing more. A vivid dream, and one of the few wet dreams I'd had in my entire life.

All I wanted to do was get cleaned up and forget the entire thing had happened. I tried to stand, but my knees gave out and I returned to the couch. I ran my hands through my hair, aware of the headache that felt like it might split my head in two.

How could I have such a headache? Despite the temptation, I'd had only one glass of wine. Maybe it had been two glasses of wine, but it wasn't the large amount of Scotch I'd been consuming lately.

Maybe the headache was withdrawal symptoms.

I headed to the bathroom for aspirin, then to the bedroom to get out of my clothing, which was damp with sweat and other bodily fluids.

But what did I expect? I didn't have sex with an actual woman. There was nothing there.

Or was there?

It all felt so real, and it was one of the best orgasms of my life.

I went out to make coffee and checked the pile of manuscript pages. I had stopped at page 60.

The face-down page was numbered 70.

A part of my mind — I would guess the weird part — reflected on what a useful collaborator Rebecca was. It's not every writing partner who knocks out ten pages of work and then provides mind-blowing sex.

I got my coffee and sat down to read.

The new pages drove the story forward vividly. Soul and Miranda struggled to recover from the harrowing aftermath of their brutal battle, tending to wounds that cut far deeper than just skin. Exhausted yet determined, they confronted their prisoner, each question laced with urgency, as they pressed him to reveal Romanov's whereabouts. The captive broke under their relentless pressure.

Armed with this crucial information, Soul and Miranda turned towards each other, trust seared deeper into their bond by shared trials and sacrifices. In silent understanding, they crafted a plan to move forward — an intricate strategy woven from desperation and courage. This danger forced them to lean on one another more fiercely than ever before, their lives now intertwined as intricately as their fates.

I took this opportunity to set up the scanner and scanned the pages onto my computer. I then emailed them to Meredith Thompson with a simple cover saying: I would like to meet with her, please share the pages with the publisher, and thank you for your offer.

Finishing up, I heard a car coming up the cabin's gravel driveway. I walked around to the front of the house to see my cousin Robert drive up in his Mercedes-Benz.

Unexpected company might not be a good sign, and he did not look happy.

"Robert," I said as I came out the door. "I wasn't expecting you."

"Probably not," he said, getting out of the car, annoyed. "But I spoke with Ashley and decided it would be best to come up here and clear up any situations."

I gestured to the front door of the cabin. "Come in. Can I offer you coffee?"

"No, I've had to cut back. My stomach can't take it anymore."

He led the way, and I followed. After all, he knew the cabin as well as I did. Robert was the oldest of the cousins, and as kids, he intimidated all of us into doing what he wanted. Except Ash, who kept him in line.

He faced me as I shut the door. "Ash tells me you were asking about Rebecca Hawthorne."

I would not let him play the intimidation game with me, and without answering, I walked to the kitchen and started a second cup of coffee for myself. "I understood that you, Ash, and Liam knew her."

"That was a long time ago."

"I know. She disappeared about twenty years ago. From what I've read, she was working on a book here at Whispering Pines."

"Why does that matter now?" he demanded. "Why even bring it up?"

For a moment, I wanted to tell him everything, the strange appearance of the pages, the ghostly woman at the desk, maybe even the strange sexual encounter that might have only been a dream.

Instead, I said. "I'm reading her books. I'd like to know more about her, about why she came here to the cabin."

He paced and finally he said, "We met at a book release party thrown by a publisher in New York. I accompanied Dad because he didn't want to go alone and Mom hated those things. I thought it would be fun."

I was familiar with such events and seldom attended them myself.

Robert went on. "She was a little older than me, and at first, she didn't impress me. She wore a plain, loose-fitting dress, had glasses on, and had her hair pulled back. But when I found out who she was, I had to talk to her. I'd read both *Whispers Of Moonlight* and *Shadows Of Deception*."

"You were a fan?"

"A big one. We got to talking, and she whispered to me that her outfit was a disguise."

"A disguise?" I repeated. "What was she, a spy?"

Robert shook his head. "No, she told me she needed a disguise to wear in her regular life."

"What does that mean?"

"I don't know. She said things like that. Then, she told me she was getting ready to write her next book and was desperate to find someplace secluded where she could write it."

"You suggested the cabin."

"I did! When I told Dad who she was, he said that we could make the place available to her the following fall. She told him that the timing was perfect. She still had things to clear from her plate. I gave her my phone number and email address. After that, we'd talk or email every month, putting it together."

He sat down heavily at the table. "I remember the weekend she came up. Mom and Dad had gone back to New Jersey, but Liam and Ash wanted to meet the famed author. She came by train to Port Jervis, and that's where we went to pick her up. I expected her to look the way she did at the event, glasses and all that."

"Did she?"

"No. The woman who came off that train was completely different. She wore no glasses, her hair loose, and a brightly colored dress showing every curve. More than that, she had this… aura… around her. She got off the train with two suitcases and strode towards us, and the three of us stared open-mouthed. I think Liam almost swallowed his tongue."

"Why the change?"

"I don't know, but from the way she acted, you'd think she was just released from prison. She utterly mesmerized all of us with just the power of her presence. As we drove to the cabin, we bombarded her with questions, eager for more insight into her life. She simply laughed and instructed us not to mention her 'so-called normal life' during her stay. Her focus was to be solely in her artist persona and the experiences she would have and anything we would share."

"What happened when you got to the cabin?"

"She kind of took over. We spent days drinking, swimming, talking. Liam followed her like a puppy, and Ash felt she'd found a new best friend."

"And you?"

Robert sighed again. "I have to tell you, she was pretty eccentric."

"What do you mean?"

"Here in the cabin, you know there are only two bedrooms. The girls took the smaller one with the two beds, and Liam took the other. I slept out in the main room on a cot. On the first night Rebecca got here, I was sleeping, and a sound woke me up. It was the sound of a typewriter. I looked over at the clock, and it was two-thirty in the morning."

A shiver crept down my spine.

"I see Rebecca sitting at that desk, right there," he said and pointed at the desk. "She was typing away without a stitch of clothing on. She's sitting there in the buff in the middle of the night."

"Wh-what did you do?" I said, so surprised I stammered.

A small grin appeared on his face. "Stayed quiet. I have to tell you I got an eyeful that night. For a thirty-year-old lady with a daughter, she was magnificent."

"Did you sleep with her?"

"No, but believe me, I thought about it. After seeing her in all her glory, I was ready. But I knew she was married, and back then

I had a strict rule about not getting involved with married ladies. Besides, Liam was totally smitten, and I didn't want to get in the middle of that."

"But you all went skinny-dipping."

Robert smiled sadly. "You heard about that, did you? Yes, we'd seen the old lady with the binoculars always watching us, day after day. Then, on the night of the full moon, we had a touch of Indian Summer, and the cabin was hot. We had fans going and had been drinking all day long, but we couldn't get cool. Ash said we should all go for a swim, and Rebecca said we should swim in the nude to give the old lady something to gawk at. We were all pretty drunk, so we peeled off our clothes and walked down to the lake."

He looked up at the ceiling. "The moon was so bright, we could see the path without a problem. We must have been a sight, Liam and me carrying our towels, our dongs hanging out. Rebecca brought a towel, but carried it folded up on her shoulder, exposing her charms to the world. Ash covered herself with her towel. We got down to the dock, and Rebecca went over and just pulled the towel off Ash dramatically, which made Ash cover herself with her hands. Rebecca gave her ass a smack and told her to loosen up. We all got into the water and splashed around, then sat on the dock until we cooled off. We laughed and splashed and just had a good time."

"That was all?"

He looked up at the ceiling, his mind lost in memory. "Yes, but I could never shake the feeling that it — almost — was more. There was an intense, reckless atmosphere that night radiating from Rebecca herself. It was like she was ready to do anything with any of us."

"Ashley, too?"

He drew a deep breath and seemed to come back to earth. "At that point, even she was sitting out, not bothering to cover herself. I think she was the reason we kept control. Ash stood up and told us she could sleep now, and that broke the spell. We headed back to the cabin. That night, I heard the typewriter and woke to see Rebecca typing in the buff again."

"How long did you stay when Rebecca was here?"

"That was the last day. We all woke up with hangovers, except Rebecca, who appeared undamaged by all the drinking. We loaded up the car, said our goodbyes, and all of us hugged her. The next time I went to the cabin was to see Liam."

"I read in the news coverage that he was the one who reported her missing."

"He called me right after he made that report, and he was losing it. I came up — driving these roads in the late fall — to be with him and help him deal with it. He confessed he'd been coming up every other weekend to visit and that he'd slept with her — or rather, she slept with him. From what Liam told me, she took charge of the sex, but Liam was a willing participant. He kept repeating, 'Why did she do it, to leave me like that?' over and over."

"Do you know anything else?"

"What else is there to know? The lady came, used the cabin, banged my brother, wrote her book, and took off. Simple as that. Look, Joey, there's no big conspiracy or anything. She was flighty, and she took off, leaving Liam a mess. Of course, Liam has been a mess most of his life, but this was one more thing he didn't need. I told him that sleeping with a married woman always goes wrong."

I nodded. "Thanks for telling me. I think I know her better now."

"Well, I'm glad to hear that!" he said with sarcasm. Then his tone became serious. "Look, I came all the way out here to tell you just to drop it. Liam went through therapy and bouts of depression over that lady for years, and I don't need you to bring it back up."

"But Liam was coming up here. Maybe he knows where she went or what her mindset was—"

Robert stood. "Damn it, Joey, she's gone; it's ancient history. And I'm telling you, bringing it up will only cause trouble. Liam was in love with her, and even Ash felt Rebecca was a friend, and maybe a mentor. Whatever happened, we all knew once her book was done, she was going to go back to her old life."

I nodded, trying to appear I agreed with my older cousin.

I escorted him to his car, apologized that my investigation had forced him to drive all the way up here, and sent him on his way.

But I was more determined than ever to find out what happened to Rebecca Hawthorne.

Ten

First Dates Are Awkward

I spent the rest of the afternoon writing and getting ready for my date. I was in luck, as the sequence I worked on involved both Soul and Miranda being nervous and on edge. That reflected my own feelings perfectly.

What would we talk about? I mean, she was a librarian, so she liked books. But I wasn't knowledgeable about many writers, only the ones I liked.

Also, there was the age difference. I guessed she was thirty, and I was forty. Not exactly robbing the cradle, but I didn't want to come across as the older guy trying to recapture his youth.

With all the distractions of my own thoughts, it took all afternoon to finish the ten pages. Then I got ready, showered and shaved, to make myself look acceptable.

I mean, it was a first date, so nothing would go too far, right?

What do you care, Joey? You got laid last night.

Or did I? What had happened other than a lonely man getting off because he had a dream?

You know it wasn't just a dream.

I also know a ghost, even a female ghost, cannot become flesh and actually have sex. Nothing like that has ever happened.

Or has it? I took a few minutes and did a web search on my phone.

Succubus was the word that came up.

I found a couple of articles, the first of which claimed that men who have sexual activity with one of them would have their life essence absorbed by the spirit and die.

Not the scientific approach I'd hoped for. I continued the search.

I found medical literature exploring the connection between the succubus and incubus legends, claiming they resulted from sleep paralysis and hypnagogic hallucinations. These phenomena can lead individuals to believe they are being held down by a demon.

That would explain my feeling the weight of a full-grown woman on top of me.

The article suggested that many so-called alien abductions resulted from this phenomenon, where people hallucinated intricate stories of aliens taking them and experimenting on them.

It was all overwhelming. Either I was suffering from sleep paralysis or I'd had sex with a ghost. I had no history of sleep problems, having nothing worse than a few bad dreams. But none of my dreams ever had the reality of what I'd experienced.

With questions still running through my mind, I closed down my search, got into a suit and tie, and headed up to Milford to meet Emily.

Following my GPS on my phone, it guided me to a green colonial house in the center of town, only blocks from the library. I got out of the car and headed up the walkway. The door opened, and Emily came out. She looked different from at the library. She still wore her thick glasses, but her hair was loose. Instead of the work clothes of a blouse and pants, she wore a light blue summer dress that hugged her curves, and looked dressy without being too formal.

She raised her eyebrows at my suit and tie. "You look good."

"You look amazing," I said. "I didn't know you lived so close to the library. It's just down the street."

"I walk there most days. Shall we go?"

I went to the car and opened her door. I was doing my best to be a gentleman, but nowadays men don't know what to do about opening doors. If we open them, are we saying women are weak? If we don't, are we being rude?

Fortunately, there were no dramatics. Emily nodded in appreciation, got in, and I closed the door. We were soon driving down the street.

"First dates are so awkward, aren't they?" she said.

I let out a pent-up breath and chuckled. "I've been thinking that all day."

"If we just accept the fact that we're both going to say and do all the wrong things—"

"And make fools of ourselves—"

"Right! Then maybe we can relax and have a pleasant time."

"You are a very sensible lady, Emily."

"I prefer to think I'm realistic," she replied. "Oh, there's the parking lot."

I pulled into a space, surprised at how little I'd driven to get to the location. "We could've walked here from your place."

"You can walk me home. The sun won't set until after nine."

That was an adroit move. She was already implying our date would go well, so I could relax.

We walked to the building, which was quite impressive. The extensive structure blended Victorian elegance with rustic warmth, and featured an airy wraparound porch with tables for outdoor dining.

My palms were moist with sweat as we walked into the crowded restaurant. I glanced over at Emily, radiant in the flowing summer dress, her dark hair cascading down to her shoulders.

The hostess led us to our table, and we sat with an exchange of nervous smiles as an awkward silence filled the air. I felt my heart thud loudly in my chest. I fumbled with the napkin on my lap, trying to gather my thoughts, but everything I mentally rehearsed suddenly vanished from my mind.

"This is quite a historic place," Emily said, as a waiter brought us menus and we looked them over. "In the early twentieth century, William and Elizabeth Kensington saw the spot by the river and loved it. They bought a wooden cottage and transformed it into an inn."

"And since it was beside the water—" I began.

She smiled again. "They named it the Waterside Inn. But the place got a reputation even back then. Turns out Elizabeth was quite the chef. And back then, people didn't always accept women in that role, running a kitchen. So most of her staff was female, as they didn't mind working for a woman chef."

"Good for her!" I said.

We placed our order, and we each got a glass of wine, which helped me relax. Maybe my nervousness was nothing more than the result of reducing my alcohol intake. I would normally have had several drinks by this time of day. One symptom of alcohol withdrawal is nervousness, isn't it?

As the evening unfolded, our conversation became more relaxed, deeper, and more personal. Our initial awkwardness gave way to shared laughter, and I felt a genuine connection. I soon discovered Emily had a bit of a naughty wit, which she had to keep under control at the library.

I genuinely enjoyed her company, and she seemed to enjoy mine. It was towards the end of the meal I asked the question on my mind.

"Emily, do you mind if I ask you how old you are?"

This elicited a teasing smile. She spoke in a fake Southern accent. "Why Mister Riley, I believe that a gentleman never asks a lady her age."

I smiled back. "You're right. So how much do you weigh?"

We both laughed at this.

"Not that it matters, but I'm thirty," she said, and met my eyes. "And you're forty."

I frowned. "How—?"

"I found your birth year listed on Wikipedia. As a librarian, I can actually do math."

I grimaced. "You don't think I'm too…" I stopped talking.

"Too old? Maybe if you wanted to play in the NFL. But no, I don't think you are too old to date a thirty-year-old."

I blew out a breath. "That's good."

"But I will remind you that when you were ten, I had just been born," she said, her brown eyes bright as she teased me. "And when you were twenty, I was only a girl of ten."

I held up my hands in surrender. "Please, I'm aging rapidly right before your eyes."

After dinner, we stepped outside to take a view of the nearby Sawmill River. The gentle lapping of water against the banks as it flowed downstream and the soft evening breeze created a feeling of intimacy.

We walked the six or seven blocks back to the house with her apartment, signaling the end of our date. We paused on the walkway in front.

"I had a great time," I said, annoyed that I was saying such a trite line.

"So did I. As first dates go, I think we did okay."

We lingered, that awkward feeling coming over me again as I was unsure of the proper next step. However, Emily's eyes reflected the same uncertainty mingled with hope, and she took the initiative, leaning in for a shy, yet sweet, goodbye kiss.

"Call me," she said and headed for the door.

"I will," I said as she went inside.

I stood there for a minute, feeling pretty good about myself. The walk back to the car in the twilight left me feeling happy, and I drove home in the same state.

I arrived back at the darkened cabin and realized I had not left a light on. As I got out of my car, my heart skipped a beat. Why did the darkness seem so imposing?

Fear prickled my skin as I fumbled for my phone, desperate to pierce the ominous veil with its feeble glow. The muted light cast eerie shadows on the surrounding trees as I cautiously approached the front door.

With trembling hands, I unlocked and pushed the door open, the creaking sound echoing through the desolate night. As I walked inside, an icy shiver ran down my spine, and I knew, without a doubt, I was not alone.

I glanced over at the desk and I saw someone sitting there, silhouetted in the moonlight. There was a tiny red glowing light, like the eye of a demon staring at me.

"Rebecca?" I whispered.

Exhaling a shaky breath, I reached for the wall switch, illuminating the room in an instant. I fell back with a cry as there was indeed someone sitting in the chair I'd seen Rebecca in, night after night.

Sitting there, looking at me, was my cousin Liam, dressed in a denim jacket, shirt and pants, with tall motorcycle boots.

"Jesus Christ, Liam," I bellowed. "You scared the shit out of me."

He seemed unperturbed by my outburst. He had a lit cigarette in his hand, and I realized what I thought was a glowing red eye was merely the burning tip. "Sorry, cuz. I thought maybe we should talk."

I switched off the light on my phone and put it away. "How the hell did you get in here? Where's your car?"

"I pulled it around back," he said, taking a drag and blowing out smoke. "Come on, man, I know where we keep the spare key. I also helped myself to some of your scotch."

He picked up a glass from the desk that held an amber liquid and a pair of ice cubes, and took a sip.

"Look, Liam, it's not that you're not welcome here," I said, and found I was still angry. "But this is my home. You don't just break into it whenever you want. You call first."

He took another sip from the glass and nodded. "I had to talk to you. Ash and Robert both called me and told me you were asking about Rebecca."

He sucked the cigarette down to the filter, then tapped it out in a coffee mug placed next to the typewriter. Apparently, he found it in the cupboard and chose it for an ashtray.

"You were the one who reported her missing," I said. "I figured you have to know more than what appeared on a police report."

He slugged down the scotch and pulled another cigarette from a crumpled pack, lighting it with an old Zippo lighter. As I observed him, I realized he looked old and incredibly sad.

"That was all a long time ago," he complained. "Why the hell do you have to bring it up now?"

I looked at my cousin. Here he was, forty-eight years old and living like a bum. I was also mad as hell, since he had let himself into my house and scared me.

I had no weapon but the truth. "Because she's here."

The color fell out of his face, and now it was his turn to look frightened. "What?"

"She is here!" I yelled at him. "Every night she visits me. I came out here to find her in the chair you're in right now."

Liam jumped up as if I'd lit his ass on fire and glared down at the chair. "You see her? Right there?

"Yes, and she's naked."

Liam stumbled to the dining table and caught himself on a chair. I rushed to him and helped him to sit.

"No, it can't be, it can't," he murmured.

I helped him into the chair, and he put his head in his hands.

I immediately felt sorry for my cousin and for getting mad at him.

"It's okay, Liam," I said in a soothing tone. "I'm just trying to find out what happened to Rebecca. I don't think she ever left this place. Not alive anyway."

Liam wept, not just crying, but in huge wracking sobs, his face twisted into a mask of despair. Tears streamed down his face, mingling with the dirt and grime that clung to his skin.

"I... I've known all along," he whispered, his words carrying a dark weight. "I knew Rebecca was dead... because I buried her."

Eleven

Rebecca's Death

I backed away from Liam, my eyes searching the room for a weapon. For the first time in my life, I felt I was in danger. He'd driven up here unexpectedly, parked his car around back, and waited here for me in the dark, when only he and I would be here.

"Did you kill her?" I said, barely able to get out the words.

"I loved her," he yelled, then hung his head and wept. "No, I didn't kill her. I could never hurt her. Even when I knew she was leaving me."

I grabbed his glass from the desk, went to the kitchen, and poured another scotch. I set the drink in front of him. "You'd better tell me all about it."

I sat at the desk, several feet away, just to be safe. My fear of Liam being dangerous was passing, and he looked more like a broken man now, incapable of hurting anyone except maybe himself.

He ran a hand under his nose. "From the first time I saw her, I was in love with her."

"You met her at the train station with Robert and Ash?" I said.

"Yes, that was the first time. God, you should have seen her come off that train. It was like a movie — everything slowed down as she came down the steps with her two suitcases. She looked like a goddess."

"How soon did things turn… romantic?

He shook his head. "Not the first week, not with Ash and Bobby there. But one night, toward the end of the first week, we all got drunk off our asses and went skinny-dipping."

"I heard about that."

He lifted his head. "Yeah? Let me tell you, that was torture for me, seeing Rebecca naked. I kept getting a hard-on, and had to jump into the lake over and over to calm down. It wasn't just her body; it was this energy she had."

"But you two became lovers."

"Yes, after we all went home, I came back up the next weekend to see her. On the second night of my visit, I was staying in the second bedroom. In the middle of the night, I feel someone next to me in that tiny bed. It was Rebecca, and she was naked."

"By any chance, was it two-thirty in the morning?"

This surprised him. "I guess. It was in the middle of the night. Anyway, she comes into the room and takes charge. Right there on that skinny little bed, we made love." He sat back and took a shaky breath. "It was beautiful and the most amazing sex I've ever had. I mean, she was so sensual. We spent the next day just making love. She told me I inspired her writing.”

I frowned. “She said that?”

“I guess it was the sex that inspired her writing. I heard only what I wanted to hear.”

“You saw her often?”

“I was working back then, in construction, and could only get up here on the weekends. Then we’d see each other and spend almost all of our time in bed. We even did it down on the dock one night to give the old biddy with the binoculars a show.” He hung his head. “That’s when I told her I loved her.”

“How did she react to that?”

“She said ‘thank you’,” Liam said glumly.

“Ouch.”

“After that, I felt her pulling away. I mean, we still had sex, but she was — emotionally — far away.” He sipped at the scotch I’d put in front of him.

“Did she ever get up at night to write?” I asked.

“Every night. I’d wake up in the master bedroom and she would be gone, and I’d hear typing in the next room. Y’know, since you brought it up, when she’d get up and go type, I used to look over at that old clock radio in there. It always read two-thirty.”

I felt a chill run up my spine as he said this. A habit in life had become a habit in death. And I was the beneficiary.

“Then, one weekend, it all seemed to fall apart. I headed up, and there was a rental car in the driveway.”

“She had another guest?”

“Rebecca came out, pulled me aside, and told me I had to leave, that a friend had come by and needed her attention. I asked what it was about, and she told me it was personal. Rebecca told me to go home, and I just lost it. I started yelling at her and demanding she send her friend away so I could be with her."

"I take it that didn't go well."

"She just stood there, waited until I finished, and then just said that I knew this had to end, and that she would leave soon. I said to Rebecca that I thought I inspired her. She said that her friend inspired her as well, in different ways."

"What did that mean?" I asked.

"I didn't know then, and I still don't. But I figured it meant she was banging him, whoever he was. I asked her to run away with me, that we were good together."

"What did she say?"

"She just smiled at me and told me I was young and far too immature to have a grown-up relationship. She said it just that way. Then she told me she was finishing her novel and going back to her husband and daughter. She told me I had to know that our relationship wasn't for keeps. It was a pleasant diversion to inspire her work."

"You were just someone she used."

"Yeah, something like that," Liam mumbled.

"Did you get a glimpse of the guy who was visiting?"

"No, I drove home and walked to a bar. After consuming a few drinks and some pot at home, I fell asleep, but I felt hurt and angry."

He blew smoke into the air and went on. "The next day I called Rebecca, but she didn't pick up. Then I went back to work, expecting to hear from her. I waited all week, and she never called. I kept getting madder and madder, and finally I went up to see her."

I lowered my voice. "And that's when you killed her."

He lifted his head. "No, that's when I found her."

"Found her?" I repeated.

"Joey," he said, his eyes intense. "She hanged herself. She hanged herself right there in the master bedroom."

My mouth fell open, and I thought of the pulley I'd noticed on the beam over the bed. "She used the pulley?" I asked, my voice nothing more than a croak.

"Yeah, that thing's been there since Dad bought the place. He left it because he thought it was funny. But she'd gotten a rope from the shed and run it through the pulley and tied it to the wall. I figured she tied it there, put it around her neck, and jumped off the bed."

He sobbed again. I stared at my hands, desperate for a drink myself. No wonder the bedroom was always so cold. It was the place where Rebecca died.

"What did you do?" I asked.

"I took her down, and got her to the floor and checked her. She was dead, and I didn't know for how long."

"Did you call the police?"

"I couldn't!" Liam ranted between sobs. "I'd touched the rope, I'd touched her. She had just broken up with me. They would think I did it!"

"But you had to report it," I replied feebly.

"I couldn't; I knew I couldn't. Plus, all of us had been there, Bobby, Ashley, and me. If they checked the place, all of us might be under suspicion."

The depth of what he was saying became clear to me. "Oh God, Liam. What did you do?"

He slugged the rest of his drink, and I got the bottle and poured us both more.

"I waited until dark. Then I went to the shed, got a pick and a shovel and walked into the woods and dug a hole. It was late October, and the ground was getting hard, so it was tough work. It took me hours because I knew I had to make it deep enough. I found an extra canvas for the rowboat in the shed, and I wrapped her body and used twine to tie it closed. Using the wheelbarrow, I took her out to the hole and carefully put her in it. Then I got her suitcases and clothes and put them on top of her."

A large swallow of the scotch burned going down my throat, but I hardly felt it. The idea of Rebecca committing suicide went against everything I thought I knew about her.

Liam was still talking. "It took me until dawn to cover her up. I put everything away, put my clothes in the wash, took a shower, and collapsed in bed, crying the whole time. I waited until Monday, called in sick for work and reported her missing to the police on the Monday."

"Liam," I said, trying to find words.

"I think I knew why she did it."

I shook my head. "Why?"

"The fireplace was full of ashes, and from the amount she'd burned, it was a lot of paper. She always put her work in two piles on either side of the desk, just like you're doing."

I glanced over at the desk, and next to the typewriter were two neat piles of typed pages.

"But you see, when I was cleaning up, those pages were gone. I also found an unburned corner that had a page number, four hundred."

"She burned her manuscript?"

"I don't know. I mean, James Joyce burned his first book, right? Maybe she finished it, hated it, and burned it."

It surprised me that Liam knew any author trivia, but I also could not imagine Rebecca doing such a thing. She was a great novelist and a brilliant writer. I also believed her to be resilient enough to bounce back from one bad manuscript. Then again, the article I read suggested she dealt with mental illness and bouts of depression.

I wrote first drafts that didn't work, clumsy and ridiculous and sometimes downright incoherent. With the help of a content editor and several rewrites, the books ended up quite good and sold very well.

Yet I didn't know Rebecca Hawthorne. I read parts of her book and glimpsed her in my dreams. I even had sex with her in a dream. But I didn't know her, and everything I experienced could merely reflect my own desires.

Burning the book didn't sound like her. It could have been merely a prop for someone else left to suggest despair.

I also wondered whether Liam was telling me the truth.

"Okay," I said, trying to pull myself together. "Tomorrow, I need you to show me where you buried her."

"What good will that do?" Liam said, sniffling.

I considered this for a moment. There was an inkling of an idea, but I didn't know if it would work. "I can say I was digging and found items in the ground. That will give me a reason to bring the police in."

He rose. "They'll want to question me; they'll demand that I —"

I grasped his forearms. "You can leave. Go home before I call them."

"I don't know," Liam whined. "Why would you even be digging back there?"

"I'll say I wanted to build a fire pit."

"No, no, it's crazy. It'll open up the whole thing, start an investigation. I'm not good at being questioned."

I refilled his glass and handed it to him, and Liam took a desperate sip.

"I… I don't want to get involved in all that," Liam stammered, his eyes darting away.

"Liam," I continued, leaning in slightly, "this isn't just about you anymore. She had a husband and a daughter. They deserve to know what happened. Bringing this to the police could help you, too."

"How does it help me?"

"You can tell the police about the person in the rental car. Maybe they can find him. After all, he was the last person she saw when she was alive."

Liam looked up at me, vulnerability etched on his face. "What if they don't believe me? What if I get in trouble?"

"It's a step toward making things right," I said. "It's never too late to do the right thing."

After a long pause, Liam nodded slowly. "Okay. Let's do this."

I poured him another glass of scotch, gave him an extra pair of my pajamas, and got him set up in the second bedroom. He dutifully dressed and got into one of the small beds.

When I got to my bedroom, I paused. I picked up the old-style key from the dresser and locked the door. Guilt tightened around my chest. Never had I felt the need to lock the bedroom door until tonight. But I was suddenly more afraid of Liam than I had ever been of Rebecca.

For all I knew, Liam killed her, then buried her.

Twenty years later, if the police recovered the body, it would be little more than bones, and her cause of death would be difficult to establish.

I returned the key to the dresser and sat on the bed. My stomach churned with unease. Or maybe it was the scotch.

Trouble always haunted Liam. Was this the reason? I shut out the light and got under the covers, but shadows danced uneasily on the walls, as if in silent agreement with my trembling conscience.

I needed to find the body, bring Rebecca's death to light.

I also hoped that finding her remains would end the haunting of Whispering Pines.

Twelve

Grisly Work

I slept through the night and got up while Liam still slept. At my desk, I found ten new pages added to the piles. I was sure the air had been freezing cold and there had been typing at about two-thirty, but this time I had slept through it.

I said a silent 'thank you' to Rebecca, made coffee, and started some oatmeal. The prospect of food made me queasy, but I required it for the task that lay ahead of me.

While Liam was still asleep, I phoned Emily. I hated to call her at work, but I believed my schedule was about to get complicated, and I didn't want days to go by before I called her.

I couldn't get a signal, put the phone away, and after a moment of consideration, was thankful. Better I talk to her after I'd made the so-called discovery and brought the police in.

I roused Liam, who looked a lot worse than I did. We had the oatmeal out on the deck so Liam could smoke without filling the cabin as he had the previous night.

He ate little, mostly used the spoon to move it around the bowl. I ate all of mine, which made me feel better and solved the queasiness in my stomach.

Liam was staring out at our view of the lawn, the nearby forest and, in the distance, the lake.

He finally broke the silence. "You know, I forgot how beautiful this place is. I could never bring myself to come back here after… you know."

"Can you show me where I should dig?" I said, trying to bring him back to reality.

"I can," he said. "I'll never forget."

We got dressed and headed out to the shed to get the tools we needed. As we stepped into the darkened room, I suddenly understood the odd impressions I had felt the first time I was here. The old cover on the boat was just that — an old cover. Liam had wrapped Rebecca in the newer canvas Uncle Rick bought for the boat. He'd also used the wheelbarrow to move her, and the twine that sat in it. Also, I understood why the rope filled my heart with fear. The rope she hanged herself with came from the hank I saw on the workbench.

Even on that first day, Rebecca was trying to get my attention.

I located a pick and two shovels and piled them into the wheelbarrow.

"Where to?" I asked.

"I had to stay close to the house, but I didn't want to be near the path where we walked to the lake," he said and pointed to a place on the far side of the cabin.

He led, and I followed with the wheelbarrow. We walked to the side of the cabin that had no windows past the outhouse. When we reached the propane tank, he stopped and looked around again.

"What's wrong?" I asked.

"The propane tank didn't used to be here," he said. "Give me a minute."

My patience was waning. This was one more screw-up by my cousin. If he'd merely called the police and had them investigate, we might even know whether or not she killed herself. Burying her like he had only suggested an attempt to cover a crime.

The thought slashed through my mind again. Was Liam a murderer?

Liam got his bearings and headed down the hill.

As we stepped off the lawn and into the woods, the forest floor seemed to come alive — carpeted in layers of velvety moss cushioning each step. All around was the delicate scent of earth and dampness. Sunlight danced amidst the ferns' fronds, with delicate fingers reaching upward, seeking the embrace of the sky. Shafts of light wove through the branches, casting intricate patterns on the foliage, while patches of wildflowers added splashes of color.

I was not sure I wanted to see what awaited us.

Liam pointed to a spot not too far in. "There."

He pointed to an empty spot in the clearing. Directly in front of us was a pair of trees whose branches, alive with leaves and color, appeared to grow together to form a canopy. Looking more closely, I noticed some branches of each tree intertwined with each other. My mouth fell open at this odd case of inosculation — trees growing into one another.

"When I dug her resting place, I remembered this spot because of those trees, but they're a lot bigger now. It was October, and I saw the branches, how they linked, as the trees were losing their leaves."

I looked at the spot in the center of the clearing. The sun came down there in a steady beam, unblocked by the surrounding trees.

"You're sure?" I asked as I handed him a shovel.

He nodded, and I saw a tear trickle out of his eye that he hastily wiped away.

I used the handle of the larger shovel to draw a circle on the ground. "That should be about the size of a firepit."

We dug. I brought a pick, but it wasn't necessary. It was June, the ground was soft and gave way easily. As I removed the soil, I thought my idea of wanting to build a fire pit actually was believable. The spot was in the center of the clearing and far enough away from any of the surrounding trees to make a perfect outdoor location.

It was tough work, but I wasn't digging a grave, just the circle.

I was the one who finally hit something hard.

"Hold up," I said as Liam backed up and I dug around the object. Half-buried in the earth, with the weight of years pressing down upon it, was a suitcase. Its heavy plastic exterior, once elegant and sturdy, now bore the marks of time, cracked and weathered. I reached for the handle, and on it was a tag: Rebecca Hawthorne with a Connecticut address.

I pulled out my phone and took a picture of the tag.

"What are you doing?" Liam said.

"Getting a photo I can send to the police to ask them what to do," I said. But that was only half-true. With an address, I might track down Rebecca's husband, if he was still there and alive himself.

Liam was as pale as a ghost himself. Smoke came from the cigarette he'd lit.

"Are you all right?"

"Yeah. I didn't sleep well last night," he said, as the cigarette bounced in his mouth. "I mean, I heard typing, like when I was with Rebecca, and she'd get up and go write."

"Did you get up and look?" I asked.

He shook his head. "No. I-I couldn't."

I nodded. "Will you be okay going home?"

"Yeah, I'll be fine," he said.

"Then I have to wipe down your shovel and you need to get out of here," I said.

"What if the police ask about my being here?"

"Tell them you stayed last night and left this morning. Use the Dingmans Ferry bridge. It's a cash bridge and you won't leave an EZ-Pass trail."

"How do you know this shit?" he asked as I walked with him to his car behind the cabin.

"I write books about people hiding their trails. I've done my share of research."

We carried his shovel back to the shed, and I escorted him to his car, and he headed down the driveway.

I got a dishtowel, went to the shed and wiped down his shovel. Then I went back to the dig site, where I wiped down the tools and the wheelbarrow and then picked up everything, so if they dusted for prints, they would only find mine.

I went inside, washed my hands, and called the closest police station in Milford. Fortunately, this time my phone got a signal, and I used the local number.

I spoke to a helpful dispatcher and told her the tale, giving her my address. Using the fire pit excuse, I told her I found an old suitcase and the name on the tag. I mentioned I knew the name was a lady who disappeared and thought someone should come up and look, and that I wouldn't touch anything. I added I thought it was probably nothing, but it wouldn't hurt to check.

She said she would get in touch with the state police and see about sending an officer around later today.

Alone in the cabin, I tried to focus. I pulled out the new pages of the manuscript and tried to edit them, but I couldn't concentrate.

Why was I doing this?

If Liam had done nothing, they could investigate, and he could tell them he panicked and buried her.

I debated the pros and cons, trying over and over to be sure I was making the right decision. Who was the mysterious visitor in the rental car? Another lover?

When a knock came at my door, I almost cried out; I was so agitated.

I answered the door to find a state trooper. He was a tall white man and wore a dark gray shirt with black patches on the arms. He had a hat in his hand, and sweat on his forehead. I invited him in.

"You have air-conditioning," he said as he stepped into the main room. "That'll come in handy. Today's going to be hot."

I had grown so used to the perpetual chill in the cabin it didn't occur to me outside temperatures were normal for late June.

I told the tale, trying to keep it simple and not add to the story. That's the way to get caught in a lie, the need to embellish with details to make it sound better. I knew this from my research for my novels.

He nodded and followed me down the hill and to the place where I dug. The wheelbarrow and shovels were there where I left them, and it made a convincing scene.

He looked at the tag.

"The name on it is Rebecca Hawthorne," he said. "Does that name mean anything to you?"

"She's a writer who disappeared while staying up here," I explained. "I heard about her disappearance, and I've been reading one of her novels."

He nodded and looked around. "Mr. Riley, we're going to have to bring in a team to have a look and dig up this site."

"That's why I stopped," I said.

"Okay, let me talk to command and arrange things. Please touch nothing. In fact, if you stayed in your home, it would be better."

I nodded, and we trudged back to the cabin. He went out to his cruiser and contacted his superiors. While I still had a signal, I called Emily.

"Hello?"

"Emily, it's Joe. Sorry to call you during work."

"It's okay if we make it fast. The head librarian doesn't like personal calls at work."

"Something has come up at my place, and things might be crazy for a few days."

"Why? What's wrong?" she said, worry in her voice.

"It might be nothing, but the police are here. I'll call you when I know more."

"The police? Joe, I'll be a nervous wreck if you don't tell me."

"Don't worry, it will be all right. I promise I'll call you tonight and explain. I'm fine. I'm not hurt. No one will arrest me, and I had a great time last night."

"What? Oh… So did I. Promise you'll call me."

"I will."

I ended the call. I could've handled that better, but I was too high-strung to come up with anything.

Soon a series of vehicles appeared: another state trooper, and a large van came up the driveway. The second trooper was in uniform, but the other man wore a blue shirt and uniform pants. After a few minutes, he went to the van and came back with a huge bloodhound on a leash, and the three men headed to the site.

Cadaver dog.

I knew about those animals from my novel research. They train cadaver dogs to locate human remains, even old human remains. Although several breeds of dog do it well, bloodhounds are the first choice. Everything about them, their long ears, the folds in the skin of their faces, and their incessant drooling, helps them pull in odors.

They were gone for a few minutes, and soon returned. The trooper I spoke to knocked at the door.

"We have to get a team up here, and maybe a backhoe. Can you move your car out to the street?"

I nodded, and soon the second trooper put the vehicles in a line out on the street. Although the dirt lane I lived on wasn't a busy thoroughfare, I noticed some of the other residents came out to the street to watch things.

I got coffee for the team and tried to be a suitable host.

In about half an hour, a large step van arrived and a team of men and women came up the hill. They all wore the same blue shirts and pants as the man with the dog, and several carried shovels. They all wore masks and blue surgical gloves.

A few minutes after they arrived, a truck pulled up in my driveway. On the trailer in the back was a bright yellow one-man excavator. The driver lowered a ramp and drove it onto my gravel driveway, and then around to the side of the house.

I walked out to the street and noticed several news vans out there, and even cameramen and reporters on the scene. How did they get here so quickly?

The cameramen remained on the street but filmed the police through the trees. I don't think they got much, as the forest was simply too dense.

I headed out the back of the house to watch from a distance. Like the trooper said, it was the middle of the afternoon, and it had grown hot. I sat on the concrete base of the propane tank and watched as the group used the excavator and their shovels and dug down.

The hole now resembled a traditional rectangular grave, except larger. The machine backed away, and men and women went into the hole and dug with their shovels.

Items came up. The suitcase I glimpsed, then articles of clothing, faded and dirty. My heart was pounding with each thud of the shovels striking the soil as the team dug. I sat apart, cool and detached as all of them sweated in the heat. After a while and more digging, a second suitcase came up.

Finally, one man called out, and people got out of the ditch. Two men pulled something up, and a pair of women brought a heavy plastic tarpaulin over and placed it next to the hole.

The men pulled up a shape wrapped in canvas and covered in twine, which hung loosely in places. My first reaction was surprise at how small it looked. But of course, she was no longer the tall and vibrant woman whose spirit visited me. By this time, her remains were little more than bones.

The team carefully placed the bundle on the tarpaulin and lifted the four corners. Two men carried it away and down the hill to the van.

It felt as if the weight of the world had crashed into me, suffocating me with overwhelming sadness. I could only think of the vibrant woman she had been and how they removed what remained of her physical form, reduced to so little.

I wondered if this would end the haunting, and it left me grappling with an odd emptiness at the thought that I would never see Rebecca at the typewriter again.

But it was the right thing to do, the only thing to do. Her death and her burial here on this land had trapped Rebecca's spirit. I hoped these actions would set her free to move on.

The team collected all the pieces they uncovered, and a trooper put stakes in the ground and wrapped police tape around the pit as I returned to the house.

Soon, I saw the excavator return to the truck bed, and the vehicles pulled away and drove off.

The trooper who spoke to me first came to the door.

"Please touch nothing over there," the man said. "A detective will come by, and he'll want to speak to you."

I nodded, and he headed off. Taking the opportunity, I returned my car to the driveway and tried to review the new typed pages of the book, but it was difficult. I couldn't shake the feeling I'd lost Rebecca.

Why did it bother me so deeply?

She was dead when I got here. Our nocturnal dalliances had merely been a dream sparked by my overactive imagination and unsatisfied libido.

At about five PM, a car pulled up the driveway. It was unmarked, but obviously a police sedan. A tall man, a rather imposing figure, stepped out. He stood about six feet tall with a broad build. As he approached the door, I saw he had rugged, chiseled features with a square jawline and piercing blue eyes. He had short hair, neatly trimmed, showing flecks of gray around the edges.

He would make a great Soul Mason. He was a little older, but if he could act and they offered me a movie deal, he would be my first call.

He didn't come to the door but walked around the house, and I saw him through the various windows until he went out of sight on the side of the cabin. He was looking at the dig site before he talked to me.

After a few minutes, he walked to the front door and knocked.

"Mr. Riley?" he said as I opened the door. "I'm Detective Sullivan with the Pennsylvania State Police. May I come in?"

I stepped aside, and he walked in. His presence felt intimidating.

He retrieved a long notebook from a pocket and a pen.

"Please sit down," I said. "Would you like some coffee?"

"No thank you," he said, and pulled out a chair from the dining room table and brought it around so he sat facing me. "Seems like there was a lot of excitement today."

I sighed. "It's been a day."

"I want to go over what you told the dispatcher and the trooper, if that's all right."

"Sure," I said.

"You were digging a fire pit out there, right where the woods started, is that correct?"

"Yes."

He stared at me, and I realized I felt nervous. "Any reason you chose that spot?"

I desperately wanted a drink. "Yes. It was far enough from the cabin. Since the propane tank was on that side of the house, I wanted to be a suitable distance from that as well. The spot was a clearing, with no trees too close, and it seemed a suitable spot."

Keep it simple, stupid. Don't elaborate, my brain shouted at me.

"Were you digging it alone?"

"Yes."

He paused, looked at his notebook, and met my eyes. "Do you smoke, Mr. Riley?"

I frowned. "No, why?"

"Forensics found ash, and a recently discarded cigarette at the site." He checked his notebook. "Plus, there were two sets of footprints."

I cursed myself mentally. I should have used a tree branch to erase the footprints and made new ones after Liam was long gone.

It was good I only wrote about spies, because I made mistakes that would get someone like Soul Mason killed.

I decided it was best to come clean with the detective.

"My cousin Liam Riley helped. But only at the beginning. When I … um… uncovered the suitcase, and we realized it might be something I needed to report and that we had to stop digging, he… um… headed out."

"I see," he said, and his tone held terrible insinuations. "Would you provide me with contact information for your cousin?"

"Is that really necessary?"

He grinned, but all it did was make me more nervous. "I am never sure what is necessary in an investigation. But I need all the people who were here when you uncovered the site."

He'd put that very well, making it sound like we hadn't found a body.

"Are you the current owner of the property?" he asked.

"Yes, my uncle left it to me in his will."

"And your uncle owned the property for how long?"

"I'm not sure. Forty years or more. My family and I used to come up here when we were kids."

"You seemed to know something about the artifacts you dug up. Is that correct?"

"There was a name tag on the suitcase I uncovered. It said Rebecca Hawthorne. I was aware she'd been working here at the cabin and then disappeared."

"How were you aware of that fact?"

"I'd been doing research on the history of the cabin, and her name came up. I downloaded newspaper articles about her at the library."

I pointed to my closed laptop on the table.

He shut his notebook and fixed his eyes on me. "You don't think it's odd that you were researching this woman's disappearance and then stumbled across the place someone buried her? That's quite a coincidence."

"Synchronicity," I said.

"I'm sorry," Sullivan said, confused.

"Carl Jung believed many occurrences labeled as coincidences are not because of chance. He related such situations to the observer's mind."

"Your suggestion being that since you were thinking about her, your subconscious attracted you to that location?"

"Something like that."

My statement earned me his annoying grin again.

"All I know, Mr. Riley, is that I've got a dead body from an old cold case, and your family has been the only people on the property for the last twenty years."

Thirteen

Possession

I pointed out that there had been caretakers, property managers, and cleaning crews up at Whispering Pines often over the years, and he dutifully wrote the information into his notebook.

I also gave him Liam's phone number and address in New Jersey. At least I thought it was his current address. Liam moved around a lot.

Then, with an "I'll be in touch," he headed back to his car and drove off.

I was at a loss about what to do. Should I call or text Liam? What if they took his phone? A call or a text from me right after the detective came by looked suspicious as hell.

I finally called Ashley, not knowing what else to do.

She picked up on the second ring. "This is a bad time, Joey. It's Saturday night, and I'm getting slammed."

"Ash, call Liam and tell him a detective was by here and knows he helped me dig the fire pit."

"Wait. What? The police came because of a fire pit?"

"No. It was the spot we dug, Ash. They found Rebecca Hawthorne buried there."

I heard the sounds of Brew Haven behind her: cash registers jiggling, people talking, and the door opening and closing, but not a sound from Ashley.

I heard a door close, and the cafe noise became muffled. She must have gone into her office.

"Christ, Joey, what did you do?"

Part of me wanted to tell her the whole thing. My research, Liam's confession, everything, but that would embroil her in my cover-up, putting her at risk.

"We just started digging a fire pit, that's all," I said, sticking to the lie. "Liam was helping me. We uncovered an old suitcase with a tag that read 'Rebecca Hawthorne'. I told Liam I had to call the police, and Liam, you know, he's had run-ins with the law."

"Yes, I know. I've bailed him out twice."

"He left and told me not to tell anyone he'd been here."

"Then why did you do it?" she said, and I heard the anger in her voice.

"A detective came by, and he asked me if I smoked and said the forensics team found a fresh cigarette butt and there were two sets of footprints. I gave him Liam's cell number. Look, just let Liam know that the detective will talk to him, and he should just tell them about the firepit."

There was another long pause. "You weren't just digging a fire pit, were you, Joey?"

I couldn't get anything past Ashley. "That's what I told the detective. Liam should just say the same thing. Please, Ash, I don't want Liam to panic."

"Okay, Joey, I'll call him. But at some point, I'm coming up there, and you're going to tell me everything. Is that clear?"

"I promise, Ash. Can you call Liam?"

"I will, but this isn't the end of this."

She ended the call, and I sat down, exhausted.

I also noticed something that hadn't occurred to me before. The main room was not nearly as cold as it had been since my arrival.

It was now past seven, and the sun was dipping down over the treetops. I thought it was safe to call Emily.

She answered on the first ring. "I've been a nervous wreck all day. Are you okay?"

"Yes, fine."

"You said the police were there. What happened?"

"We found Rebecca Hawthorne."

There was a long silence. "What?"

I went through the made-up story: digging the firepit; finding the suitcase; calling the police.

"Oh my God, I didn't know you lived in the house where she disappeared."

"The same," I said.

"No wonder you were interested in her — what a strange coincidence that you found her."

"It's more involved than that," I said and summoned my courage to push on. "I... I think Rebecca has been haunting my cabin."

Another long pause. "Really? How can you tell?"

"The place has been cold, and I've sensed a presence," I said. I didn't think it would help my chances for a second date if I told her I'd dreamt I'd had sex with a ghost.

"Sounds like a possibility. No wonder you were driven to find out about her. Tell you what, I have some experience contacting spirits."

This surprised me. "You're kidding."

"Not at all. I could bring up my Ouija board and we could see if she's really there."

Seeing Emily again would be pleasant after the day I'd had. "Do you think you could do that?"

"We can try. I'll drive up."

"Do you need my address?"

"Um—no. I know that area pretty well. I'll see you soon," she said and ended the call.

I looked around the room and picked up a bit, putting away the large bottle of scotch Liam and I had worked on the previous evening. Then I took a shower and changed my clothes.

I put on the outside light so she could see her way, and as twilight fell, her car came up my driveway. It was a little car, a Kia or Toyota, but it looked new.

She came to the door, carrying a large cloth bag, and I opened the door and took it from her. It was heavy.

"What did you bring?" I asked, "Bricks?"

"Some things, candles and candleholders, as well as my Ouija board. If we're going to do this, we have to do it right."

I put the bag on the table. She took out a dark purple velvet cloth and arranged it so that it covered a square in the middle of the table. Embroidered in the cloth were intricate patterns of intertwined vines and arcane symbols.

She placed a Ouija board in the center of the cloth. It wasn't a cheap one like I'd seen at toy stores, but crafted from wood. Its surface, inscribed with delicate, weathered letters and numbers, faded as if she'd owned it for a long time.

It had the alphabet in two curved rows, and numbers one through zero in a straight line. In the upper left-hand corner, it had a sun design and the word YES and in the right-hand corner a crescent moon and the word NO. At the top of the board was the word HELLO and at the bottom was the word GOODBYE.

She placed the planchette on the Ouija board. It was a small heart-shaped piece of wood supported on casters with a clear glass disk on the pointed end so that if it slid to a spot, you could see the letter through the glass.

She took out a pair of large candlesticks and planted pillar candles on each. They were thick and tall and had a fragrance I detected from several feet away.

"Where did you get all this stuff?"

"My mother handed it down to me. She was into the occult."

I looked over all the paraphernalia. "Do you think you can contact Rebecca?"

"I've had luck contacting spirits the other times I've done this. I think if she is here, we should be able to get her attention."

I nodded, feeling nervous about the whole thing. Rebecca's spirit may have gone with her body, and I didn't want her to remain if she could be free. Then again, there was my book, with still less than a hundred pages written.

She lit the candles, went around the room, turning off all the lights. I was nervous as it was growing dark rapidly, and the candles seemed to create a bubble of light in the darkness and shadows of the room.

A sliver of light glowed under my closed bedroom door. I had left the lamp on in there, but it did little to dispel the gloom outside our candlelit circle of light.

She returned to the table and closed her eyes as if in silent meditation.

When she opened her eyes again, I asked, "Prayer?"

"Preparing myself. I try to get out of my own way when I do a reading."

"Is that what it's called? A reading?"

She smiled, her brown eyes magnified by her glasses. "Take my hands."

I gently grasped her hands. They felt warm and soft.

"Now close your eyes and take a deep breath. Let everything go."

I didn't know if I could let everything that had happened go. I doubted I could even let the last twenty-four hours go. But I did as she asked, took several deep breaths and let them out slowly, trying to clear my mind.

God, I wanted a drink.

She released my hands and asked me to come around to her side of the table. I slid in next to her, feeling her warm body next to mine, and sensing the scent of a lovely fragrance she was wearing.

"Now we put our hands on the planchette," she said, and placed her fingers on the left side of the heart-shaped board. I followed suit, putting the tips of my fingers on the right-hand side. "Don't put any weight on the planchette, just hold your fingers there and allow the energy to work through you."

I nodded, as if I knew what she was talking about. I had never done a Ouija board before, and always thought them silly. But the events of my life since I arrived at Whispering Pines made me willing to try something new, if it would work.

"Spirit," she said aloud. "Are you there?"

The planchette changed position under my fingers. I didn't do it at all, but I kept my fingers on it as it slid up the board to the word, HELLO.

Emily and I exchanged a grin, and we returned our attention to the planchette.

"Is this the spirit of the cabin?" she asked.

The planchette slid quickly to YES.

She went on. "Are you Rebecca?"

The strong sliding motion back to 'YES' practically pulled me from my chair.

"Why are you here, Rebecca?" she asked, then added, "Why do you stay?'

The planchette slid quickly from place to place, spelling out, W-A-N-T.

"What do you want, Rebecca?" Emily asked.

Once again, the planchette quickly slid about the board to spell out: H-I-M.

"Him?" I said, frowning. "Who does she mean, me?"

"You're the only him in the room, Joe."

The planchette was on the move again and spelled out N-E-E-D, paused, and flew to H-E-L-P.

"Need help," I repeated. "What help does she need?"

"If I can help you, Rebecca, let me help," Emily said, looking around the empty room into the darkness all around us.

An icy wind blew through the cabin, extinguishing the candles in an instant. Emily grabbed me for support, almost convulsing, and I put my arms around her protectively.

Just as quickly, the flickering candlelight returned; the candles burned again by themselves. I looked at Emily to see her smiling at me with an unsettling hunger in her magnified eyes.

She shifted her body to face me and pressed her lips to mine. This wasn't an innocent peck, but a full-mouth kiss that locked onto my lips as if she wanted to suck the life from me, her tongue playing feverishly in my mouth.

I pulled back, more out of surprise than anything else. "Emily, are you all right?"

She rose to her feet, grabbed my hand, and pulled. "Come with me," she said, her voice a deeper register.

"But the candles, the Ouija board…" I said, as she all but dragged me toward the bedroom. How did she know which room was my bedroom?

She opened the door, pulled me in, and brought her mouth to mine again. This time, however, one of her hands went lower to touch me intimately, rubbing against my pants. As this got the desired effect, she gripped me with her hand.

"That's what I need," she gasped. With her free hand, she pulled off her glasses and placed them on the dresser next to the door.

I pulled back and pushed her hands away. "No, Emily, there's something wrong."

Yet, I felt a force, an erotic energy moving through my body. Though I fought to restrain myself, I was rock hard as a teenager.

"Come on, lover, I need this!" she growled and took my hand to guide me to the bed. I could not resist. I knew something was wrong, but my body, flooded by desire, was outside of my control.

She sat me down on the bed and unbuttoned her sensible blouse.

"Emily — this isn't you — this isn't me. It's—" I stammered.

Her blouse floated down to the floor, quickly followed by her bra. She took my hands in hers and pulled them to her breasts.

I looked at my hands, and they seemed to belong to someone else. As my fingers acted on their own, caressing the firm flesh, she threw her head back and hissed, "Yesssss!"

While I massaged her, she unbuttoned my shirt, all but ripping it off my body. She pulled me to my feet and into another embrace, her bare chest against mine. Her hands went to my belt as she opened my pants and pushed them down past my hips, along with my underwear.

In a move that was eerily familiar, she pushed me, and with my legs trapped in my trousers, I fell onto the bed. She grabbed my legs and pulled my pants all the way off.

"Let me take charge," she said, in a voice I had heard before, but only in my dreams.

It wasn't Emily's voice.

"No, Emily — something wrong. We have to stop—"

I tried to sit up, but with one arm, she pushed me back with remarkable strength. She stepped out of her own pants, then climbed on top of me, completely naked. In a moment, she straddled me, rubbing her pelvis against me, her gaze fixed on mine.

I looked up into her eyes and saw that they glowed — or appeared to. They were no longer brown, but green. Not just green, they had light brown coloring around the iris.

Hazel. Like Rebecca's eyes in my dream.

"Rebecca?" I said, amazed. "No, you can't—"

"Stop talking," she said and pressed her mouth to mine. As she did, she raised her hips and slowly lowered her body onto me, pulling me into her warm flesh. I gasped during the kiss, and she made a throaty grunt of pleasure.

I wanted to protest; I wanted to stop, not do this — try to figure out what was happening. But I was helpless, the sensations overwhelming me as Emily/Rebecca pressed herself against me and into her.

At that moment, lost in sensation, I felt like a passenger in my body as her warm, firm hips slid up and down with enthusiasm.

Emotionally, I was in turmoil. I cared for Emily, yet this wasn't really her; it was Rebecca pulling the strings. She had ensnared both of us, using Emily as a puppet while manipulating me as well. We had become her marionettes, and I felt powerless to break free.

The room grew colder, and I glanced over at the radio-clock to see the ice crystals appearing in the clock face.

Watching myself as if from far away, I kissed her and suckled her breasts, which made her groan and mumble words of encouragement. With a fervent yearning, my hips surged upward to meet hers in a sensual rhythm. The pace increased as the world faded into a hazy blur, leaving only the warmth of our bodies.

By now, she thrust against me with a frenzied fervor, just as Rebecca did in my dream, and I felt my grip on self-control slipping away like sand through my fingers.

Our bodies surged against each other, each moan escaping my lips, blending harmoniously with Emily's breathy grunts. As she pressed urgently against me, I found myself powerless to halt the momentum. Our breaths mingled and quickened, every nerve ending ignited with an electrifying intensity, creating a symphony of sensations that swelled toward an inevitable climax.

Finally, as in my dream, she suddenly stopped moving, as her face twisted in an expression of surprise and amazement. She raised her head, opened her mouth, and made a guttural moan, blowing out her breath in a thick, white fog. Her entire body convulsed, her pelvis vibrated on top of me, and her eyes rolled back into her head.

I have been with maybe a dozen women in my life, and I've seen them in various stages of sexual enjoyment — but I have never seen a woman climax like she did at that moment.

She arched her back, lifting us both off the bed for a moment, and flopped on top of me, which pushed me over the edge. It was all in a sudden rush, like a wave crashed over me. It began deep within and surged upwards, breaking against the edges of my consciousness. I had no choice but to surrender, and I released a sound that was part moan and part scream.

We lay together gulping air in ragged breaths, exhaling thick mists of fog in the frozen air.

I gently wove my fingers through her hair as she lay against me, our bodies still intertwined, pulsing with the remnants of our shared ecstasy. Waves of sensation cascaded through her, causing her pelvis to quiver softly, tender aftershocks from our union. Her breath came in soft gasps, punctuated by delicate, melodic whimpers.

Finally, I slipped out of her and pulled the afghan over us, concerned about how cold the room had become.

At that moment, I would have been content to fall asleep with Emily in my arms, her body pressed against mine. I felt more peaceful than I had for many months.

In an abrupt motion, Emily's head snapped up as though jolted from an electric shock. She scanned the dimly lit room, illuminated by the single lamp.

I could see that her eyes were brown. Just plain brown.

She couldn't quite focus on her surroundings.

"Are you all right?" I said, trying to think of how to explain what we'd just experienced.

She pushed herself off me. "What did you do to me?"

I was stunned by this. "We — made love. I don't completely understand it myself."

She pulled the afghan off the bed and stood up on the cold floor, and I saw her eyes glancing around blindly. "Where are my glasses?"

"By the door on the dresser," I said, and pointed.

She stumbled over to the dresser, her hand searching for her spectacles. After a moment of fumbling, she found them and slipped them onto her face with shaking hands.

She spoke almost in a whisper. "How could you do this to me?"

I rose from the bed. "Emily, something happened. We were both overcome or something. We were at the Ouija board and you—"

"Don't come near me," she shouted, her face a mask of fear and anger.

I sat back on the bed.

"Where are my clothes?" she demanded.

In our haste to remove them, we'd scattered them around the room. I looked around and picked up her bra and blouse, holding them out to offer them to her.

She yanked them unceremoniously from my hand and said, "Get my pants, socks, and shoes and hand them through the door. Don't come into the main room."

I nodded, dumbstruck, and she went out of the room and slammed the door.

"She doesn't remember," I muttered to myself. This wasn't good. I liked Emily and even believed we might have a relationship. But now she thought I had taken advantage of her.

Not knowing what else to do, I threw on my pants and shirt, shivering in the cold. I gathered the requested items, walked to the door, and knocked on it, then held her pants, socks, and shoes out through a gap in the door just large enough to fit my arm.

She took them, and I closed the door, trying to get my head around what to say. I waited a couple of minutes, then opened the door a crack and asked, "Can I come out now?"

There was no response, and I stepped out. The lights in the room were on, and Emily angrily packed things away into her cloth bag, fully dressed.

I stayed in the bedroom doorway.

"So what did you do, drug me?" she demanded, her eyes intense behind her glasses.

"Emily, I wouldn't do something like that," I said. "You've had nothing to eat or drink since you got here. Don't you remember? We were using the Ouija board, and you kissed me. Then we — I mean — it was like I wasn't even me anymore—"

She paused and looked at me with suspicion. She seemed to recollect what I said, but wasn't sure.

I went on. "You pulled me into the bedroom and took off your glasses. I kept telling you to stop, but neither of us could."

She shook her head. "I never take off my glasses unless they're right nearby. I'm blind without them."

"You pushed me onto the bed and pulled off your clothes," I said.

But I knew the truth. The entire thing was Rebecca's idea. Rebecca wanted to make love — no, Rebecca wanted sex, straight down and dirty sex. She used Emily's body and mine to make her desires come true.

She put the last item into her bag, doubt written all over her face.

"Emily, I promise, I would never trick you or force you to go to bed with me," I said. "It was like we were possessed."

She looked at me with a strange expression as if she remembered what had happened, then looked away, shaking her head. "No. I could never let go like that. That… freely."

"Emily, I like you. I want to date you. I didn't plan on this happening — I mean, at least not this soon."

She picked up the bag. "I have to go."

She walked out the door and to her car without a look back.

Fourteen

Aftermath

I didn't know what to do, so I found the large bottle of scotch, which still had a jigger or two in it, and finished it. I considered pulling out the vodka as well, but I was too tired.

Who knew being a ghost's sex puppet would be such hard work?

I could understand Liam's infatuation with Rebecca, if that was a sample of her prowess. But he'd been a young man in his early twenties. I was forty, though I was still slim and didn't have a gut like a lot of men. I also had only been along for the ride, not the one in control of my body.

The propane heater came on in the corner, demonstrating how cold the cabin had grown.

I finished my drink, my mind racing with what I could do to soothe Emily. What if she never wanted to see me again? This came with the realization that I valued her opinion of me. Had I behaved badly? Neither of us were in control of our bodies, but at least I remembered everything.

It all happened so fast…

With these concerns spinning around my head, I fell into bed fully clothed, only kicking off my shoes. I was certain I wouldn't sleep a wink.

I was wrong. In a few brief moments, I was out.

I woke to hear typing.

Glancing at the clock — two thirty once again.

I rose, my breath misting, put on my slippers, and went out into the main room.

The table lamp silhouetted Rebecca as she typed away.

"Go away. I'm working," she said.

Once again, I was not sure she actually said it or if her voice appeared in my mind.

"Why did you do it?" I said.

She didn't turn around. "I needed to take charge, so I helped myself. What are you complaining about? You enjoyed it."

She spun around, the chair with her, which startled me. If she had no substance, why did the chair spin?

She was nude, as usual, but seemed more voluptuous than I recalled. Her curves were even more appealing, drawing my gaze toward her with an almost magnetic pull. Her green-brown eyes glowed with the inner fire I'd seen in Emily's eyes. It was as though the lovemaking session had wrapped her in a mysterious aura that simultaneously fascinated and unnerved me.

Succubus…

"She thinks I did something to her," I said.

She smiled. "Afraid you'll lose me?"

This angered me. "Emily's not a plaything. She's a person."

She ignored this. "Don't worry, you'll get yours."

Again her mouth moved, but the words came into my head, without the use of my ears at all. It also didn't seem like she was talking to me. Her words didn't really match what I had said. It was more like she had this conversation with someone else and I was merely receiving it.

"Why are you doing this?"

She rolled her eyes. "I have a book to finish."

"The book?" I said. "What does the book have to do with this?"

She returned to the typewriter. "I need energy to work. Sex has always been the best inspiration for me." She looked at me over her shoulder. "I need your energy, and you're young and can spare it."

"Rebecca, you're dead."

She spun around again. "You can leave if you don't want to take part."

I didn't know what else to say. I was arguing with a ghost. Again, her part of the conversation seemed detached from mine. "This is my house. You need to move on."

"I need to finish the book," she spat angrily. "Now, either help me or get out of the way." She returned to the typewriter. "Go to bed. I've got work to do."

I woke up in bed.

I sat up quickly, and my head hurt so much I immediately regretted it. I realized I had not changed out of my clothes from the previous night. The sun was pouring in the front-facing window. I glanced at the clock — it was nine o'clock.

I tried to understand what had happened. I had been in the main room, talking to Rebecca. Then, it felt like someone removed a splice of tape, and I found myself in bed.

Or had I dreamed the entire thing?

Was this what happened to Emily? Was her recollection that she was at the seance table and then suddenly was lying on top of me naked in bed? If so, I understood her assumption I had drugged her.

I went out and got some aspirin and started coffee. As the cup brewed, I went to the desk and picked up the face-down top page.

During the night, Rebecca added twenty new pages.

Was this my reward for being a part of her erotic tableau the previous night? Or was it like she said — that sex gave her the energy to write?

I tried to think about what I could do to reach out to Emily.

The twenty-first century may have a lot of advantages over previous times, but being a straight male was as confusing as ever. And being a twice-divorced forty-year-old guy with his own personal ghost made a difficult situation worse.

Maybe if I showed up at her house with flowers…

There was a knock at the door as I grabbed my coffee. I stumbled over, annoyed I hadn't heard the car come up my driveway, probably because of the pounding in my head.

I opened the door to Detective Sullivan.

He looked at me and asked, "Am I catching you at a bad time?"

It took me a moment to speak. "No, come in. Would you like coffee?"

I stepped aside, and he came in, scanning the room. "Coffee would be great, thank you. Black."

I went to the coffeemaker and started a fresh cup.

"I'd like to review parts of our discussion from the other night,," Sullivan said and pulled out his notebook.

I sighed. "If it will help."

"I haven't been able to get in touch with your cousin, Liam Riley. He doesn't appear to be answering his phone."

This worried me. "He left here early yesterday, right after we started digging the firepit."

He looked at his notebook. "And you're sure that is what you were doing? Digging a firepit?"

I stared at him. "Of course we were."

"The reason I ask is you seemed ill-prepared, if that was your intention."

I got his mug and handed it to him. "What do you mean?"

"You didn't have any of the things you would need to construct one. Paver stones, gravel, paver base, not even a tamper to flatten the soil." He went to the table and sat down, mug in hand. He took a swallow and went on. "Plus, I thought you'd lived in the city and the suburbs all your life. Do you have any experience building a firepit?"

"I… uh… saw a video online. It seemed to be easy enough."

He nodded. "I watched some of those videos last night just to refresh my memory. All of them recommend digging down about a foot. You went down three feet."

I was sweating now. "I figured I would dig deep and then even it out."

I shut my mouth, annoyed with myself. I was falling into the trap an experienced cop can put you in. You make things up to validate your actions, and the added detail only creates more suspicion.

He took another moment to look at his notebook. "The medical examiner has classified the case as a homicide."

"Really?" I said. "So quickly?"

"He had little to work with, but he could easily recognize a perimortem hyoid fracture. That kind of fracture means—"

"I know what it means," I replied. "It suggests strangulation."

He sat back in the chair. "Interesting that you know that."

"Detective, I am a novelist, and I write thrillers."

"I know. I downloaded one of your audiobooks. I was listening to it in the car."

I ignored that tidbit. "I've done extensive medical research to give my books an air of authenticity. From my studies, I know perimortem hyoid fracture could be strangulation, or it could be from someone committing suicide by hanging themselves."

He nodded and sipped his coffee.

"Have you identified the body?" I asked.

"We are working from the assumption that it is Rebecca Hawthorne. The ME said the skeletal remains were definitely a female who had at least one child, which matches Ms. Hawthorne's history. We are getting the dental records. I tracked down her husband."

"You did?" It shouldn't surprise me. The police have many more avenues than a simple internet search.

"Yes, he lives in Connecticut and remarried. Apparently, he had Ms. Hawthorne declared dead years ago, so he controls her estate."

I nodded. I wanted to get a name and ask about the daughter, but I thought that would only create more questions in the detective's mind.

He sat back in the chair. "Where were you in 2004, Mr. Riley?"

"I was living in New York." I stopped to meet his intense stare. "Why are you asking?"

"Anyone who had access to this cabin needs to be investigated," he said, his eyes still fixed on mine. "Did you come up here at all that year? Perhaps you met Ms. Hawthorne?"

The room seemed to shrink in that instant, and my perception of reality distorted. In the penetrating stare of Detective Sullivan, beneath his calm exterior and veneer of professionalism, I saw suspicion reflected at me. I was not an ally but a potential suspect.

"I… believe I should contact my lawyer," I said.

He attempted a friendly smile. It was not pretty. "Why, we're just talking? If you have nothing to hide…"

And there it was, the technique the police always use. The claim is that if I have nothing to hide, I should tell them everything. That ploy was as old as the hills, and I used it in one of my early short stories about a policeman.

I stood up. "Detective, I don't mean to be uncooperative, but any further discussion will have to be with my attorney present."

"If that is how you would prefer it, Mr. Riley," Sullivan said, swallowing the last of his coffee and standing. "But I should let you know, the Pennsylvania State Police are taking this seriously."

I nodded, keeping my big mouth shut.

I watched as he pulled his unmarked police car down the driveway and back onto the dirt road. I had the feeling that this wasn't going away soon.

I thought finding Rebecca's body would solve things, bring some closure, but it only made things more complicated. Of course, the police were going to look into it. A writer at the peak of her career disappears, and then someone discovers her body twenty years later? It was the stuff that made headlines and—

Headlines…

I grabbed my phone. The internet was blowing up with stories about Rebecca Hawthorne.

It had not only hit the local news, but the Associated Press had also jumped on it, and it had gone national.

Body Found Outside Cabin In The Poconos

Was Body In Poconos Famed Writer?

And on and on. All I wanted to do was end the haunting, and instead I opened Pandora's box and brought the troubles of the world pointing at me and my family.

The phone rang in my hand, and Ashley's name appeared.

"Hey Ash," I said.

"What did you do?" She yelled so loudly that I yanked the phone away from my ear. "I've been getting calls all morning from reporters. If I were a nasty lady, I'd have given them your number."

"Thanks for that. The police are trying to find Liam. He's not answering his phone. There's a detective, and he's smart and suspicious and very thorough."

"This is the last thing I need right now. You weren't around after Hawthorne disappeared the first time. They put the family through hell. Even Dad and Mom, who barely even met that damn woman."

"I thought she was your friend," I said.

"She was a troublesome bitch who only thought about herself."

I saw that myself. At first, I welcomed the mysterious pages appearing like a gift. Now I was aware they had a cost. The cost was giving power to the ghost and allowing her to use me and Emily.

Ashley went on. "I thought your going to that cabin would be a good thing, finally ending the guilt and worry all of us had after the bitch disappeared. But here you have brought it all up again. Liam went into hiding because of this. I hope you're happy."

"Ash, I didn't plan any of this—" I stopped, realizing it was the same thing I said to Emily.

"Just keep me out of it, Joey. I was done with that damn cabin twenty years ago."

She ended the call.

Leave it to cousin Joey to bring peace and love to the family. Maybe Robert was right, and I should've sold the place. If I did, I could buy something — a condo maybe — far away from mountains, buried bodies, and ghosts.

A memory from my dream came to me. Rebecca Hawthorne, staring at me and saying, "I have a book to finish."

I grabbed the new pages that had appeared in the night.

Yes, I wanted the book finished. Yes, having Rebecca and me taking turns was creating an excellent book that would sell very well, make my publisher happy, and induce agent Meredith Thompson to sign me.

It all depended on getting the book done.

I focused on the last page I had typed and onto the new material. Rebecca was imitating my writing style to an impressive degree at this point. But it was more than that. The new pages were very good — no, great. It was plain to see why Rebecca was on the best-seller lists. The pages sounded like me working at a level I had not yet attained.

The plot proceeded on. Soul and Miranda were on a merry chase, deep into a world of hackers and criminals, and handling themselves as best they could. Soul pulled out of his depression from the loss of his partner to operate on as high a level as ever.

Miranda helped him, but didn't coddle him. She wasn't the awe-struck type of woman character I used in previous books, but an agent as strong as he was, and as good at kicking ass. However, their fight scenes and interrogations were realistic. Miranda didn't beat up three hundred pound men, like many popular movies show women characters do these days. She just shot them.

I read the last page and went to the typewriter, inserting fresh paper with a carbon and started typing.

It was funny. Almost any little turmoil in my regular life kept me from writing, and I spent my time focusing on the problem. Now, the story pulled me in, and I wanted it to continue.

At about noon, I finished my tenth page and placed the original and the carbon on the piles. Looking at myself, still in yesterday's clothes, I felt like I was coming out of a dream. I quickly showered, dressed, and ate a bit of lunch.

I wanted to call my lawyer, but that would have to wait until Monday.

I needed to face the Emily situation first.

I thought about calling, but decided it might work better if I showed up in person. Taking a detour to the nearby Weiss Market, I found flowers. With them in hand; I drove to Milford and pulled across the street from the house with Emily's apartment.

I figured if she wasn't there, I would leave them on her doorstep.

I walked up and pushed the bell, and I heard it ring on the second floor. I was tall enough to peek in the small window built into the door and saw Emily come down the stairs. When she saw it was me, her expression grew hard, but she opened the door.

She glared at the flowers in my hand. "Supermarket flowers?"

"It was all I could get on a Sunday," I confessed and offered them. She took them and sniffed the blossoms.

"Look, Emily, about last night—"

She cut me off with a hand gesture. "I've been thinking about things… and remembering. I don't think you attacked me."

I released a pent-up breath. "That's good."

"But there are things you didn't tell me, and things I need to tell you. There's a coffee shop about five blocks that way," she said and pointed north. "The Cafe Wren. I am going to put these in water and walk over."

"I could drive you," I offered.

"No, I need to think about what I want to say." She raised the flowers. "I'll put these in water and meet you there in twenty minutes."

Cafe Wren stood out from the coffee chain stores, as it was an establishment that actually was charming. Its spacious interior boasted large multi-paned windows adorned with lush hanging plants, with seating options ranging from comfortable armchairs for relaxation to simple wooden chairs around round tables. The walls displayed an eclectic mix of artwork, much of which local artists had made and sold. The subdued ambiance and the lack of a crowd made it the perfect place to have a conversation with Emily.

I got a cappuccino and sat far away from the other patrons in one of the comfortable chairs, and in about ten more minutes, Emily came in.

I stood. "Can I get you a coffee?"

"I've got it," she said, and headed to the counter to place an order.

She returned moments later with a steaming cup and sat across from me.

"Thank you for agreeing to see me," I said. "You were pretty mad last night."

She nodded. "Mad and confused. I... remember... what we did... what I did, but it's like I wasn't in control. The whole thing was like a dream."

"I had the same problem. I think Rebecca Hawthornes's spirit possessed you, maybe possessed us both."

She sat back in the chair, her brow creased in thought. "How is that even possible?"

"You're the one who said you'd had experience with the occult. Can you explain it?"

"I believe my offer to help Rebecca allowed her to use us. Like inviting a vampire into your house."

"Can she do that again anytime she wants?"

"I don't think so. But I can see why she might choose to use me."

This surprised me. "Why?"

"Because I knew Rebecca when she was alive."

Fifteen

Emily's Story

I sat back, stunned. "What?"

She looked at me, her eyes big behind her glasses. "I said there were things I need to tell you. First, until yesterday, I didn't know you lived in the cabin Rebecca used up here. Believe me."

"I… I do," I replied.

"Good," she said, and grappled with what she wanted to say before she went on. "I grew up across the street from Rebecca and her husband. Her daughter, Elora, was my best friend growing up. Rebecca used to call us the twins — Emmy and Ellie. I was ten when Rebecca went missing. Ellie was really upset. She said she spoke to her mother on the phone, and Rebecca told her she finished her book and would be home in a few days."

"Really?" I said, but this made me wonder. Why would she kill herself if she said she'd finished the book and was heading home?

"The police came by and talked to her and her father, and even came over and asked my parents questions. Elora told me that someone named Riley filed a report of her missing. Was that you?"

"No, I never met Rebecca."

Not in life, anyway.

"It was my cousin, Liam. He's the one who filed the report."

And buried her.

She shook her head. "I should have connected with the name Riley."

"It's a common enough name," I said. "My uncle owned the cabin, and we all went up to it as kids."

"How did Rebecca end up using the cabin?" she asked.

"My cousin Robert met her at a book event." I explained their meeting and the invitation to use the cabin.

"That was Rebecca," she said. "As a kid, she always insisted Ellie and I call her by her given name. She was always doing things, writing, painting, making stained glass. There was one room in the house dedicated as her workroom, and we only went into it with permission. Dozens of journals she'd written over the years, as well as half-finished projects, filled the room."

"You can remember that?" I asked.

"Sure! She was always talking about the next book she wanted to write and saying she had to get away to write it. She left for four months one time and six months another time. I know because both times, her aunt moved in to help. Rebecca came back with a finished book both times."

"Must have made life difficult for Elora."

"Yeah, I think that's why she was an only child. I had two sisters, and all of us kind of adopted Ellie, watched out for her."

"What happened to her?"

"Ellie? She's still in Connecticut, but she's married and has two kids. Her mother always seemed annoyed by children, but Ellie loves having kids. On a good day, Rebecca was fine, but if she was dealing with her depression, she was moody. Ellie and I always walked on eggshells when she was in one of her bad phases, and Ellie would spend a lot of time at my house."

"I read she dealt with depression."

"Yeah. Looking back, I'm sure she was manic-depressive. You could see it in her clothing choices. On days when she felt depressed, she wore nothing but gray and black. Then, during her manic episodes, she became a whirlwind of color and patterns."

"I guess my cousins met her during a manic phase."

"A few years after Rebecca went missing, Ellie wanted me there when they cleaned out her workspace for emotional support. It must have been five years after Rebecca was gone, because both of us were teenagers. I helped her and her dad organize what we could, her journals and all, but we threw away so much. We all cried when we did it, because it meant we knew Rebecca wasn't coming back."

She looked so incredibly sad. I wanted to take her in my arms.

"How did her husband cope with Rebecca acting the way she did?"

"He indulged her as much as he could. I hope I haven't given you the wrong impression. Rebecca handled things as best she could most of the time. But every few years, she needed to go on a writing retreat, as she called it. It was later, when Ellie and I were eighteen, that she told me her mom's retreats were a vacation from her marriage as well."

I exhaled heavily. "At the cabin, she slept with my cousin, Liam."

Emily sighed. "She was a different person when writing. I remembered as a kid, right before she went on her last retreat up here, I had a sleepover at Ellie's. I woke up in the night because I heard a noise and went downstairs, following the sound. When I got to the first floor, the door to her workspace was open. There was Rebecca, typing away, but she was completely naked. It shocked me. I mean, I had never seen a grown woman naked before. She didn't notice me. Whatever she was writing completely engrossed her. I backed out of the room and went back to bed, but I remember that."

I nodded, knowing all too well what she was talking about. I saw it night after night. "You said your mother was interested in the occult?"

"Yes, ghosts and haunting and ESP. Rebecca loved it and invited my parents over all the time to use my mom's Ouija board. Rebecca always said that if she died, she would stick around just to mess with people's minds."

More than their minds, I thought. "How did you end up in Milford?"

"I've always loved books, so I figured, become a librarian. In college, I studied library and information science. Then, looking for work, I found the job in Milford, and Ellie reminded me that Milford was near where her mother disappeared. So, I took the job and moved here. I wanted to see the place where she disappeared. I'll be honest with you. I knew the way to your cabin last night because since I started living up here six months ago, I've been there almost a dozen times."

"What?" It seemed like I was going to be surprised over and over. "What did you do?"

"Don't worry, I didn't break into the house or anything. I just walked through the woods with a pair of copper dowsing rods my mother owned. She helped a friend find water for a well with them. I thought it would help me find her."

I nodded. "But they didn't lead you to the site where she was buried?"

She shook her head. "No. They kept guiding me to the cabin. I walked around those woods for hours and all I got was a pull to the cabin." She lowered her head. "It made me mad. One time I felt like I wanted to blow up the damn cabin."

"I'm glad you didn't," I said. "I would be homeless."

"I cooled down, came home, and went to bed. The destructive impulse was gone once I got some sleep."

"Sleep," I repeated. "I think Rebecca was sleeping, and I woke her up."

She frowned. "How do you know that?"

"I've seen her almost every night. And she talks to me in my dreams."

She sat back in her chair and sipped her coffee, troubled. "So it was her last night."

"I… I think so," I said. I wanted to take her hand, but I didn't know what she was feeling, and I didn't want to do the wrong thing.

She paused, made sure people were not nearby and spoke in a low tone. "She wanted to have sex with you." Sitting back, she studied my face. "But that wasn't lovemaking, what she did with us. That was… angry and… it wasn't giving. It was taking."

"I don't think you should go anywhere near the cabin. We can meet here in town, where she can't control you."

She was staring at her coffee. "But you're not safe either."

"I am if I'm alone. She has done nothing to me."

"Except last night," she replied cryptically. "You said you weren't in control either."

"It was the only time. Last night, we were an outlet for her desires. I think your offer to help let her in." I glanced around again, making sure myself that no one was nearby. "In my dreams, she told me she needs energy, and that sex gives her the power to write."

"Write?" she replied, confused. "How could she write?"

"That's the thing," I explained. "I came up here to write a novel, and, well, Rebecca has been adding pages every night."

"Adding pages?"

"I go to bed, and the next morning there are more pages than I wrote. It's in my style and follows my plot line. In fact, she's improved it."

She made a little noise, like "Ah!" then added, "That's what Rebecca did when she wasn't writing her own books. She took on work as a ghostwriter."

I felt an unearthly chill go up my spine.

"I don't understand how she could work on your book," Emily said, frowning. "She never used a computer."

"No, I'm typing the story. There was a typewriter in the cabin."

She snapped her fingers. "That's right! You said that the first time I met you. Is it a portable?"

"Yes, it came in a big case. An Olympia Traveler."

"Blue and White?"

"Yes. It was out on my desk last night."

"I didn't notice it. But if it is a blue and white Olympia Traveler, then that was her typewriter."

And suddenly it all became clear to me. I assumed that removing Rebecca's remains would release her, but her spirit didn't remain within the long, decaying body.

The typewriter held Rebecca's spirit.

It made perfect sense. I discovered the old machine and used it. That gave her the ability to manifest. I wrote my story and pulled her back to awareness. That's why her page number increased each day. As I gave her more, she gave more, and that increased her power.

Enough to control Emily and me.

Emily looked at me, confused by the strange expression on my face. "What is it?"

"It's the typewriter. You couldn't find the grave because Rebecca's spirit didn't have a connection to it. She's haunting the typewriter. It's what gives her the power to make us do things."

"The typewriter? How is that possible?"

"How is any of this possible?" I asked. "But I've been writing every day, putting my energy into creating a story—"

"You think that's how she made us... uh... do the things we did last night?"

"She told me that sex gives her inspiration, that she needs it when she's writing," I said. "She used Liam, but wait! Liam told me he had a big fight with her because he showed up and there was a rental car in the driveway and Rebecca told him to go away. That was right before she disappeared."

"Rebecca was seeing multiple men at your cabin?" she said. "You think it was the guy in the rental car who killed her and buried her there?"

"It's a possibility," I said. I knew Liam buried the body, but I wasn't sure about her hanging herself. If there were someone else, it could have been murder. Then again, Rebecca had a history of depression. She could've finished her novel, read it, and hated it, despaired that it wasn't good enough, burned it and hung herself.

Or Liam could have killed her. All of it was possible.

"From what you know about the occult," I said. "How do we disconnect Rebecca from the typewriter?"

"You want to cast her out?" Emily said.

"I want her to move on, to be free."

"Do you think that's what she wants?"

I sat back and considered this. "She said she wants to finish the novel we're working on."

"If you finish it, maybe that will release her."

I sipped my cappuccino. "I don't know. She controlled us. I don't want to be used like we were last night — against our will."

She leaned forward. "It was weird. It was like I wasn't there for whatever amount of time it was. Then this morning, I woke up and I could remember everything we did. All of it."

"I'm glad you're not mad at me anymore. But as far as an out-of-body situation, Rebecca's doing that to me as well. I go into a trance when I write these days. It's when I review the pages that I see what I wrote."

"Do you think you're in danger?"

"I don't think so," I said. "She needs me, needs my energy. Once the book is done, though, I don't know. Do you have any occult books?"

"Several."

"Could you look up how to remove a ghost?"

"I'll see what I can find. What will you do?"

I sighed. "I've got to keep working on the book. My publisher wants it soon. But, I'd also like to see you, but only in a place where you'll be safe. I like you."

She took my hand. "Joe, I like you as well. I want to go out with you again."

I smiled. "That's good."

With a twinkle in her eye, she added. "After all, you have seen me naked."

I felt my cheeks grow hot. "That's true. But I'm willing to take things slow. I don't want you to feel pressured. Even after… what happened."

"I'm glad you came by, and thank you for the flowers."

"Thank you for seeing me. Can I drive you home?"

"No, I want to walk. And I'll look through my books for information about ghosts. I can also look in the library."

I nodded. "Okay, I'll head back to the cabin."

"If you feel you are in any danger, I have a sofa I can put you up on."

I smiled. "That's good to know."

We parted, and I drove back to Dingman's Ferry, our discussion running through my mind. Why didn't I get it sooner? The typewriter was the focus of Rebecca's power. If I used the scanner and saved a digital copy of the book into my laptop, I could finish the book on that machine, disconnected from Rebecca.

Of course, all the appearing pages would cease, but I felt the story was far enough along that I could complete it.

It's not like I hadn't finished a book before.

It was a balmy day as I drove up the road, through dense forests and rolling hills. I inhaled the scent of freshly bloomed wildflowers on the breeze. I was pleased Emily would see me again, and since she remembered our encounter, she knew I hadn't forced myself on her or drugged her. That truly improved my mood.

I slowed down for a deer crossing the road and saw a rabbit darting into the undergrowth. Untamed beauty surrounded me.

I pulled up the driveway and parked my truck; the cabin looked harmless on such a clear day. Instead of going in, I walked past the house and caught a view of the lake in the distance, its water shimmering like diamonds under the midday sun. The reflection of the sky painted a kaleidoscope of blues, and I paused for a moment, taking in the view.

Only to find Liam's car parked behind the house.

I frowned. What was Liam doing here, and why hadn't I taken in that damn spare key?

I went inside, and he wasn't in the main room, and with my temper rising, I called out, "Liam!"

A noise pierced the air, coming from my bedroom. I froze. The sound—like a desperate gasp—sent a jolt of dread through my veins.

"Oh God," I gasped, plunging through the door.

Dangling a foot above the bed, Liam's body swayed from a hastily made noose. I saw the rope knotted cruelly around his neck, its fibers biting into his skin. The kitchen step-stool lay askew on the floor beneath him.

He'd tied one end of the rope to the wall cleat and used the pulley, and was hanging with his eyes closed.

Heart pounding, I lunged forward, grasped the cleat with trembling hands and yanked the rope free as quickly as I could.

With a rattle from the pulley overhead, Liam plummeted onto the bed, falling flat. But the remaining tension of the rope still constricted his neck.

With shaking fingers, I rolled him over, fought against the binding grip of the rope, and finally loosened it. Flipping him onto his back, I watched, breathless, as he coughed violently, and drew struggling breaths that rattled like thunder in the stillness.

Almost in a daze, I grabbed my phone, grateful I had good reception, and dialed 9-1-1. As the ringing echoed in my ear, my gaze shifted upward, an icy chill creeping down my spine.

"Rebecca, was this you?" I shouted into the expanse above, my voice trembling with fear and accusation.

The dispatcher answered, but my focus remained on Liam, desperate to secure help for my cousin.

The shadows in the room appeared to deepen, as if they too held their breath, waiting for the next move in this twisted game.

Sixteen

Trance

I sat on the bed next to Liam, waiting for the ambulance. He was still unconscious although he was breathing evenly now, but my hands were shaking from the adrenaline rush.

What would have happened if I had stayed in Milford longer, or stopped off at the grocery store on my way home?

Liam's neck had a dark red line around it that would soon be purple bruises.

What made him do it? I knew from personal experience Rebecca could possess people and make them do things. After all, she'd done it to me.

But why? Vengeance for his burying her? Or was it more than that? Was Liam experiencing so much guilt he couldn't bear it because he killed Rebecca?

I heard the ambulance pull up the driveway.

Two men came in and maneuvered Liam onto a gurney as I stood watching helplessly. One man put an oxygen mask over his face, and they wheeled him out.

I asked, "Where are you taking him?"

"The Bon Secours Hospital in Port Jervis. It's the closest," the leader of the pair said.

"Can I come with you?"

"Not enough room," he explained, and they headed to the waiting vehicle.

"I'll follow you," I said, grabbing my coat and heading for the door.

The ambulance drove away with lights flashing, and I pulled my truck behind it to follow. The sun was still out, and I tried to recall if the bedroom was cold when I saved Liam.

I was still so pumped with adrenaline, I couldn't recall.

With a deep sigh, I focused on the road and used my Bluetooth connection to make a hands-free phone call to Ashley.

"Yes, Joey," she said, not pleased to hear from me. "What now?"

"Liam's on his way to the hospital," I stated flatly. "He tried to kill himself at the cabin."

"What?" she gasped.

I told her the story. She listened silently, adding nothing as I spoke.

Finally, she let out a long breath and said, "That damn cabin. I thought with you there, I wouldn't have to deal with anything about it anymore."

"What do you mean?" I asked.

She sighed again. "During Mom's death and the last few years, I took over the arrangements for the upkeep of Whispering Pines to take it off Dad's plate. He even offered to leave the place to me."

I didn't know this. "Why didn't you take it?"

"I hate that place, Joey. There's something — I don't know — dark there. That's why I've only been up to the place once or twice in the last few years. I was the one who told Dad to leave it to you."

This resolved the mystery of my inheritance. Ashley, as she had done so many times in our youth, took charge of the situation and took care of me.

"Ash, you need to know the truth. It wasn't an accident that I found Rebecca's remains. Liam led me to the spot."

"I know. He told me the whole thing," she said. "He's been staying at my house for the last few days. I told him he should just talk to the police, but he wouldn't listen."

"Do you think Liam could have killed Rebecca?"

"What? That's crazy! Liam?"

"I know. He doesn't seem like the type. But I've been doing research on Rebecca Hawthorne. I don't think she would have killed herself."

"This is from your up close and personal knowledge of the woman?" she spat.

"I just have a feeling."

"Liam was head over heels in love with Rebecca. He would've done anything for her. I think she wrote her damn book and found out it wasn't any good. Look, Joey, she was mercurial and could be pretty wild. I don't put it past her to kill herself. She probably even knew Liam would discover the body."

"Did you see her much while she lived here? Robert said you felt like she was a mentor."

"Now you're interrogating me! Joey, I didn't even own a car back then. Look, I have to call the hospital and make a plan for

Liam. I doubt he has any health insurance, so there goes a chunk of his inheritance."

She ended the call before I could ask another question. Her timing was good, as I pulled into the driveway for the hospital. I pulled my truck behind the extensive building and into the parking lot.

I stepped through the automatic doors of the hospital, my nerves frayed and heart hammering in my chest. The harsh fluorescent lights cast cold, sterile shadows, making everything feel distant and unreal.

Approaching the receptionist with trembling hands, I fumbled out my cousin's name. She offered me a measured glance, efficiently yet impassively directing me to wait outside the emergency ward.

Taking a seat among strangers whose drawn faces mirrored my fear, I felt each painstaking second tick by like torture.

A nurse came out and handed me a form, which I filled out. I put down my name and number as well as Robert's and Ashley's. I filled out what medical history I knew, which wasn't very much.

The restless murmurs and faint coughs around me melted into a bleak background hum that only intensified my anxiety.

Hours trudged past; the waiting became unbearable, the not knowing tearing me apart from within.

Finally, after what felt like an eternity, a man in a crisp white coat emerged, his eyes scanning the waiting area. "Mr. Riley?"

I rose unsteadily, heart pounding like a drum, and walked towards him.

He was of average height, clean-shaven and wore thin-framed glasses. His features hinted at Indian heritage — his tanned complexion faintly illuminated by stark hospital lights. The badge pinned precisely to his chest read 'Dr. Singh.'

My voice cracked slightly as I spoke, desperate and fearful of the answer. "How... how is my cousin, Doctor?"

He studied me intently, his gaze softening slightly. "You were the one who rescued him? Who called in the paramedics?"

Swallowing hard, I managed only a brief nod.

His eyes held mine a moment longer, filled with quiet sincerity. "You likely saved his life."

Despite his reassurance, an unexpected wave of guilt hit me then, far heavier than relief or gratitude. If it hadn't been for me, Liam might never have made that dreadful choice in the first place.

Struggling to steady the tremor in my voice, I asked urgently, "What else can you tell me, Doctor?"

He glanced down briefly at the clipboard in his hands before he lifted his eyes again, mingling cautious optimism with tempered seriousness. "There's some promising news. When Liam arrived, he was breathing spontaneously. I've just tested him, and his pupils showed a response to light. All good indicators at this stage."

A fragile flicker of hope sparked inside me, warring immediately with stubborn, heavy dread. "Do you have a treatment plan?"

Dr. Singh nodded thoughtfully, eyes returning to his notes. "We're preparing him for hyperbaric oxygen therapy now, hoping it will aid his recovery. But—" he paused, weighing his words carefully, "at the moment, he's still comatose. Unfortunately, there's nothing more you can do here tonight. I suggest you get some rest and return in the morning."

Feeling numb, I stood rooted to the spot, the reality of my cousin's uncertain future hitting me like a physical blow. As Dr. Singh returned through the double doors into the maze of medical equipment and hushed voices beyond, I realized I had never felt so helpless — or so painfully aware of my responsibility in the tragedy unfolding before me.

Driving home, my phone in my shaking hands, I was desperate to call Emily and hear her voice. But I let the phone fall onto the passenger seat. Emily didn't deserve more heartbreak, not yet. Her quiet life had already twisted into enough darkness.

My thoughts spiraled chaotically, relentlessly circling back to Liam. Could Rebecca have manipulated him into doing something so horrific?

A chill slid down my spine at the thought.

I couldn't remember a single encounter where Rebecca had appeared during daylight — her presence always arrived under the shroud of darkness, at two-thirty in the morning or invading my vulnerable dreams. Could her powers now extend beyond nightfall?

Liam's troubled mind always balanced precariously at an edge, long before Rebecca ignited my nightmares. Had Detective Sullivan's relentless pursuit finally pushed him to a breaking point? Or had it instead been Liam's own suffocating guilt, finally erupting, pulling him into a darkness deeper than I could imagine?

Each unanswered question clung heavily to me, weighing down my chest as I drove, uncertain if the coming answers would lift the burden or shatter me completely.

It was dark by the time I arrived at the cabin.

I made it a point to clean up the place, as I needed to do something. I put the stepladder back where it belonged and rolled up the rope to return it to the shed.

As I walked outside, I found the shed door open and the padlock on the ground. This made me pause. Did Liam know about the ring of keys in the kitchen drawer? I guess he had to know.

I went into the dark room as the creaking door swung closed behind me with a haunting groan. The air inside was hotter than outside and hung heavy with the acrid scent of mildew. My footsteps echoed in the silence as I placed the rope on the workbench where I had seen it before. I considered hiding it, but what good would that do?

Finding I was hungry, I went back inside to make dinner, just as Detective Sullivan's unmarked police car pulled into my driveway.

This was the last thing I needed.

I opened the door for the tall man. Gazing up at his movie-star good looks just pissed me off.

"I thought I made my position clear," I said, not caring if I sounded rude.

"I got a call about your cousin," Sullivan said. "We put out an APB on him, and the hospital called me. Have you been hiding him here?"

I glared at him. "What? No!"

"The doctor said he tried to hang himself, is that right?"

The hospital freely shared information about my cousin, which annoyed me. "I found him here, hanging by the neck in the bedroom. I figure he came here and used the spare key to let himself in."

"How is he?" he said, compassion in his voice.

I shook my head. "The doctors are evaluating him, but he hasn't regained consciousness. I should be with him."

"You could do that. Why don't you tell me what happened, the whole story?"

I gritted my teeth. I didn't like it, but it made sense for a policeman to come by after a suicide attempt. We sat at the dining room table and I told him what happened, as best as I could remember.

"Over the last few days, your cousin wasn't responding to phone calls," Sullivan said, as he finished writing his notes. "We also sent some patrolmen to monitor his apartment. He hasn't been home."

I nodded. I certainly didn't intend to tell Sullivan that Liam had been staying with Ashley. "He's been troubled for a long time."

"I know; I've reviewed his police record," Sullivan said, flipping through pages of his notebook. "Driving while under the influence — he lost his driving privileges for a year when that happened. Arrested for possession with the intent to distribute, petty theft, and more. It seems like your uncle got him some good lawyers, so he didn't do any jail time. He's been in and out of trouble for about the last twenty years."

He raised his head to gaze at me with his intimidating stare.

"Twenty years, about the time of Ms. Hawthorne's disappearance," Sullivan said. I could tell he was choosing his words with care. "Do you think there might be a connection between your finding the remains the other day and his attempt at suicide?"

I swallowed hard. That was what I was considering.

Finally, I spoke. "You'd have to ask Liam."

"It's just odd," Sullivan went on, ignoring my answer. "The pair of you set out to dig a firepit, without any of the things you might need to build one. Then, a few days later, he comes back here to hang himself. The coroner believes Ms. Hawthorne may have died the same way."

"Really?"

He nodded. "Yes. By the way, we received the dental records, and it is definitely Mrs. Hawthorne."

I looked at my hands, not wanting to make eye contact, not wanting to meet those eyes that seemed to peer right through my lies. "At least you've solved that mystery. What are you trying to say, Detective?"

He shrugged. "Why did your cousin come all the way up here to hang himself? He could have done it anywhere."

I had enough. "If you're trying to suggest that my cousin killed Rebecca, I'm going to tell you no."

His mouth twisted in a rueful smile. "So, it's Rebecca now, is it?"

I set my jaw. "I told you, I've been researching the woman. In a sense, I feel like I know her."

He rose, snapping his notebook closed. "I have what I came for. I'll talk to your cousin once he's conscious. If I feel you haven't been up front with me, I'm going to call you in for a formal interrogation, so I would advise you to contact that lawyer."

"Is that a threat, Detective?" I asked.

"Just sound advice, Mr. Riley."

I sat there, my mouth a tight line as he drove away.

I thought about calling Emily again, but felt I had burdened the woman enough for one day.

I had finished the scotch, and I wanted the vodka. Instead, I grabbed a bottle of wine and poured myself a tumbler, filling it to the top. I looked at it for a good long while before I finally took a sip.

I glared at the typewriter. Rebecca's spirit cursed the machine. It was her physical link to this world. I wondered what would happen if I took the damn thing and threw it in the lake?

I paused. What about the book? *Lost Soul* was going so well, and if I did something, anything that would prevent the book from being finished, it would anger my publisher and a next book deal might not come to fruition. And the stuff Rebecca was giving me was gold.

My resolve crumbled. If I lost her, could I finish the book? I had felt so confident, but now I wasn't sure.

In a daze, I sat at the desk as the story unfolded in my mind. Without even thinking, I put paper in the machine and my fingers went to the keyboard.

Almost in a trance, I watched my fingers dance on the keys and saw the words appear on the page. It was like there was a movie of the events playing in my mind, pulling me deeper in than ever before.

The ringing of my phone startled me, pulling me back to reality.

"H-hello," I said and leaned back so I could see the clock on the stove. It read 11:30. I had been writing uninterrupted for over three hours.

"Joey, is that you?" Robert's voice was abrasive. "You sound like you're a hundred miles away."

"I might be," I said, feeling like I'd just woke up. "Sorry, I was writing."

"I'm in Port Jervis at the hospital. I thought I'd see you here."

"The doctor told me to go home, as Liam hadn't regained consciousness. I thought I'd head back tomorrow."

"Maybe that's for the best. He's still unconscious," Robert said, and his voice shifted. "I was wondering if I could stay in the cabin with you. It's getting late and heading back to New Jersey on those back roads—"

"No, that's fine. I've got plenty of room. We could go up together and see Liam tomorrow. I'll make up the second bedroom for you."

"I'll be there in about half an hour."

I set my phone aside, a sudden unease tightening in my chest. Doubt twisted my thoughts, making me question if I'd made the right choice by agreeing.

Would Rebecca still come tonight? Would she appear at her customary two-thirty? My pulse quickened as uncertainty spread through me, the quiet darkness around me amplifying the dread pooling inside my stomach.

No matter what happened, he was family and needed a place to stay. If we could help Liam, that is what we needed to focus on.

I walked over to the typewriter and found my empty tumbler without even remembering drinking it. Looking at the half-finished page in the machine, I observed I had added thirty pages to the manuscript.

I half-sat, half-fell into the chair and pawed through the pages to make sure I hadn't jumped the page number at some point. But the stack had grown, and the page numbers were correct.

I read a few lines from the pages, but I couldn't recall writing them. The story was clear in my head, and had progressed to the next part in the narrative, but I couldn't actually recall typing the words.

The word choices and sentence structure also impressed me. I usually spent a lot of time checking my thesaurus, as I had the bad habit of using the same word more than once in the same sentence.

There was none of that in what I typed. The writing was clean and strong, and at the level of the stuff Rebecca wrote.

Rebecca.

Had she possessed me like she had done the previous night?

If so, she was getting stronger.

And what would that mean for me?

I had to make changes. So far, these strange events had carried me along, much like Rebecca used me to experience sex with Emily. I'd been so caught up in the extra pages and my interactions with Rebecca that I didn't see just how dangerous she was.

I now saw that I was in a battle, perhaps a battle for my very soul.

Seventeen

Reacquaintance

Less than an hour later, Robert pulled his Mercedes up the driveway and parked next to my truck. He was wearing a suit, no tie, and a tired demeanor.

"You look like crap," I observed.

He nodded as if his head weighed eight hundred pounds. "You, too. What do you have to drink?"

"Wine and vodka. I finished the scotch."

"Wine will do," he said and sat heavily on the sofa.

"How's Liam?" I poured wine into a water glass for him.

"Still unconscious," he said. "The doctors say he's in a coma."

I handed him a glass, and he took a deep drink, then asked, "Are you having any?"

"I've had enough," I said.

"So what the hell happened?" Robert asked after draining half the glass. "Why did he try to kill himself?"

"That's what I'm trying to figure out," I said. I went through the story of arriving and rescuing Liam again. I was getting good at telling it as I'd repeated it to Detective Sullivan and the EMTs.

When I finished, he shook his head. "Any idea why he did it?"

It was my turn to sigh. "Actually, yes, I do." I met his eyes. "Rebecca Hawthorne."

"You think the police finding her body set him off?"

I refilled Robert's glass. "Bobby, he's the one who buried her."

I used his childhood nickname, hoping it would help him open up to me.

I carefully went through the story Liam told me about finding Rebecca hanging in the bedroom and how, in a panic, he buried her and her belongings.

Robert sucked down his wine. "Jeez, what a clusterfuck."

"Yes, and there's a Pennsylvania state detective named Sullivan, who feels that I was not completely forthcoming about my explanation of locating her remains."

"I spoke to him," Robert replied. "He asked me questions about that summer and about you."

"Anything I should know?"

"As far as I know, you were in Manhattan that summer." His eyes grew narrow. "You didn't tell him about Liam, did you?"

"I only said that Liam was here helping me dig the fire pit, but that he left as soon as I dug up the suitcase. Sullivan's been trying to track him down with no luck. Ash told me he's been staying with her."

"Is that where he's been? I've been trying to reach him myself."

"The problem is that Detective Sullivan knows I didn't tell him everything, and keeps coming back to talk to me." I asked the question that troubled me the most. "Bobby, do you think that Liam could have killed her?"

His eyes grew wide, and he sat back in the chair. I could tell he was seriously considering it. "I don't think Liam is violent. He was crazy about Rebecca, kept talking about how they were going to run away and be together, that kind of stuff."

"If he pinned all his hopes on being with her and she rejected him…"

He shook his head.

"Bobby, admit it; his actions are highly suspicious. I mean, he buried the body, and besides that, he's a person of interest. He was coming up here every weekend to see her."

"There were others, from what I understand," Robert said.

I nodded. "Liam said there was a rented car in the driveway and someone came up to see Rebecca, but he didn't know who. Liam said they had a fight. Then the next time he came up, she was dead."

"Pointing suspicion at Liam. No wonder he didn't want to speak to the cop." He gulped the rest of his glass of wine. "My troubled brother—what a fuck-up."

"Maybe Liam didn't see a way out," I said. I gestured to the almost empty bottle of wine. "You want more? I have other bottles."

"No, I'm all in. If Liam regains consciousness, I'll convince him to talk to the police. I'll also get him a good criminal lawyer. One of Dad's friends must know someone."

"It's good of you to take this on."

"I've been rescuing Liam his whole life," he said, weary. "He's a mess, but he's our mess." He rose from the table. "You got any pajamas I could wear?"

"There's a pair in the second bedroom."

He stopped, glancing at me. "I have to ask you, why did you bring all of this up?"

"What?" I said.

"I mean, asking about Rebecca, looking into her. You had to know it was a sore spot. Why ask about it?"

I wanted to tell him it was because she was here. She was haunting this place and writing my book. I wanted to free her, but I also wanted to keep her around until I'd finished the book.

I could tell him one thing that was true. "I wish I'd never brought it up."

"That makes two of us, Joey. See you in the morning."

He walked into the second bedroom and closed the door.

I shut off the lights, put our glasses in the sink, and with a glance at the typewriter, went into the master bedroom.

As I lay down, I wondered if she would manifest at her usual time, and if so, would Robert even see her?

The sound of typing woke me. In a way, I'd been waiting for it, drifting in semi-consciousness.

I sat up in bed and saw my breath as I exhaled. It was even colder than last time. Was she getting stronger?

The cold air in the room seemed to linger, thin and crisp, almost frosting on my skin. Every breath felt biting, creating a cloud of icy vapor with each exhale. I pulled open the door with numb fingers and stepped into the main room.

There was a layer of frost on top of the stove, and an icicle dripped out of the kitchen tap.

The desk lamp cast Rebecca's shadow across the floor as she typed maniacally.

My God, she was casting a shadow now.

The soft curve of her hips and breasts mesmerized me until a voice coming from across the room broke the spell.

"Oh, my God."

Robert stood in the open doorway of the bedroom with a blanket wrapped around him. He gaped wide-eyed at the woman typing.

"R-Rebecca?"

Rebecca pulled the page from the typewriter as she rose from the chair, and instantly she wore a loose white blouse and jeans. The change was so startling, I couldn't understand how it had happened.

"Bobby, what are you doing here?" she asked. She wasn't staring at my shivering cousin in the bedroom doorway. Instead, she fixed her eyes on the front door.

She went on. "So your brother sent you to plead his case?"

"What?" Robert said, frowning, but she continued to stare at the front door, and I realized Rebecca was not aware of me or Robert in the flesh, but was reliving something that had happened in the past.

She shook her head. "I tried to explain to him it's about the book. Once it's done, I am going back to my husband and daughter. He was great fun, but I only needed the extra stimulation while writing."

Robert twisted to me, and in a loud whisper, said, "It's Rebecca."

"I know," I said, watching my breath come out in a fog as I spoke.

"Don't act innocent with me, Robert Riley." Rebecca stepped away from the desk into the center of the room. "I know you watch me work at night, pretending you're asleep. I know you want me."

She stared at the space, apparently listening to someone who wasn't there.

"How is this possible? She's dead!" Robert stepped toward her, the blanket wrapped around him tighter. "Rebecca, can you see me?"

She ignored him, continuing the conversation with her invisible companion. "I'll tell you what I told him. Once the book is done, I'm gone. Thanks for the use of the cabin. It's a great place to work. But I am going back to my old life."

Her eyes grew wide, and she suddenly grabbed a chair from the dining room table and flung it at the door. It flew, and both Robert and I ducked and covered our heads.

The chair crashed into the front door, and we both looked up, but Rebecca had vanished. It was just Robert and me standing in the room, lit only by the lamp over my desk.

In the corner, the propane heater came on full blast.

"My G-God!" Robert said, staggering slightly.

"Go stand by the heater. It'll warm you faster."

"You s-saw her, right?" he hissed. "She was there?"

"Yes, but who was she talking to?"

He walked across the room and stood in front of the heater, the blanket still clutched around him. "Me, I guess. I visited Rebecca here at the cabin. It must have been a few days before she died. I told her she needed to let Liam down easy. Then she threw a chair at me."

I looked at the chair lying on the floor near the front door. "Why did she do that?"

"I may have called her a whore. But the crazy woman threw a chair at me, just like what happened now."

I carried the chair back to the table. It was undamaged from its flight across the room, so I sat on it. "We heard her end of the conversation she had with you?"

"Yes. I didn't think she knew I saw her at night — y'know, when she was writing."

"Which she does in the buff," I said, as Robert raised an eyebrow. "I've seen her every night since I got here."

"So that's why you wanted to find out about her." He walked toward me. "Look, we have to get out of here. Lock this place up and run."

"I can't," I said, annoyance creeping up inside of me.

"You saw her. There's a goddamn ghost in this place."

Avoiding his stare, I said, "I can't leave. I'm working on a book."

He frowned. "You can do that anywhere."

"No, I can't," I said, and my voice rose. "I've had writer's block until I got here. I've been using the typewriter."

"Her typewriter?"

"Yes. If I leave, it might break the spell."

Robert's brow furrowed with concern. "Joey, I get you want inspiration, but the house is haunted. She just threw that chair across the room. It's dangerous to stay here."

"You don't get it," I said firmly. "Rebecca has been helping me."

"Helping you?"

I didn't want to tell him she co-wrote the book with me. "Yes, helping me."

"I'm getting dressed and getting the hell out of here."

"Robert, it's the middle of the night."

"If she can throw chairs and God knows what else, I'm not going to risk my life." He walked to the bedroom and opened the door. "If you had any sense, you'd come with me."

He slammed the door as I sat there. A part of me actually agreed with him. This whole thing was getting out of hand, between her adding pages and me falling into that strange fugue when I was writing today. She could now manifest and move solid objects. She had controlled Emily and me to have a romp between the sheets and empower herself.

I wanted her to be put to rest, but what if she didn't want that? What if she wanted to stay in this cabin, remaining here until it crumbled from neglect?

And what about my book?

I had not reviewed the pages I had written that day, and had no memory of them. Rebecca was doing her nightly typing when Robert and I interrupted her. How much had she achieved?

I needed that book; I needed it for my career, and yes, for the damn money. Rebecca needed me to feed her energy. I believed we could get the book done and lay her to rest. Happy ending all around.

Isn't that why I wrote fiction? To end everything with all loose ends tied up.

Trouble is, life rarely ties up the loose ends. I had so many hanging down, it's a wonder they didn't strangle me.

Robert came out of the bedroom completely dressed. The cabin was warmer now, and I was a bit too warm in the heavy flannel pajamas.

"I'll come by the hospital tomorrow," I said as he made a beeline for the door.

"I'll let you know where I'm staying," Robert said, with a glance over his shoulder.

He stepped outside into the dark night, and a few minutes later, I watched his car drive away from one of the front windows.

Robert had confronted Rebecca years ago, and she had thrown a chair at him. He says it was because he called her a name, but I didn't know that for a fact.

What if he had tried something physical?

Robert could have killed Rebecca and staged her hanging body for Liam to find. He could do it, especially twenty years ago when he wasn't even thirty. Using the pulley in the bedroom would make it easy.

I stepped away. What was this place doing to me? I was looking at my cousins as if they were all murderers.

But Rebecca ended up dead. And I still did not know why, or how to free her.

I went back to bed, and as I lay down; the sound of typing began again.

Eighteen

In The Hospital

The next morning, everything appeared fine. Warm air filled the cabin, and the sun shone through the windows. Pages were quickly accumulating on both sides of the typewriter.

I wanted to read them, to go through what I wrote yesterday, as well as any new pages Rebecca added, but I promised Robert I'd be at the hospital, so I got coffee and headed into the shower.

Half an hour later, dressed and ready to go, I quickly sent a text to Emily:

My cousin tried to kill himself last night

Going to the hospital

Call you later

She replied as I got in my truck.

Please take care.

Do you think it had something to do with Rebecca?

I knew it did, but telling Emily would only upset her. Instead, I drove off to Port Jervis.

As I headed north through Milford, I wondered if I should call Robert and talk to him about the incident the previous night. But what could I say?

After thirty minutes of driving, I pulled into the lot for the hospital and made my way through the main entrance and into a well-lit lobby.

The hallways of the hospital were wide and organized, and as I walked, I saw the walls adorned with posters on health and wellness, and demanding if I had my current flu shot.

I knew I had reached the correct place when I saw Robert sitting in the waiting area.

I sat down in the chair across from him.

"Nice to know you didn't die during the night," Robert said.

"Where did you end up?"

"The Best Western in Matamoras. The guy screwed me on the price, but I have a bed. Tomorrow I have to head back."

"Is Ashley coming up?"

"Yeah, this afternoon at some point, if she can get away from her coffee place."

"How's he doing?"

"As of now, he's still in a coma," he said and glanced at his watch. "The doctor is coming by to give me the latest."

"Does the doctor think he'll wake up?"

He sighed. "Anything could happen. I've been looking into long-term care if he stays in the coma, and let me tell you, it isn't cheap."

We sat quietly as Robert sent texts on his smartphone. I read through an old magazine I found nearby.

Dr. Singh arrived, and recognizing me, he came up to us. "Mr. Riley?"

We both rose, and I indicated Robert. "Hello, Doctor. This is my cousin, Robert Riley. He's Liam's brother."

"What's his condition, Doctor?" Robert asked.

He looked at the clipboard in his hand. "He still has not regained consciousness, but we're continuing the hyperbaric oxygen therapy. Gradual progress towards neurological recovery is the best choice. We don't know whether there is permanent damage. He might slip into apallic syndrome, which is a vegetative state, but so far the tests look good."

"You have my number to call me with updates?" Robert asked.

"Yes," Singh said, looking over the sheet of paper on his clipboard. "It's all on the patient form. I'll keep you informed."

With that, the doctor headed off.

Robert and I sat side by side, and my cousin looked at me. "So every night you've seen that thing—"

"Rebecca," I snapped, and I found it offended me he'd called her a 'thing'. "Her name is Rebecca!"

Robert glanced around because I was loud. "Okay, calm down. Do you see her every night?"

"Yes, usually at two-thirty in the morning. She's always typing."

"Naked?" Robert asked.

"Yes," I said, feeling I was revealing more than I wanted to admit.

He shook his head. "She did that every night. Working on that damn book of hers."

"You're the one who watched her do it when she was alive."

"Yes, but that was a long time ago. It was weird. I mean, watching her was kind of sexy, and yet not really. She wasn't typing naked to have sex or anything; she seemed more natural that way, relaxed."

My experiences were different, but I would not share those with Robert.

"Do you think you can get rid of her?" he asked. "Call a priest, do an exorcism — something?"

I couldn't tell him I needed her to help me finish the book, but I could come close. "No, Robert. I'm on a hot writing streak. I need to keep everything the way it is until the book is done."

"Wow," he said, frowning. "That's almost word for word the same thing Rebecca said." He shook his head. "That crazy book she was writing. I heard she burned it in the fireplace."

I looked at him. "How do you know that?"

"What do you mean?"

"Liam told me he found papers burned in the fireplace when he found her. How do you know?"

Robert glanced around, not meeting my eyes. "I guess it was in the police report after Liam claimed she went missing."

I wanted to pursue it, but a voice called out. "Good, both of you are here."

We saw Detective Sullivan plop himself in the middle chair across from us, facing us.

"Detective Sullivan," I said, not trying to hide the exasperation in my voice.

"Oh?" Robert said. "You're the detective I spoke to?"

He pulled his notebook from his wrinkled suit coat and a pen from his pocket. "Yes. I was hoping to follow up on what we spoke about last time concerning what you know. Do you have a few minutes?"

Robert glanced at me and saw I wasn't pleased about the detective's visit.

I spoke up. "Really, Detective, don't you have better things to do than harass my family?"

He glared at me. "I am trying to find out how a thirty-year-old woman at the height of her career ended up buried in the ground outside of the cabin your family has owned for forty-odd years." He shifted his eyes from me to Robert. "My first choice would be to speak to Liam Riley. Since I cannot and you are here, I am speaking to everyone who could have visited the cabin during the time in question."

I wanted to object, but Robert raised a hand to silence me. "I'm willing to talk to you, Detective. Can we go over there?" He pointed to the corner.

I fumed, but Robert and Sullivan walked to a corner of the room away from me.

I announced, "I'm getting coffee," and headed to the elevator, back to the first floor.

Despite my dislike of Sullivan's interference, I had to admit he had reasons to reexamine the case. It didn't help that Liam was doing everything to suggest guilt on his part. As far as Robert or Ashley dealing with the detective, I thought they each could take care of themselves.

I wondered if Robert would mention the incident we saw reenacted the previous night, where Rebecca threw a chair at him. Could Robert have rented a car instead of driving his own? Was he the mysterious person Rebecca wouldn't let Liam see? That made sense if she was bonking both of them and knew Liam wanted an actual relationship.

Emily mentioned Rebecca told her daughter she wanted to 'come home.' Why would she then hang herself?

Nothing seemed to add up.

This made me question the novel again. Did she finish it and then burn it? Or did someone else destroy it because it revealed something about them?

With a cup of coffee from the downstairs cafe in hand, I returned to the waiting area, and Robert was sitting back where he'd been when I arrived, but was looking paler.

Sullivan was standing, leaning against a wall, writing in his notebook. He raised his head as I approached. "Mr. Riley. I was planning on taking another look at the scene today."

"Not without me there," I insisted.

"That's fine. I was going to head out there now."

I looked at Robert, who said, "You might as well go, Joey. I'll call you if there are any changes."

"But you'll be here alone," I said.

"Ash is coming up. She'll spot me. Besides, there's nothing we can do for Liam right now."

I nodded and returned my gaze to the detective. "Fine, I'll meet you there."

I went back to the parking lot, got my truck, and headed toward home. I felt annoyed, but I understood why the detective was doing what he was doing. He had a case that looked like a murder, involved a celebrated writer, and had been a mystery for over twenty years. I was sure there was a lot of pressure on him to find answers.

But what did I know? It wasn't like Rebecca was telling me whether she had killed herself or someone else had killed her. In fact, our only interactions were working on the book or attempts at being sexual. Her growing ability to manipulate people and objects was troubling, but so far, she had done nothing violent or dangerous to me.

Yet.

I pulled into the cabin's driveway and saw Sullivan's unmarked state car waiting. I parked on the far side of his car. I got out of the truck and noticed that the bird sounds were quiet, and there was an odd hissing noise in the air.

Sullivan got out of his car and walked over to me. "I waited until you got here. You know, I didn't have to wait for you. It's an active crime scene at this point."

"I appreciate that, Detective," I said, trying to like the guy, but I just couldn't.

"Your cousin recalled a visit to the cabin he'd failed to mention before."

"Did he?"

"Yes, said he had forgotten, but he'd had an argument with Ms. Hawthorne and she threw a chair at him."

"Really?" I tried to keep my poker face.

"He said he stayed here last night and had a dream where he remembered."

"He stayed last night, but headed to a hotel early this morning." At least I was telling the truth. I didn't mention how early.

"Seems odd to pay for a hotel when you're only a half-hour away," Sullivan said. "And you have plenty of room."

"I'm sure Robert had his reasons. Now, do you want to see the scene?"

The sharp crack of gunfire pierced the stillness, shattering the tense atmosphere like glass. In a heartbeat, the world slowed to a surreal crawl. Sullivan dropped into a low crouch and reached under the fabric of his coat to get his weapon, and I fell to one knee as well.

Then, the surrounding air seemed to vibrate, and a wave of heat hit me. I instinctively shielded my face with my hands as the force of a shockwave threw me backwards to the ground.

A brilliant ball of fire and billowing smoke rose into the sky, lighting up the forest with an ominous glow. The earth trembled beneath my feet, a deep, resonant pulse that sent vibrations rippling through the ground and into my bones. The sharp, acrid odor of burning fuel, a stench that clawed at the back of my throat and made my eyes water, assaulted my nostrils.

A mushroom-shaped cloud of smoke and debris rose into the sky, billowing out high above — right where my propane tank had been.

Nineteen

Fire in The Forest

I threw my hands over my head as falling metal and debris filled the air. The pieces bounced off the roofs of our vehicles in a rhythm that sounded like hail. A fragment landed on my arm, scorching a hole through my shirt. I brushed it off, but winced at the nasty red mark it left.

A thick haze of smoke filled the air. Peering around, I saw a terrifying sight — fire engulfed the forest just past my cabin. The building obscured my view of the cabin's far wall, so I couldn't see if my home also was ablaze.

Sullivan was crouched between his car and my truck. He pulled the door open, grabbed the radio handset. "10-13, 10-13, shots fired. Contact the Dingman Volunteers. The fire is located at—" and he rattled off my address.

His voice seemed distant, and I realized it was the aftereffects of the explosion, leaving a distinct ringing in my ears.

There was also the sound of the crackling of flames and billowing plumes of smoke in the air. I got to my feet.

Sullivan gestured at me to duck, shouting, "Shots fired, get down!"

"My house is on fire," I yelled back, running for the door. "I have to get an extinguisher."

I burst into the house, which was filling with smoke. I stopped to look at the far wall, but the fire hadn't burned through yet.

Yanking the small fire extinguisher off the wall next to the stove, I ran back out the front door. By this time, Sullivan had grabbed a much larger fire extinguisher from the trunk of his car and joined me as I ran around the side of the house—

—and into hell.

The spot where the tank had been was a flaming heap of debris, and the trees closest to the house were aflame. At first, I backed away from the heat. But looking at the cabin through the smoke, I saw crackling flames dancing on the logs, casting an ominous glow on my home's wooden façade.

The power of the explosion had knocked over the old wooden outhouse. It lay on one side; the door hanging askew on its hinges. Fire raged on it and in it, leaving little more than charred fragments, disappearing into the flames.

"Don't worry about the outhouse," I yelled.

"Too late for it anyway," Sullivan shouted as he took the lead.

We approached the blazing wall. It wasn't one large fire, but multiple small fires started by the burning debris. Heat radiated all around me, and the smoke and haze stung my eyes and made it hard to see.

I pointed my extinguisher at the flames, and a powerful burst of foaming agent erupted, covering the flames and smothering them. The adrenaline coursed through my veins, and I acted swiftly, targeting the flames methodically to douse them.

I looked over and saw Sullivan doing the same as me. Sweat dripped from his brow, mingling with the ash-covered lines etched on his face. His extinguisher was a CO_2 type with a large funnel, and he sprayed the flames with the cold mist using a sweeping motion.

It shocked me to see pieces of metal embedded in the log wall, the remains of my propane tank, propelled with the force of a bullet. I kept applying my extinguisher's contents to the burning debris, trying to be thorough and dousing the embers, but I was rapidly running out of foam.

The smoke thickened, obscuring my vision, and my breathing grew heavier, the heat taking its toll.

Sullivan stood a dozen feet from me, focusing his spray on the wall of the house. The cabin was still in danger from the nearby burning trees, but we had to quench the flames on the building itself.

Fear gnawed at my gut, threatening to undermine my resolve. I thought of my manuscript inside and cursed myself that I hadn't scanned the latest pages into the computer or saved it up to the cloud. If my house burned down with the manuscript in it, I didn't know what I would do.

The sound of sirens blaring in the distance eclipsed the crackling of the burning trees, growing louder with each passing second as my extinguisher ran out of fluid. After a moment,

Sullivan stopped shooting blasts of CO2, his own extinguisher empty. We had subdued the flames on the house, but fire swallowed up the nearby trees, and would soon start the house burning again.

I heard the huge vehicle before I saw it, as it rattled up the gravel driveway and past my truck and Sullivan's car to pull up on the grass near where we stood. The first responders, dressed in their protective gear, leapt out and grabbed their equipment.

One man waved us to get out of the way as they unraveled hoses, attached them to the truck, and sprayed powerful jets of water on the cabin, wetting the walls down so they would not burn again.

One firefighter came over to us and ushered us away from danger and around the back of the house.

"Stay back, please," he yelled over the sound of the water and flames. His voice sounded odd in my head, my ears still ringing.

I sat down heavily in the grass nearby to catch my breath and glanced over at Sullivan. The pair of us were sweat-soaked and covered in soot. Smoke hung in the air, drifting lazily as wood burned and water sprayed.

"Do they have enough water?" I yelled to Sullivan.

He pointed at a pair of men in gear as they dragged a bright yellow hose toward the lake.

Sullivan coughed and spoke. "They're going to draft the water from the lake using a pump in the tanker, and send it to the guys at the fire."

The firefighters directed powerful streams at the flames, fueled by the continuous supply of water from the lake.

As the flames dwindled, wisps of steam swirled in the air, blending with the dense smoke to create a surreal mist that veiled my surroundings. The smoke possessed a thick, acrid aroma mixed with the smells of damp earth and the scent of burnt wood.

The encounter would scar my cabin, but it survived the ordeal in one piece.

"How could this have happened?" I said to Sullivan.

"Did you hear a gunshot before the explosion?" he asked.

I frowned. "Yes, but it sounded far away. I thought it was a hunter in the woods." I looked at the man. "You think someone shot my propane tank, and it exploded?"

He shook his head. "You can't set fire to a propane tank with a bullet, even an incendiary bullet. But something is wrong here. Propane tanks don't just explode." He rose. "I'm going to talk to the battalion chief."

He walked away, and I sat, feeling a mix of emotions, primarily shock. My body trembled from the adrenaline rush as I considered the severity of the situation. A part of me felt numb, unable to process what had occurred.

I glanced over at the remains of the outhouse. It was nothing more than a burnt-out shell. The smoldering wood simply fell to pieces from the power of the multiple water sprays.

I struggled to make sense of how close I came to losing everything, including my half-finished book.

I sat there for minutes, trying to recover, when Sullivan walked back into view, appearing out of a cloud of smoke. "The fire chief will let me know once he finds the cause." He looked at his grimy clothes, and his hands spotted with soot. "The place where we found Ms. Hawthorne's body is completely corrupted and filled with water."

I stared at him, baffled.

"I'm going back to the station and get cleaned up and change. The fire inspector will come out here later. I'll come back then."

I nodded.

He snapped his fingers in front of my face, which made me blink.

"You all right?"

I looked up at him. "Fine… just tired." He held out a hand and helped me to my feet. Standing, I said, "Thanks for helping and calling the fire department. I don't think I would've come through this if you hadn't been here."

He nodded. "Remember that the next time I want to talk to you."

He headed toward his car. The firefighters, tired but determined, worked fast, ensuring no embers remained to reignite the blaze. They wandered about the scene, the fluorescent yellow stripes on their black protective gear contrasting with the surroundings.

Others meticulously combed through the remnants, sifting through the rubble. With gloved hands and special tools, they sought any hidden hot spots or buried items that might rekindle the flames.

A man removed his helmet and walked towards me. He was a heavyset man about five feet-five and his brown hair was gray at the temples. "Are you the owner?"

I nodded. "Joe Riley."

"I'm Joe, too, Joe Santiago. I'm the Battalion Chief."

"Thank you and your men for saving my house," I said.

"You own the place now?" he said. "Oh yeah, Riley, that was the family that owned it as long as I can remember."

"I just inherited it. Any idea what caused my propane tank to explode?"

"Not my job," he explained. "But I'll tell you, you were lucky. It looks like most of the explosion was on the side of the tank that faced the woods. That's why it set the trees on fire. If the brunt of the blast hit your cabin, it would be nothing but a burning wreck now."

He eyed the wall nearest him and nodded. "It helped that it was log construction. Solid."

I followed his gaze.

He went on. "The fire inspector will be out later. He'll want to talk to you and maybe take a statement."

"That'll be fine," I said. "Is it alright if I go inside? I would like to get cleaned up."

"Sure, go ahead. We'll just make sure everything is under control and head out."

"Thanks again," I said, and went in the back door.

The main room had a haze in the air; the smell of smoke still lingered. The ringing in my ears had faded, and I heard the men outside yelling to each other and putting equipment away.

The light came into the room in an eerie pattern as soot covered the outside of the windows, displaying haunting streaks of sunlight. One window had a large crack running down the glass. The view to the outside blurred and distorted, mirroring the disarray I felt inside.

I went to the bathroom and saw my face dirty with sweat and soot. Taking off my clothes and leaving them on the floor, I climbed into the shower. Standing under the warm water, I washed away the grime on my hair and skin. I washed carefully, avoiding the fresh burn on my arm that, by this time, had swelled into a blister.

What could have caused the fire?

Had Rebecca lashed out and somehow ignited my propane tank? The idea seemed both plausible and terrifying all at once. If she did, it meant she now had incredible power to influence the world around her. After all, I'd seen her throw a chair.

Considering it further, I dismissed it. She tied her existence to the typewriter and wanted to finish the book. Blowing up the cabin wouldn't help that.

I grabbed a bath towel, and I walked to the bedroom and pulled out fresh clothes.

As I got dressed, a memory flashed into my head. I was sitting inside the Cafe Wren with Emily across from me. We both had our cups of coffee, and Emily revealed to me that before I moved into the cabin, she came to examine the grounds several times — but she said one thing that hadn't registered the previous day.

"One time I felt like I wanted to blow up the damn cabin."

Could Emily have done this? I was taking the woman as she presented herself, but what if I was wrong? Could she have lied to me about everything, about being Rebecca's neighbor and her daughter's friend?

In fact, could her entire 'possession' by Rebecca have been nothing but an act, bringing the Ouija board and paraphernalia along to set the scene?

I doubted that as I became possessed as well, and her shock and anger coming out of it had appeared genuine.

I grew angry with myself because I doubted her. But I knew I would have to look into her, run a background check and try to find out if what she said was true. If she wasn't who she claimed to be, I was dealing with a psychopath.

And a dangerous one at that.

Twenty

Confession

By the time the fire crew packed up and left, it was late afternoon, and I was doing the best I could to clean the windows and rid the cabin of the smell of smoke. I put my smoke-damaged clothes in the washer, feeling like the shirt with the burns on it was a lost cause.

As I cleaned up, I knew what I needed to do. I hooked up the scanner, and without reading the most recent work, I scanned the pages into the machine in groups of fifty. There were now over two hundred manuscript pages. Between Rebecca and me, the book was getting done.

I combined the pages into one PDF and sent it up to my cloud storage account. It pleased me the fire had not taken out my new satellite dish, and I still had service. Soon, I sent the book safely to the cloud, so that I couldn't lose it, even if I lost my laptop.

With things cleaned up and my laptop working, I wanted to check Emily's story, now I had names to do it with. I typed in Elora Hawthorne and Rebecca Hawthorne.

I went through a few sites until I discovered Rebecca's husband's name was Michael Hawthorne, and the couple had one daughter, Elora.

I heaved a sigh of relief. That part of Emily's history was true.

I kept searching, switching to images. I finally pulled up an article from over twenty-two years ago that appeared in the New York Times Sunday Magazine, a puff piece. In one photo was Rebecca, a face I clearly recognized, and in the background was her daughter, Elora. Eight-year-old Elora was a cute girl, but that didn't answer any of my questions.

I closed my laptop, trying to convince myself I was simply being paranoid.

Eating dinner as twilight fell, I saw a pair of cars pull into my driveway, followed by a knock on my door. I opened it to Detective Sullivan and a rail-thin man with white hair, who wore a suit.

"Detective Sullivan," I said.

"This is Fire Chief Carter," Sullivan said by way of introduction. "May we come in?"

"Sure," I said, and stepped aside to let the two men in.

"Young man," the white-haired man began. "We need to talk to you about your propane tank."

"Any idea how it exploded?" I asked.

They exchanged a glance that was telling, and the white-haired man went on. "Mr. Riley, do you know anyone who might want to injure you?"

This question took me aback. "Um — no, not anyone I can think of. Could you tell me why?"

Sullivan took over. "We located a large section of the exploded tank."

"The bottom half, which was important," Carter added.

"What did you find?"

"There was a bullet hole near the bottom of the tank, fired from a high-powered rifle," Carter said.

I frowned. "Is that what made the tank explode?"

"No, no, that wouldn't do it," the older man corrected. "However, it could cause the tank to leak. The men also did an on-site test of the concrete pad your propane tank was on. We do that in case there are chemicals that might re-ignite. I won't bore you with the details, but the entire test is self-contained and only takes a few minutes to do."

"Anything I should know about?"

"They found traces of ammonium nitrate and aluminum on the cement pad under your tank," Carter said. "That's what caused the explosion."

I fell into a chair at the table. "Someone put a bomb under my propane tank?"

Sullivan and Carter exchanged another telling look, and Sullivan spoke. "That's what Mr. Carter thinks. But not a bomb. It could have been something as simple to get as an exploding target—"

"A what?" I asked.

Carter took over. "An exploding target. It's used for target shooting. The chemicals come in separate pouches, and you mix them into a small box with a bullseye painted on it. Once mixed, if you fire at it with a bullet, the target explodes."

"Oh my God," I said. "Is that even legal?"

"Completely," Sullivan said. "It's pretty common and easy to get."

I sat there in shock.

Carter went on. "I would like to assure you, we are going to do more thorough testing. This was just a preliminary. Our concern is that if someone put this mix of chemicals under your propane tank and set it off. You could be in danger."

Sullivan said, "We want to find the location from which the shots were fired. The state police will bring troopers with dogs to search the woods tomorrow."

I nodded, trying to comprehend what they were telling me.

"You were enormously lucky that the force of the explosion went towards the woods," Carter said, almost as an afterthought.

"I've ordered troopers to monitor your house for the next few days," Sullivan said.

I frowned. "What should I do?"

"You should take precautions," Sullivan said. "If someone targeted you today, so soon after the news of the body being discovered, I have to assume there is a connection."

Once again, the memory of Emily talking about blowing up the place passed through my mind.

"I need to get home," Carter said. "I'll leave the two of you to discuss the arrangements." He went to Sullivan. "I'll get back to you once all the tests are completed."

"Goodnight, Chief," Sullivan said and rose as Carter went out the door and headed to his car.

Sullivan met my eyes.

"Look, if you want to interrogate me again..." I began.

Sullivan held up his arm and looked at his watch. "Actually, I'm off duty. I was going to ask you if you had anything to drink."

"Just wine or vodka," I said, surprised.

He sat at the dining room table. "Wine is fine. I have to drive home myself."

I opened a bottle of a good red blend, one that had a lot of flavor but was inexpensive, and pulled out a pair of wineglasses. I poured us both a glass and handed one to Sullivan. He toasted me and took a sip.

"Very nice," he said, and glanced over at the typewriter on the desk and the two piles of papers beside it. "How's the book coming?"

I followed his gaze. "Good, very good."

The truth was, I couldn't remember what I'd written the previous day, not to mention the pages Rebecca added.

"Good thing the house didn't burn down. You could have lost what you wrote," he said.

"I scanned the book and put it up on my cloud account."

He sipped his wine and nodded. "That's good." He looked around the room. "So, do you have any idea who would want to blow up your house?"

"I know for a fact it wasn't Liam," I said.

Sullivan nodded with a grin. "He's the last person on my suspect list for that crime." He looked at his wineglass. "By the way, I checked on him. He's still unconscious, but the hyperbaric treatment improved his condition."

"Thanks. That's good to know."

"It's strange. Hawthorne's disappearance happened so long ago. You come up and in just a few days, you find her body and someone tries to blow up your house."

"Just my luck, I guess."

"Could you think of anyone who might have a grudge against you? Maybe you've pissed off a publisher?"

Now it was my turn to grin. "There's always my ex-wife. She took my other house; maybe she wants to see me homeless."

"Seriously?" he asked.

"No, I don't think even she'd be capable of such an overt act. As far as anyone else is concerned, I have annoyed several publishers over the years. I don't think any of them are seeking vengeance."

"It's just odd. You locate the body, and then this happens. I find it hard to believe it was some long-forgotten Rebecca Hawthorne fan who wanted to take revenge."

Emily's voice was in my head. It made me mad.

One time I felt like I wanted to blow up the damn cabin.

"What's your theory?" I asked. "After all, you're the professional."

"It's only guesswork," Sullivan said. "But then there's your cousin trying to commit suicide. Could you tell me why he would do that unless he felt guilty?"

"Maybe there was another reason," I said.

"If you want to tell me anything, now would be a good time."

I shook my head. "I don't want it to hurt my family."

"Telling the truth won't hurt anyone. But I have to tell you, after today, keeping secrets might get you killed."

Hesitantly, I went through the story Liam told, finding it easier as I went along. I mentioned the burnt manuscript pages and how he found Rebecca. I finished with the idea for the fire pit and the hope I could keep Liam out of it.

"I guess you'll want to arrest me for lying to you," I finally said.

"Lying to a police officer? It happens every day, and I can understand your motivation." He sipped his wine. "Besides, I knew the story was bullshit the first day."

"So much for my powers of persuasion."

"It's not that. You're not used to lying, and you're not good at it. Do you think Liam killed her?"

"I don't — well, I didn't. Liam trying to kill himself makes me wonder. Are you going to arrest him?"

"I'll have to interrogate him once he's conscious. If she was already dead, and all he did was bury her, that's a different story. Still illegal, but not as serious."

"Liam's been troubled for a long time."

"He also gave a report to the police that sent us searching for a woman who was already dead."

"I honestly think he didn't want people to know she killed herself."

"If she did," Sullivan said and gazed at the fireplace. "The ME knows from the damage to the bones in the neck that she died of strangulation. That could have been from hanging herself, or someone did it to her. We just don't know."

"I'm sorry I kept it from you. I wanted to protect Liam."

"I get that. I've looked over the police report from back in 2004. They found the remains of a burnt manuscript in the fireplace, so part of his story is true."

"There's that."

He looked over at my desk. "I've used a typewriter in my time, but I noticed that you have two piles of paper. Could you tell me why?"

"One is the carbon."

He frowned. "The what?"

"The carbon copy. It's the way novelists used to write books before computers and copy machines. You type the story with a sheet of carbon paper under it and make a copy as you go."

"May I see a page from the carbon stack?"

I went over to the desk, pulled a sheet, and handed it to him.

He looked it over. "Is it normal that it has all these smudges on it?"

"Usually. The rollers cause the smudges on the paper as the two pages go through the machine together. Also, as you use the carbon several times, parts of each letter end up missing on the carbon, because of the sheet wearing out."

He nodded. "I've seen photos of what they found in oh-four, and none of them had marks like this. Do you think Ms. Hawthorne didn't use a carbon?"

"I'm sure she did. There was carbon paper here when I arrived."

"How could you tell if it was a carbon copy or not?" he asked.

"That's easy. The carbon is darker and blurrier. And as I said, running it through the rollers would leave faint, wide black stripes on both sides of the page."

"The scene photos showed the remains of typed pages, mostly edges and corners, and the occasional heading with the page number. None of what they found had the markings you mentioned."

He handed it back to me, and I returned it to the pile, considering what he'd said. "Do you think she didn't burn the carbon copy?"

"There weren't any pages in the buried belongings we dug up. We went through them."

I sat in the desk chair, and it creaked under me. "Do you think it's possible that the carbon is here? In this cabin?"

"I don't know about that. But if it is, that could be the reason someone wanted to blow up your house."

Twenty-One

Emily Attacked

Sullivan left soon after, and taking his suggestion, I searched my cabin. If I wanted to hide a manuscript, where would I put it?

I went through the bedroom furniture first. As I did, I contemplated why I didn't mention that a friend of Rebecca's daughter was in town and once thought about blowing up the cabin.

I mean, I took it as a joke, an expression of frustration, not as an actual threat.

Maybe I should have?

As I pulled out the drawers of the cabinets in the bedrooms, even checking to see if someone had taped an envelope to the bottom of the drawers, I couldn't get the idea out of my head. If Emily were a crazy psychopath, Sullivan had the resources to do a serious background check on her. Why didn't I bring her up?

I decided it made little sense. Even if Emily lied to me about everything, it's not like she could have taken Rebecca's life. She was a kid, and there was no way she could've killed her.

But blowing up the cabin, perhaps to take revenge for the death of her friend's mother? That made no sense either.

As I finished with the cabinets and furniture in my bedroom, I went into the spare bedroom, where I did an even more thorough job. I pulled the sheets — I had to wash them anyway. I also flipped the mattresses and box springs as they were a pair of single beds.

I found nothing in any of the drawers and pulled them out to look under them and to see if anything was stuck to the bottom. That's when another idea hit me. There was the person in the rental car. What if that had been Michael Hawthorne, Rebecca's husband? What if he flew here, rented a car, murdered Rebecca, and left her hanging for Liam to find?

Could Emily know about it, and the reason she came here was to make sure no one found out?

I was grasping at straws. According to Liam, Rebecca told him she was planning to return to her husband.

But what if he was jealous, and violently so?

Emily said that Michael Hawthorne was still alive and had remarried. My guess is that he would be in his fifties or sixties. Could he be the one to come up here and try to blow up my house? Or Elora? What if Emily disclosed the discovery of her mother's body to her friend and the location of my cabin?

I wanted more wine, but put my empty glass into the sink. I needed to keep a clear head, even though what was running through my mind seemed like pure paranoia.

Continuing my search, I checked around the washing machine before I started the sheets to washing and put my clean clothes in the dryer.

I wanted to call Robert and ask about Liam, and I went for my phone, but I couldn't find it. Retracing my steps, cleaning up as I went, I still didn't locate it.

Thinking back, I recalled the last place I used my phone was my truck, right before the explosion.

Annoyed, I went out to my truck and there it was, right where I left it. With the explosion and all the trouble afterwards, I completely forgot about it.

The battery was dead. Cursing under my breath, I brought it in and plugged it into the charger.

I waited for it to charge enough to work so I could see messages. Robert or Ashley might have been trying to reach me all day.

As I waited, I heard a car pull into my driveway and saw flashing police lights.

Emily's car pulled up next to my truck. Directly behind her was a state trooper with his lights flashing. He stepped out of his vehicle and approached Emily's car, his hand near his sidearm.

I opened the door, raised my hand, and called out, "It's all right, Officer. I know her!"

He looked at me, smiled, and stepped back. Emily got out of her car looking flustered. She was wearing a white tank top and jeans with sandals and, oddly, a necklace of black beads. She grabbed her purse and a shopping bag from the front seat.

The trooper waved and headed back to his car. As Emily walked toward me, he pivoted the cruiser around and headed back to the street.

Emily glanced back out after the car, then drew close and hugged me.

I was a bit surprised and pulled back a little.

"What happened?" she asked, concern in her voice. "I've been texting and calling since I got off work."

"I left my phone in the truck, and the battery died," I said and backed away.

She looked at my yard; the grass ripped by large tire treads and the aftermath of the hoses and equipment. Even in the floodlight from my front door, it was obviously a mess. "What happened here?"

"It's been a day. Come inside; it's cooler there. I'll tell you everything."

We stepped out of the sultry night and into the coolness of the cabin. She put her bag and purse on the floor near the dining room table as I poured her a glass of the red wine.

"Oh my God, did you have a fire? The entire place smells of smoke."

I brought her the glass and steered her to a chair away from her purse. It annoyed me I'd become so paranoid. I felt a need to keep her away from her belongings in case she had a weapon.

We sat across from each other, and I quickly related the story of how I found and saved Liam and what they said at the hospital.

She sipped the wine and listened raptly. When I finished, she asked, "Why do you think he did it?"

"I don't know," I said truthfully. "It could have been the finding of the body and bringing up all of this stuff around Rebecca. He wanted to run away with her."

Her mouth fell open. "You didn't tell me that."

"I didn't think it was relevant. I mean, it was twenty years ago. But it's worse than that. Today, when I got back from the hospital, someone tried to blow up Whispering Pines."

"Your cabin?" She was shocked, and I could tell it wasn't fake. "What are you talking about?"

"Someone put an explosive device under my propane tank. You can't see it here in the dark, but it set the woods on fire and a wall of the cabin as well."

She stared at me. "That's insane."

I leaned in closer. "Emily, is there anything you haven't told me?"

Her eyes widened behind her glasses. "You think I had something to do with it?"

"You told me you thought about blowing the cabin up."

"Thought about it? Yes, but that's all. I'm a librarian, not a terrorist."

"I just want to be sure you've been honest with me."

She got up from her chair. "Have you been completely honest with me?"

I frowned. "What do you mean?"

"Everything you told me about Rebecca appearing to you."

"Emily, you saw the Ouija board the other night. You were there when you — when I — when we…"

She shook her head. "I know I was there — mostly. Just not totally in control."

"Neither was I. I'm sorry if it was an unpleasant experience—"

Her cheeks became bright red, and she looked away. "No, it wasn't unpleasant. In fact, I've thought about it... a lot... since it happened."

At least now I could be honest. "So have I, but not like that. I want it to be us, not something using us as puppets."

"Agreed," she said with a slight grin. "I brought some things to help with that." She pointed to the shopping bag under the table. "Look in that bag."

I walked over and picked the shopping bag up from the floor and glanced into it, but it seemed to contain a variety of items. They didn't look dangerous, so I put it on the dining room table, and she came over.

She pulled out what looked like a collection of twigs, but they transformed into a small carved wood tripod stand. An abalone shell followed, and I saw the mother-of-pearl finish inside. It fit perfectly on the stand. She pulled out a four-inch bundle of dried leaves wrapped with string.

"What is all this?" I asked.

She held up the packet of dried leaves. "This is called a smudge stick. It's made of sage, and you set it on fire and then let the smoke waft through the home."

"It couldn't hurt. The cabin was already full of smoke today."

"But this is to cleanse the place of negative energy. Also, I found this for you." She reached into the bag and pulled out a thin black cord with a black disk the size of a silver dollar.

She placed the cord over my head; the disk hanging down on my chest. I felt my heart skip a beat, captured in a whirlwind of desires that made me yearn for more than a simple touch.

"What's this?" I asked, trying to keep my mind on what she was doing.

"It's shungite. It's a black mineral that protects you from ghosts. I'm wearing one myself." She held up the necklace of beads that hung around her neck. "These beads are shungite, and the purple ones are amethyst."

And as I looked into Emily's eyes, the only thing I could think of was the taste of her lips pressed against mine.

I focused my attention on the smudge stick instead of how much I wanted to kiss her. "What will any of this do?"

"If we can cleanse the cabin, perhaps it will set Rebecca free," she said, and gazed around the room. "I have to tell you, I would like to actually see her."

"She manifests only in the middle of the night, usually at two-thirty."

"Where?"

I pointed at the desk. "At the typewriter. She's usually writing, and she's naked."

"Like when I saw her in her office as a child," she whispered.

"If you wanted to, we could wait for her." I touched the medallion around my neck. "I mean, if you think these crystals will protect us from falling under her control like last time."

"Joe, I have a job, remember? I can't stay up all night waiting to see her."

"This place has more than one bedroom. You could sleep and I could wake you when she shows up."

She glanced over at my closed bedroom door. "Let's burn the sage and see how we feel."

"You could lock the door if you don't feel safe. I could give you a key."

"Good to know," she said, and returned to the table. She reached into the bag and pulled out several more items. A small, smooth purple stone with veins of white running through it, followed by a pink one, and a small Tupperware container. She opened the container and poured white sand from it into the abalone shell sitting on the tripod. She put out a pair of candlesticks and inserted candles into them.

"What are the stones?" I asked.

"Crystals. The purple one is amethyst."

"Like on your necklace?"

"That's right. It helps to reconnect with our intuition, and you use it with a protective stone like shungite if you sense a presence." She retrieved a long-stemmed lighter from the shopping bag and ignited the candles. "The pink stone is rose quartz, the heart stone. It offers love and peace. Rose quartz has the power to act as a protective shield and transform negative energies into loving vibrations."

Using the candle, she ignited the sage smudge stick. Flames appeared on the bundle of leaves, and she quickly extinguished them in the sand in the shell. Smoldering, she held up the sage bundle, releasing aromatic smoke. It was a unique blend of earthy and herbal notes, reminiscent of pine or cedar. The fragrance made me feel calmer.

She placed the smoking sage stick in the shell and held the shell in her hand. As wisps of smoke curled and danced in the air, she pulled her last item from the bag, a feather from a large bird. Using the feather, she fanned the smoke into the room ahead of her.

She walked around the room waving the feather. Tendrils of sage smoke spiraled towards the ceiling as she walked about.

"It smells a lot better than the smoke from the fire," I said.

"Sh!" Emily chided. "Focus on cleansing the cabin, freeing Rebecca."

I shut my eyes tightly and put my intent on purifying the cabin. I didn't see any potential negative consequences. If Rebecca were to depart, I could still complete the book.

I mean, I could, right?

She walked around the main room, then went into each of the bedrooms and the bathroom. Nothing unusual happened at all, and I relaxed. Maybe there was something to this after all.

She continued walking around the main room, fanning the feather to spread the smoke. She stopped and looked at my desk and took a deep breath. "And now, the typewriter."

I stayed where I was as Emily waved the sage fumes over the typewriter. With each pass, she spoke out loud, "Any negative energy present, I release you. This space is now cleansed and filled with positive energy."

Suddenly, a chilling breeze ran through the room, snuffing out the candles, blowing the smoke wildly and causing the windows to rattle with its strength.

"Emily, back away," I called out.

"Rebecca," Emily said firmly, "I understand you might be upset or restless, but we are trying to help you."

I took a step toward her when, with a 'thud', something hit me in the back of my head, pitching me forward. I fell past Emily and crashed into the desk, tipping it back so it slammed into the wall. The typewriter and the pages shifted a bit and became disheveled, but stayed on the desk.

I was on my knees and in pain, and reached instinctively for the back of my head. My hand came away with blood on it, and I felt the warmth of the blood trickling down my neck. I saw the amethyst on the floor and glanced up to see the rose quartz shaking on the table, creating a rattling noise.

I pulled myself to my feet as the quartz flung itself into the air. I got between Emily and the projectile and swatted the crystal out of the air, crying out as it smacked against my palm.

It fell to the ground, and I stood, breathing hard, my hand stinging from the pain.

I turned to Emily and saw her eyes widen in fear.

"What is it?" I said, my voice tight with tension.

She pointed at her neck, and I could see that the protective crystal beads on her necklace were constricting tightly around her throat, choking her. As I watched, the beads pulled closer together, embedding into her skin.

The abalone shell holding the smudge stick slipped from her grasp and fell to the floor, shattering into pieces. The feather fell from her hand, spiraling to the ground as the air filled with the powerful scent of burnt sage.

Emily's hands went to her throat, clawing at the beads, fighting to pull them loose, to release them and get some air.

Frantically, I grabbed at the necklace. I tried to pry the crystals away from her throat, desperately attempting to free her from their suffocating grip. With each passing second, Emily's struggle for breath became more desperate, her face growing red.

"Rebecca," I yelled at the ceiling, "Don't. This is Emily, your daughter's friend. Don't hurt her."

Suddenly, the beads on Emily's necklace loosened their grip, releasing the pressure on her throat. I yanked the stones off her neck. A magnetic clasp only held them together, and it easily came apart. I threw the necklace to the ground as Emily coughed, sucking in deep breaths.

I pulled her over to the chair. She gasped as if each breath carried weight. Her breathing hitched and wheezed, and I hugged her against me.

Emily slowly regained her composure, her fear mingling with determination. She looked up at me, her eyes gleaming.

"Why would she attack me?" she said, her lip quivering.

"I guess she doesn't want to leave, and she didn't know who you were or that you were trying to help."

I met her eyes, and her face suddenly relaxed, and her eyes became unfocused and blank behind her glasses.

"Emily, are you okay?" I asked, feeling a hint of unease as I saw a mischievous glint come into her expression.

She sucked in a breath and pulled my face to hers, pressing her lips against mine. Not that she wanted to kiss me, she seemed to want to devour me. The effect on me was instantaneous, despite the lump on the back of my head.

But this time, I knew it wasn't Emily. It had to be Rebecca. Emily was not the person who could go from fear for her life into a sexual frenzy.

"Stop," I said, pulling away and grabbing her wrists to push her off me.

"Come on," she hummed, with a lusty grin on her face. "I want you so badly."

I grabbed both of her wrists in my right hand, took the cord with the medallion off over my head, and hooked the string over her head, allowing the black crystal disk to fall between her breasts.

The change was immediate. Emily blinked, and her eyes became clear and focused again. She drew back. "What was I doing?"

I relaxed and released her hands. "A repeat of our previous encounter. But this time, I knew it wasn't you."

She looked down at the shungite disk lying on top of her tank top. "I guess these things really work."

"Are you alright?"

"I-I think so," she said, her voice strained and hoarse.

Her hand went to her throat, and I saw the red line in a circle around her windpipe. It was a series of small, red, interconnected dots I knew would be bruises tomorrow.

I got out the dustpan and cleaned up the broken shell and the sand. I placed the smoldering sage outside. When I came back in, Emily was at the table drinking her wine and rubbing her throat.

I went down on one knee in front of her. "Em, you can't stay here. It's not safe."

"She hasn't hurt you."

I shook my head. "She seems to need me, or at least my energy. But if anything happened to you, I-I don't know what I'd do."

She nodded, but set her jaw. "I want to see her."

"Emily—"

"As long as I'm wearing this, I should be fine. Besides, she didn't attack me until I tried to cleanse her from the space. It was my fault; she was only defending herself. She didn't know who I was, and I was doing things to exorcise her."

"I just want you to be safe."

"Please? I'll keep the medallion on the entire time."

I met her eyes, and I saw she wanted this despite the fright she had.

"All right. But I'm worried about your being alone in the spare bedroom."

"We could sleep in your room. We'll just stay dressed, so nothing happens."

I thought about this. "That might work. I would feel safer knowing you were there."

"Then it's decided. Tonight I will see Rebecca."

Twenty-Two

Face To Face

Emily bandaged up the wound on the back of my head with some gauze pads and tape she found in the bathroom. My lump had grown into an impressive goose egg.

Once she had bandaged it, the pair of us went into the bedroom and kicked off our shoes. I felt safer with her. There was no way she could have faked what I witnessed in the main room when she approached the typewriter with the smudge stick.

I also was glad she was there, and with the state troopers watching the place, I decided we were safe from outside intervention.

As she lay on the queen-size bed, I brought my phone into the bedroom, plugged it in, and set an alarm for two-thirty.

We lay together on the bed, and I instinctively rolled over, believing that adopting a back-to-back position was the wisest decision. Her mere presence ignited a fire within me and created an obvious physical response.

I focused on my phone and my missed messages.

There were multiple messages and voicemails from Emily, starting at five, like she'd told me. There were also texts from Robert giving me updates. He let me know Ashley had arrived, and she was sharing his suite at the Best Western. He also said the hyperbaric chamber treatment helped, and Liam showed significant progress. The doctors hoped Liam would regain consciousness the following day.

That was all good news.

I put the phone down and tried to relax. However, the room was thick with an almost tangible tension. The only sound was the gentle creaking of the old cabin settling into the night.

Emily shifted slightly as I lay rigid beside her, my eyes fixed on the windowless far wall. I could feel her warmth so close to me, and the atmosphere felt electric.

"Are you asleep?" she said.

"No."

She rolled over to face me, our bodies grazing against one another in tantalizing closeness. The moment hung heavy with an intimacy that swirled around us like a potent perfume. "You know, if anything happened—"

"What do you mean?"

"I mean, with you and me. As long as it was us, really us, it wouldn't be so bad." Her voice was soft, but filled with intensity. She pressed her lips against mine, and I melted into the kiss, feeling the warmth spread through me. It was as if the world outside ceased to exist; it was just her, just us.

She rolled over, getting on top of me. As I held her and kissed her, the weight of my day settled in. The stress and hard work of battling the flames to save my home tightened my chest. I could feel myself fading, the exhilarating adrenaline giving way to an overwhelming fatigue.

"Are you falling asleep?" Emily teased, and I heard her chuckle in the darkness.

"Huh?" I mumbled, struggling to pull my thoughts together. "No, I'm just — it's been a really long day…" My words trailed off, swallowed by the heaviness in my eyelids.

She slid back to her side of the bed. "It's okay. You've done so much today. Get some rest; I'm right here." Her voice was soothing, like a gentle lullaby that wrapped around me.

Despite the fire raging in my heart, the exhaustion finally caught up with me. I wanted to stay awake, to treasure this moment, but sleep's pull was too strong. As my eyes fluttered shut, I focused on the feeling of her hand in mine.

It seemed as if I had only closed my eyes for a minute when the alarm on my phone went off, pulling me awake. I groaned as I reached over to silence the alarm and felt disoriented in the darkened room.

I grabbed my phone — now fully charged — and was aware of the frigid air all around me.

Two-thirty.

"Come on," I said to the body next to me.

"I'm up, I'm up. Damn, it's cold. Where are my shoes?"

I used the light on my phone to find our shoes, and we put them on, exhaling clouds of vapor. I went to the closet and got my robe and put it around Emily, who was shivering.

"Do you think she's here?" Emily asked.

"I'm sure of it," I said, as I opened the door.

The gooseneck lamp arched gracefully over the desk, its warm glow casting light on the keyboard below. There was Rebecca, as familiar to me as the rising sun. Her figure was bare, yet exuded a captivating intensity as she immersed herself in her work. She was a vision of concentration and determination, absorbed in the task at hand.

I heard Emily gasp when. she saw her. "Oh my God, it's her. It's really her."

"I know."

"She looks real, I mean, like she's alive and actually here." She frowned. "How is she typing?"

"I don't know, but if she can throw rocks and choke people, she can type."

"Why is it so cold?"

"It's part of the manifestation."

She pulled my robe around herself tighter and stepped toward the desk, her breath visible in the crisp air. My heart pounded with equal parts excitement and trepidation.

Emily gestured for me to move back. I did as she asked.

She took a deep breath, and spoke softly, "Rebecca? It's me; it's Emmy."

This got no reaction from Rebecca as she kept typing.

Emily took another step closer and said, a little louder, "I was Ellie's friend, back when we were kids. Do you remember?"

Rebecca rotated the chair and rose. Once again, as with Robert, she stood before us fully clothed. This time, she wore a sweatshirt and sweatpants, both a bit rumpled. Her hair, which had been hanging to her shoulders, was now pulled back in a ponytail and looked dull and unwashed, and her face looked tired and careworn.

Rebecca spoke, and like every other time she did, the words appeared directly in my mind. "Emmy, I'm glad we had time to talk, just the two of us. I need to go away for just a little while. I have a book I have to write."

The transformation surprised Emily, as did the words Rebecca spoke to her.

"What?" Emily responded.

Rebecca went on. "I need you to be there for Ellie. I know how you and your sisters watch out for her. She'll really need you for the next month or so."

"What are you talking about?" Emily said.

Rebecca leaned forward and her speech pattern was as if she were talking to a girl and not a woman. "I'll only be gone a couple of months, and Ellie's Aunt Karen will be down to help. But you're her best friend, and she'll need you."

I stepped up to Emily. "Do you know what she's talking about?"

"That's right." Rebecca went on as if I hadn't spoken. "It'll only be a little while and I'll come back in a better state of mind."

Emily frowned. "I think this was a conversation we had before she left. She took me aside and — my God — I didn't realize how worn-out she looked."

Rebecca looked past us and spoke. "Ellie, you and Emmy go downstairs and play. I need to take a shower after I get done with some rewrites I promised."

She looked at Emily, but her eyes focused on Emily's waist, as if she were still a little girl. "I'm doing rewrites on a man's book, and I want it done before I start on my own."

"That's right," I said. "You told me Rebecca worked as a ghostwriter when she was at home."

"Right," Emily said, watching as Rebecca returned to the chair. "For her own stuff, she always left. But she could write for other people all the time. And always on that portable typewriter. She would handwrite things in her journals, but the typewriter was the primary tool."

As Rebecca reached the chair and sat, she began typing again. As she did, her clothes faded away and her hair hung free, straight and clean again.

"What just happened?" Emily asked.

"I'm not sure. The same thing happened when my cousin Robert was here last night. She replayed a conversation she had with him before she died."

"Was it significant?"

"I'm not sure. She threw a chair at him."

She met my eyes. "Do you think he killed her?"

"I don't know what to think. Sometimes it seems like Rebecca is talking to me, and other times, she is just repeating old conversations from the past. I'm never sure which it is."

"Then you should talk to her."

"Do you think it will help?"

"She told you she needed your energy. There must be a link between the two of you."

I saw Emily's point. Everything began when I started typing my book on Rebecca's typewriter. I put energy into it, and it gave her the ability to manifest. The problem was, she was manifesting more powerfully than ever.

Emily whispered, "You should ask her what happened the night she died."

I took a deep breath and gathered my courage. Finally, I spoke. "Rebecca, can you talk to me?"

She didn't turn around, but I heard the words in my head. "I'm working."

"I know, but I need to know what happened to you."

Rebecca stopped typing and heaved a sigh. Turning in the chair, Rebecca faced me and leaned back, her bare breasts gleaming in the dim light. She grinned. "Sorry, dear, I'm working. But I'm almost finished." She spun back to the typewriter and typed again. "Tell you what, let me finish and we can celebrate."

"Rebecca, I want to help you."

"I told you," Rebecca said, not aware of my words. "You can read the thing yourself." She paused, listening. "Oh, you did read it? I hope you enjoyed it."

"Rebecca, can you hear me?" I asked.

"So you don't like the title. It's just a title," Rebecca said, and glanced over her shoulder at the table, talking to someone who wasn't there. "Yes, it's about you, and then again, it's not about you."

"It's like what happened to me," Emily said. "She can't hear you. She's repeating an old conversation."

"But with whom?" I said, frozen by the sight.

Rebecca stood, still completely naked and faced the table. "Oh, don't be such a baby. I'll dedicate the book to that name, and no one will know it's you. Relax."

She headed for my bedroom and then spun around as if someone had grabbed her arm.

Rebecca pulled herself free from her invisible adversary and gazed into the empty air. "I told you all along, I'm finishing up the dedication and the quotes, and then I'm going home to my husband and my daughter. That's the plan; that was always the plan, and you damn well knew it. Now, you can be an asshole about it if you want, or we can have some fun before I go back to being Mommy."

She put her hands on her hips, facing someone who was about eye-level to her, or maybe a little taller.

She went on. "Don't say that. You know nothing about love. Look, you were a good lay and great research, but that's all it ever was. I don't know what you're complaining about. You got your jollies as well."

In a sudden movement, she shifted her face to the right, and a red handprint appeared on her left cheek.

Someone had slapped her.

"That's it!" she said and headed to the bedroom. "I'm locking the door. You can sleep by yourself."

She spun around again and her hands went up as if grabbing two invisible arms. Indentations in the shape of fingers appeared around her throat. Emily and I stood frozen, shocked by what we were seeing.

"Wait — stop," Rebecca croaked, her face twisting in agony and desperation. She clawed at her throat, attempting to loosen the grip slowly suffocating her. Her gasps and wheezes echoed through the air, intensifying the nightmare unfolding before our eyes.

"Oh my God, we have to do something," Emily said, her eyes welling up with tears.

I clenched my fists, unable to turn my gaze away from the spectacle. "There's nothing we can do. This all happened twenty years ago."

Rebecca's naked body trembled, and she slammed herself against the wall in an attempt to break free. She fell down on one knee, but the fingers digging into the flesh around her throat were unrelenting.

The sheer helplessness of the situation was overwhelming. All we could do was watch as Rebecca's face grew red and she struggled, slamming herself against the wall again and again, striving to break free.

Rebecca fell to the ground, her face becoming purple, making terrible choking sounds as she writhed, still clinging to life. She gestured and struggled for air, clutching at the invisible hands around her neck. Her face contorted in agony, and her eyes desperately searched for help that never came. Finally, her eyes rolled up into her head, and her eyelids closed.

After a few minutes, her movements ceased, and an eerie silence fell upon the room. Her body simply faded away, the way her life had twenty years earlier.

Someone mercilessly took Rebecca's life right in front of our eyes.

"That was horrible," Emily said, her voice cracking as tears streamed down her face.

I pulled her into my arms and held her as she cried. A part of me wanted to cry as well, seeing how Rebecca's life ended.

"At least we know she didn't commit suicide," I said.

"Of course not," Emily said between sobs and lifted her eyes to mine. "Why would you even think that?"

I couldn't tell her it was because of what Liam had told me. But he still could have killed her, and it seemed like the killer was someone she knew and had slept with. Then again, with what I saw acted out with Robert the previous night, there was the possibility he had been the perpetrator.

I no longer thought Rebecca's husband had anything to do with it. Rebecca wouldn't talk about returning to her husband if he was the perpetrator.

No, this narrowed it down to Robert, Liam, or the person in the rental car — and I did not know who that could be.

Emily snuffled and got control of herself. She looked up at me through her thick lenses. She mumbled. "I want to stay with you."

"Sure, Em."

"I don't want to be alone."

I led her into the bedroom, and she took off the robe. The pair of us, still fully dressed, got under the covers. We lay cocooned in the flickering shadows, her body trembling in my embrace. After a fleeting moment, her lips grazed mine, and I kissed her, needing her, wanting her.

"Joe, make love to me," Emily murmured, her voice a soft plea that resonated deeply within me.

"Are you sure?"

"Yes," she whispered.

Our clothing fell away like the petals of a flower, piece by piece, each layer discarded to the floor. The covers remained in place against the unnatural cold, but within its confines, we burned with desire.

We had witnessed a life taken away, and in this moment, we needed to grasp at the strands of life and pull them together.

She positioned herself above me, and then, in a gentle but intense exchange, she enveloped me. Our bodies came together in a dance older than time itself. In this embrace, sounds emerged — half-whispers of both joy and sorrow.

We slid, rolled over, ebbing and flowing like the tide, pressing against one another in a celebration of life. As we surrendered to the rhythm of our hearts, the boundaries of ourselves dissolved, and we both released with sighs and moans, leaving us both breathless and fulfilled.

She lay next to me, warm and alive. After a moment, I heard her breathing shift and become steadier. Sighing in relief, I was glad to see her find some peace. I brushed a stray strand of hair away from her face, watching her tranquil expression.

As the minutes passed, exhaustion overcame me. My mind slipped toward sleep, and just before I faded away...

I heard typing coming from the next room.

Twenty-Three

Searching

The next morning, I stirred awake at eight-thirty to find Emily getting out of bed, blissfully naked. The cabin had warmed up in the night, and caused us to push the covers aside and onto the floor.

As she stepped across the room to grab her glasses and my robe, I couldn't help but admire her flawless body in the soft morning light. But my breath caught in my throat when I noticed the purple bruises encircling her neck, a stark reminder of the night before.

She pulled on my robe as I pulled the afghan up to my waist to hide my state of excitement.

She smiled at me, but I could see she appeared tired. "Good morning. I could really use a cup of coffee."

"Yeah, I'll get it for you," I said, and paused, not sure where my pants were.

"Don't worry about hiding that," she said. "It's been poking me in the back for the last half-hour."

I hurriedly got up, threw on my pants, which were hard to close because of the state I was in. Going to the kitchen, I started the one-cup coffeemaker brewing, and used the bathroom to relieve myself. As I glanced at the mirror, I saw that although battered; I was none the worse for wear. The bandage on the back of my head was a reminder of the rock that had hit me.

Emily went into the bathroom as I came out, and I called through the door, "How do you like your coffee?"

"Just cream," she said. "Could you put it in a to-go cup of some kind? I've got to get home to shower and change. I'm going to be late for work as it is."

I had a metal travel cup, which I quickly located, filled with coffee, and added cream. She came out of the bathroom looking beautiful — how do girls do that?

I handed her the cup. "I'll need that cup. So, you'll have to come back."

She smiled. "I was planning to anyway."

I smiled as well. "I'm glad. Will you be all right today?"

"I'll be dragging," she said, and her hand touched her throat. "And I have to wear a blouse with a high collar. I'll try not to fall asleep while working at the reference desk."

"What about your stuff?" I said and pointed to the paraphernalia from our attempted exorcism.

"Could you throw it in the bag and hold it for me? I really have to run."

She got up on tiptoes and planted a perfectly acceptable kiss on my lips.

"I hope to do more of that later," I said.

"I look forward to it as well. But we'll have to wait until the weekend."

"I can wait."

She took the cup and headed for the door, grabbing her purse as she went.

I started coffee for myself and walked to the window to watch her turn her little car and head down the driveway. She pulled out of sight, and I got my coffee, hoping it would help me feel better.

My muscles were sore from all the lifting of fire extinguishers and helping keep the fire from consuming my house, as well as the confrontation with Rebecca.

I booted up my laptop, picked up the items Emily had brought the previous night and returned them to the shopping bag. I went online to my cloud account and checked the last page number of the scanned copy of *Lost Soul* I had there.

I went to the desk and looked at my page count. It appeared Rebecca had added over fifty pages since I scanned it the previous day.

I fed the pages into the machine, formatting them into a PDF file I marked as *'Lost Soul 2'*, and sent the file up to be with the first part in my cloud account.

Now that I had safely stored the pages, I took the time to actually read what she wrote.

I didn't know how much was Rebecca and how much was me, and at this point it didn't matter. Our writing styles blended so well that it made the story easy to follow.

The story was building to its climax exactly as I had seen it. Miranda and Soul were in Saint Petersburg and chasing down the hacker at the State Hermitage Museum, more commonly known as the Winter Palace.

Rebecca captured the amazing spectacle of the multiple rooms filled with masterpieces that sounded like she had been there herself. I did extensive research, but how did Rebecca know to describe the various exhibits: the Room of Ancient Egypt, the Room of 17th Century French Art, or the Kutuzov Corridor? Yet she did it with amazing accuracy. I could only speculate that our mental link allowed her to tap into my knowledge gained about these places.

The ultimate confrontation took place in the Ilya Kabakov Room of the museum. Kabakov was a conceptual artist, and it contained two fairly small installations in a mostly empty room: Toilet In The Corner and In The Closet. In my concept, Romanov had placed a transponder into the In The Closet artwork, as it had electricity connected to it, and blended it with the items inside the display. Soul had to disengage it before it sent the nuclear codes for both Russia and the United States to every country in the world.

As I went through the pages, I realized the novel was almost completely finished and it was some of the best writing I had ever done. If I had done it, that is.

Rebecca's skill as a ghostwriter captured my style and improved it. I knew now I would have little or no trouble at all writing the finale and finishing the book.

I gazed up at the ceiling, the pages in my hand. "Thank you, Rebecca."

My phone rang in the bedroom.

I ran to get it, worrying it might be news about Liam.

It was Ashley, who was all but breathless. "Liam's awake. He recognized me and Bobby, and he can talk."

"That's great news," I said.

"Can you come?"

I paused. Could I go? I wasn't sure. After the situation yesterday, I didn't know if I should leave the cabin alone for any length of time.

"I don't know…"

"What are you talking about?"

"Ash, someone tried to burn down Whispering Pines yesterday."

There was silence on the other end of the phone for a long moment. "What? How?"

"Someone blew up my propane tank. A few minutes later, and they would've taken me with it."

"Oh, my God! Where are you? Where are you staying?"

"I'm here at Whispering Pines. There wasn't much damage to the cabin; in fact, the woods got the worst of it. It took the firefighters a while to get it under control."

Another long pause. "Well, that's good."

"The police staked out my place. I think I could come by for a little while this afternoon, but I want to be back before nightfall."

"Are you okay there all alone?"

"I've had people come by, especially that police detective."

"Sullivan? He asked the doctors about talking to Liam, but so far they've told him he has to wait. Now, he wants to talk to me and Bobby again."

"Ash, I told him the truth."

"What truth?"

"Liam was the one who buried Rebecca here at Whispering Pines."

"What? That's crazy!"

"He found her here, strung up as if she had hanged herself. But I found out the truth. Someone strangled her."

There was a sharp intake of breath. "Do you think Liam did it?"

"I don't know, but it was someone she was intimate with. Someone who stayed with her in the cabin. Ash, do you have any idea if she was seeing someone other than Liam?"

"Joey, how the hell would I know?" she snapped, then took a moment to consider. "Is this what Bobby told me about when he stayed there? You see that woman's ghost?"

"Yes."

"Do you know how insane that sounds?"

"I know, and I'm living through it."

Ashley exhaled heavily into the phone. "All right. Come by this afternoon, and you, Bobby, and I can try to figure the situation out."

"Okay, see you later."

She ended the call, and I sat heavily on the bed. All I wanted to do was lie down and go back to sleep.

But the suggestion Sullivan made last night went through my head. "Do you think she didn't burn the carbon copy?"

Although Sullivan and I bumped heads, the man helped save my home and had great instincts. He knew I was holding back the entire time.

I gave the cabin the once-over last night and went to all the obvious places. I focused on the desk, where both Rebecca and I worked on my book. That was the place we'd both spent our time.

If she wanted to hide something, near the desk would be the obvious place.

Next to the desk were the bookcase and cabinet. I'd gone through the books with no luck. Now I pulled out the drawers one at a time, going through them and flipping them over in case she had taped something to the bottom of a drawer.

I pulled out the bottom drawer and peeked into the emptiness of the cabinet. Since legs lifted it off the ground, I put my hand under the piece of furniture and rubbed it along the bottom, finding nothing except a splinter.

"Ow," I muttered and brought out my hand with a large sliver of wood stuck in the index finger, which I quickly removed with my teeth. I went to the medicine cabinet and found some rubbing alcohol, which I poured on the wound, hissing from the sting.

I went back and replaced the drawers with the items in them, disgusted with the entire thing. Other than Sullivan's guess, what made me think there was a carbon copy? If someone burned the manuscript, they probably destroyed the carbon along with it.

I sat in the banker's chair and looked at the typewriter in the middle of the desk with the two piles of paper on each side.

I had fallen into that habit so easily, and Rebecca did the same with her pages. Did she copy me, or had I done the obvious thing she did?

I rubbed my thigh where I felt a bruise. I must have it from when I crashed into the desk when Rebecca belted me in the head with the crystal. Why had she reacted so violently? Especially considering the violence against her we saw played out a few minutes after that?

My gaze went to the floor, and I saw the corner of a paper barely sticking out from under the right side set of drawers for the desk.

I bent over and gently tugged the page. My mouth fell open when I read:

Loving Lilliana

A Novel

by

Rebecca Hawthorne

I stared at the page in my hand. The edges of the paper were yellowed, and I could tell it was indeed a carbon copy. It had the same faint, wide dark lines running up and down every one of my carbon pages.

Sitting in the chair, I put the single page on top of the typewriter and looked down at the bottom drawer.

I should have thought of this. It was such a logical place to hide something.

Yet, it worked as a hiding place for twenty years.

I pulled the bottom drawer out until the metal stop wouldn't allow it to go any further. I examined it and felt around until I found the release catch. Once I pushed it, the drawer came out completely.

I put it on the floor and stared into the well. The trim on the front of the pedestal created a space under the drawer. I reached in and carefully lifted out a collection of loose pages.

The stack in my hands was at least three hundred letter-size pages, all carefully typed, and the print had dark roller lines from the carbon paper.

I looked over at my laptop, lying out on the dining room table and still connected to the scanner. I added the title page to the stack and walked over to the table.

I separated the pages into groups of about fifty, put them into the scanner, and pushed the button so it scanned the pages one by one.

I pulled the pages as they went through and glanced at the second page. It was the dedication page and read:

To my own Lilliana

With affection

I frowned. That meant very little, as I did not know who the character was. She could be a friend, an acquaintance, or a lover. I would have to read the book to uncover who Lilliana was to the main character. Or she could've been the main character for all I knew.

Glancing at the clock, I knew I would have to get to the hospital instead of reading. But I scanned the manuscript completely before I did anything else. It was Rebecca's last book, and I wanted to make sure I stored it on my cloud account where it was safe.

Maybe I could figure out how to get it published. I thought about my soon-to-be new agent, Meredith Thompson. I had a feeling that if I let her know I found the last novel of Rebecca Hawthorne, she'd be able to get a pretty penny for it. That money would go to Rebecca's estate, which would help her daughter, Elora.

I kept scanning the pages, putting it all into a folder I called 'Lilliana'. Once the machine finished, I put the individual files into the folder, which I stuck up to my cloud account.

My internet service worked well, and within an hour of starting, I had everything scanned, filed, and uploaded.

I looked around the room to see where to put the manuscript, but the answer was obvious. I returned it to the well under the bottom drawer, slipped the drawer back into place, and hid it once again.

Showering and shaving, gulping down a second cup of coffee, I was ready to leave when a white van pulled into my driveway. I glanced out the window and saw my caretaker, Dan Stevens, walking toward the door.

Today he was in overalls, but with a light work shirt under them, and held a clipboard in his hands. He scratched his short beard as he knocked on my door.

"Mr. Stevens," I said. "To what do I owe this visit?"

"We heard about the trouble you had yesterday, Mr Riley," he said, a pleasant enough expression on his face. "Pocono Pines sent me up to look at any damage, and see about getting someone out here to fix anything that needs fixing."

Pocono Pines Property Care took its job seriously.

"That's great, Mr. Stevens," I said. "But my cousin is in the hospital in Port Jervis—"

"Nothing serious, I hope."

I decided that an easy lie was better than a complicated truth. "Just elective surgery, but I want to see him. But I have a few minutes now. I can show you the damage."

"Good, good," he said, and I led him to the side of the house and pointed to the spot where the propane tank used to be.

"Oh my," he said, taking out a clipboard and making notes. "I'm afraid a new propane tank is going to cost you."

I sighed. What didn't cost me?

I spoke up. "I'm just glad the propane connections to the house didn't blow."

"No, they wouldn't," Dan said and pointed. "Those yellow valves on the cabin shut off automatically if there is a drop in the pressure. It's a good thing, or the explosion would have taken out the entire wall."

I pointed at the damage to some of the roof shingles, and the pieces of metal embedded in the logs from the explosion, and Dan nodded. He walked around, looking at the wall up and down.

"So you want someone to get up on that roof, and you want to see about a new tank before the cold weather comes," he said.

"The cabin is cold almost every night," I told him. "If I'm going to price out a new tank, I want someone who can give me a quote on the price of a second propane heater for the bedroom."

He nodded. "That's right. You told me you wanted that. I figured with this warm spell we've been having that it wasn't so bad." He peered down at the burnt trees and the ditch that was Rebecca's grave. The fire had melted the yellow police tape, and the firefighters filled the pit with water.

"I have to tell you, Mister Riley, Pocono Pines wanted to drop you as a client."

This surprised me. "What? How come?"

"All the publicity about finding that body. Of course, I sided with you and informed management that you just inherited the cabin and they couldn't hold you accountable for things that happened in the past."

"Thank you, Mister Stevens."

"But if I might advise you, I'd keep a low profile for a while."

"Mr. Stevens, that is the only thing I want. To be honest, I'm a writer, and I don't like attention."

"Well, Mrs. Kinney saw you swimming the other day, and she asked if you were going to be trouble, like the others."

"Wait," I said. "Mrs. Kinney? Is that the same Mrs. Kinney, who watched my cousins with binoculars?"

He smiled. "The same. She's about ninety years old by now, but still as sharp as a tack."

I felt myself getting excited. "Could I see her? Talk to her?"

He shrugged. "If you want. She lives over on Scout Resident Road. You go up Saw Creek Road and turn left, and she's the first house on the right, back a bit."

"With a splendid view of the lake, no doubt."

He chuckled. "No doubt. Yeah, the old lady still lives there, all by herself. I pick up her groceries and check on her every time there's a snowstorm or anything. Tell you the truth, I worry about the old girl."

"Would it bother her if I visited her? I mean, unannounced."

He smiled. "I doubt it. She doesn't leave the house much. She might like the company."

We talked for a few more minutes, and he told me he'd turn in a report to Pocono Pines, and someone would be out to look at the work and give an estimate. He got into his truck and headed out.

I got my laptop and locked up the cabin. Instead of heading for the hospital, I went up the side road toward Scout Resident Road.

It took only a few minutes. After all, Mrs. Kinney's house was just on the other side of Sandy Rock Lake.

I pulled into the driveway and up a hill, and I saw the lake open out in front of me. It was a charming cabin, offering a cozy and serene retreat. The spacious front deck housed a pair of rocking chairs.

I knocked on the door, and a petite woman with a slight hunch answered it. She possessed a weathered appearance and wore an array of earth-toned clothing reflecting the woods around her home. Her eyes, blue and piercing, remained unyielding behind the lenses of her eyeglasses.

"Yes?" she said, her voice dry and faint.

"Mrs. Kinney? I hope I'm not bothering you. I'm Joe Riley, and I live on the other side of the lake."

"I know who you are," she said, a glimmer in her eye like she knew a private joke. "I've seen you swimming on the dock. You're the new owner, aren't you?"

"Yes, but I used to come up here as a child."

She looked me over, her lips tightly pressed together. "You were the youngest, weren't you? Little Joey, right?"

I couldn't help but smile. "That's right. You have quite a memory, Mrs. Kinney."

"Don't stand there out on the porch, come in," she said, and opened the door.

I stepped into the cabin to find an open floor plan that seamlessly connected the living and dining areas, just like at Whispering Pines. Although her place was smaller, there was a cozy living room with a rustic stone fireplace. The furniture was simple but comfortable, and panoramic windows captured views of the surrounding wilderness, and a bay window looked down upon the lake. I saw a pair of binoculars on a small table near that window.

"If you don't mind, I wanted to ask you about something that happened twenty years ago."

"You mean that trollop who stayed at your cabin that ended up disappearing?"

My mouth fell open. "How did you—?"

"It's been all over the news. The police dug up her body. I've been thinking about her ever since, remembering the nonsense she got into when she was here. Were you the one who found her?"

"I was — uh — digging a firepit, and I found an old suitcase."

"So, someone buried her in your backyard, eh?" she said. "I'm not surprised. That woman was trouble. I saw what she did with your relatives, all of them running around naked during the full moon."

I raised my head and felt a twinge of interest. "So, you saw them."

"Brazen as they could be. And then she brought the skinny fellow down one night, and she had her way with him right there on the dock for the entire world to see."

"The skinny fellow?"

"Yes, he was one of the Riley boys."

"Liam?"

"I suppose."

"I see. I'm sorry if that upset you."

She waved a dismissive hand. "I've seen a lot more things than that in my time, let me tell you. It was the foolishness she got into with the girl that I find annoying."

"Girl," I asked. "What girl?"

"The tall one. It was dark that night, and I couldn't see them all that well. But I could see what they were doing, the pair of them naked. Now, I have nothing against homosexuals, mind you, if it's what you do in private. But out there on the dock?" She shook her head.

"You mean Rebecca was having an affair with a woman?"

"Of course, that's who I mean. And the girl was young, maybe seventeen or eighteen. I mean, if she's gay or bi or whatever, fine. But seems like she was taking advantage of that girl."

That's when it all came together in my head. Rebecca was having an affair with both a woman and with Liam. Her paramour could have driven the rental car. A woman in love with Rebecca.

And that woman could have killed her.

Twenty-Four

Under Suspicion

I thanked Mrs. Kinney and soon was on my way to Port Jervis, thinking about what she told me.

A young woman, perhaps seventeen or eighteen? What if she were someone younger? That could have led to trouble. Could Rebecca have found a local girl to 'get her energy' from? That made little sense and wouldn't explain the rental car.

Could she have been someone Rebecca knew from her home, and could only meet in the clandestine safety of the cabin?

It suddenly became clear to me. I would have to read *Loving Lilliana* if I wanted to understand the situation and the players involved.

Rebecca was a sexual force of nature. I knew that from experience. To think she would limit herself only to males was an assumption. With her forceful personality and incredible natural allure, she could easily attract all genders.

As all of this reeled through my mind, I arrived at the Bon Secours Community Hospital, made my way to the front desk to get a visitor badge, and was soon on the floor where Liam was staying.

I walked into the small waiting area to find Ashley and Robert, both of them looking unhappy. There were several other people there, so I kept my voice down as I sat down across from them.

"Is Liam all right?" I asked, worried.

"Fine. We'll be able to visit him soon," Ashley said.

I felt myself relax. "That's good. I was concerned when I saw you both looking so upset."

Ashley clenched her jaw. "We're upset because we just had a chat with Detective Sullivan."

"Is he still here?"

"No, he left," Robert said.

"After questioning us," Ashley said. "Honestly, that man is relentless. He thinks we had something to do with Ms. Hawthorne's death."

"What?"

Robert held up a hand to get my attention. "He thinks we're holding something back. That we know more than we're telling."

"What did you tell him, Joey?" Ashley demanded.

I leaned in close and lowered my voice. "Exactly what I told you, Ash. Liam confessed to me he had buried Rebecca and her stuff. He found her in the bedroom and thought she had hanged herself."

Robert rubbed his face. I noticed he was getting jowly now that he was fifty. "Great. Now he'll never leave us alone."

I confronted him. "Did you tell him about the meeting you had with Rebecca when she threw the chair at you?"

Robert nodded. "There really wasn't much to tell."

Ashley glared at him. "When did that happen?"

"A few days before she disappeared," Robert said. "I was just trying to get her to let Liam down gently. It's not important."

"We don't know what's important and what isn't," I said. "However, I now believe that someone murdered Rebecca."

Ashley and Robert exchanged a glance.

"Do you think Liam killed her?" Robert asked. "Because that's what the detective thinks."

"I don't know."

"Never mind that," Ashley said, taking over like she did when we were kids. "Bobby said you saw Hawthorne's ghost?"

I nodded. "I've seen her almost every night since I moved in."

She shook her head and glared at Robert.

Robert shrugged. "Look, he's right. I saw her too. It was scary as hell."

"It's not possible," Ashley hissed. "Ghosts aren't real."

"Tell that to Rebecca," I said.

"I think I will," she said, undaunted.

"What are you saying?" Robert said.

"I should spend the night at Whispering Pines," Ashley said. "That way I can see this so-called ghost and end this foolishness."

"You can if you want," I said.

Ashley went on. "Look, it's all over the media about the woman's body discovered there, and some people are trying to attach Dad to her disappearance."

"That's crazy," I said.

"Look who's talking about crazy," Ashley said. "Haven't you been listening to the media?'

"No, I've been writing," I said. "And trying to save the house from burning down."

"What?" Robert said.

I quickly told Robert about the propane tank and the fire at the cabin. Ashley listened as I went into details I didn't tell her when we spoke on the phone.

"My God," Robert said. "Do you think it was some crazed Rebecca Hawthorne fan?"

"Robert, she's been dead for twenty years, and she only published two novels. I doubt there are any remaining Rebecca Hawthorne fans."

"You might think that," Robert said. "But there is stuff online with all kinds of conspiracy theories. What if people think I killed her?"

"That's not true," Ashley said, annoyed.

"Like crazy theories need to be true?" Robert said. "But this is going to make trouble for me. What if the detective charges Liam? Now we really need a lawyer who can guide all of us through this and protect our interests."

I nodded. "You're right, Robert. We need someone to help us navigate the situation. We shouldn't take any chances."

"I agree," Ashley said, and glared at me. "The first thing is to stop talking to the detective."

Robert sighed. "I've been doing some research, and I spoke to that estate lawyer, Mr. Clark. He made a few recommendations. I would like to discuss our options further."

"We should act quickly and find someone who specializes in this type of situation," Ashley said.

Robert set his jaw. "One thing we need to keep in mind is avoiding any more media attention. The last thing we want is to have this blown out of proportion in the public eye. We have to handle this matter discreetly."

"After the fire yesterday, I don't know if that will be possible," I offered.

"The most logical thing is to get away from Whispering Pines," Ashley said and met my eyes. "Look, I've got space. You can come crash with me."

"I can't," I said. "I'm working on a book."

"Joey," she said. "You told us someone tried to blow up the place. Like Bobby said, it might be a conspiracy nut or — who knows — someone from Hawthorne's family."

"She has a point, Joey," Robert said. "I mean, who knows what crazies are out there these days?"

"Can't you finish the book somewhere else?" Ashley said.

I considered this. I read the most recent pages, and she was right. Finishing up the book on my laptop wouldn't be hard. It was far enough along, so the last ten thousand words would be a breeze. Plus, I could handle all my rewrites on the computer, and send a more perfect version to the editor.

But what about Rebecca?

My energy kept her going and allowed her to create. If I left, she would remain trapped there, in the same shadow existence she had inhabited for over twenty years.

"I can't. I owe Rebecca. I can't just leave her without helping her find peace."

"And how are you going to do that?" Robert asked. "Bring in a priest? Maybe an exorcist?"

"I have a friend. She knows about occult things."

"Look," Ashley said, and I saw this annoyed her. "I'll go to the cabin tonight and kick out anything that's there. How's that?"

Now it was Robert and I who exchanged a glance.

"You're more than welcome to try," I offered.

Doctor Singh arrived and told us we could visit Liam, but only for ten minutes.

As we entered Liam's hospital room, I felt a heavy cloud of worry in the air. The room was fraught with tension as Robert and Ashley, their faces wearing expressions of deep concern, came in quietly after me.

The hospital room itself was dimly lit, adding to the atmosphere of solemnity. Medical equipment and monitors beeped softly in rhythm, reminding us Liam's battle was far from over.

As I approached Liam's bedside, I saw the signs of his struggle etched into his pale face. His body lay motionless under the sterile white sheets, connected to various tubes and wires.

"Hey Liam, how are you doing?" I said.

"I've been better." He spoke in a gravelly voice, then attempted a grin that was more like a grimace. "I heard you saved me."

"A little. The EMTs did most of the work."

"You should have left me there," Liam said.

"Don't say that, Lee," Ashley said, coming forward and taking his hand.

"I've been a fuck-up my entire life," he said, and I saw tears in his eyes. "I can't even kill myself right."

Robert came forward next to Ashley. "Liam, we love you. We don't want you to go."

He looked at us standing over him. "Did Joey tell you what I did?"

"Yes," Robert said. "You found Rebecca and buried her."

"It's my fault she died," Liam said, and the tears flowed. "I should have been there to support her when she needed help."

"It's not your fault," Ashley said. "She was a selfish person. All you did was try to give her some rest."

Liam leaned back and shut his eyes. "You might as well let the police have me. Stick me in a cell somewhere. Maybe there I can do some good."

"Liam, don't talk to the police," Robert said. "We're getting a lawyer for you. If the police want to know anything, they go through your lawyer."

"And it can wait, Lee," Ashley said. "Until you're better. Then, we'll fight this thing. You'll see."

A nurse appeared at the door. "I'm sorry, but he needs his rest."

We all headed back to the waiting area.

Robert turned to Ashley and me, and said, "I'm going back to the hotel and make calls until I have a lawyer."

"I'll head back to Whispering Pines," I said.

"I'll be there after dinner," Ashley said. I want to meet this ghost of yours."

As I headed home, I went through Milford.

I had to talk to Emily.

"You found the manuscript!" she squealed. Her eyes sparkled, and her hands waved animatedly. "I want to see it."

"Sh! You're working. Library, remember?" I said, trying to calm her down.

She went on, her voice getting faster with every word. "I mean, just imagine, Joe! This manuscript was Rebecca's last novel. It's like you discovered a time capsule or the Holy Grail." She was almost dancing with joy. "Maybe it's a masterpiece that the world needs to read. We could get it published, share it with everyone, and honor her talent."

"I agree," I said. "But it's more than that."

"What could be more than that?" she whispered, turning red because she realized she was being too loud.

"I think it may hold a clue to who killed her. I won't know until I read it."

"Do you think it's any good?"

I took her hand. "Emily, the one thing I've learned since I got here is that Rebecca was a brilliant writer."

She squeezed my hand. "Wait until I tell Ellie; she'll flip out. Does that mean she'll get royalties?"

"She should. I want you to know I ran it through my scanner and put it in my cloud account, just to be safe."

She frowned. "Was that really necessary?"

"Emily, someone tried to blow up my house."

"I see your point. Besides, it's not the actual typed pages; it's the words; it's her story. Could I come by tonight?"

"No, my cousin Ashley is staying at the cabin tonight. After last night, I think you should go home and get some rest."

She sighed. "I am tired. But why is your cousin visiting?"

"She wants to meet Rebecca."

"Do you think Rebecca will manifest for her?"

"I don't know why Rebecca does anything she does," I said. I looked around to make sure no one was close by. "Emily, you've been up here for months, and you were looking into Rebecca's disappearance, right?"

Emily repeated my glance around the room. "Yeah."

"Have you heard anything about a young woman visiting Rebecca? Maybe a local?"

"How young?"

"I don't know. I spoke to Mrs. Kinney. She's got a cabin on the other side of the lake from me, and likes to look at people through binoculars."

Her eyes widened. "Really?"

"Yes, she's about ninety, and she saw my cousins and Rebecca the night they went skinny-dipping under the full moon."

She shook her head. "That sounds like Rebecca."

"Yes, but she says on a different night, she saw Rebecca with a young girl on the dock. She was sure that they were making love."

Emily frowned. "I don't know. I didn't think Rebecca was into women. Our little possession episode suggests she preferred men."

"Then again, there's the title of her book."

She shrugged. "*Loving Lilliana*? It's possible. I don't know."

"I'm on my way home to read it. I'll let you know what I find out."

"Please do."

I drove the final half-hour to my house, and I saw several state trooper vehicles on my road. I pulled into the driveway and found Detective Sullivan at my front door.

"Detective," I said, trying not to sound annoyed he was here once again.

"Mr. Riley, where have you been?"

"I was in Port Jervis visiting my cousin."

"I needed to let you know I have men going through the woods today. We're trying to find the firing location for the shots that blew up your propane tank."

"Thank you. That would be good to know."

"We have dogs with us, and we'll try to pin down a site, see if we can find any shell casings, footprints, or tire tracks from a vehicle."

"It's reassuring to have your troopers nearby."

"I spoke to your cousins this morning. They are both tight-lipped about their knowledge of Ms. Hawthorne."

"They probably would prefer the whole situation just went away. My cousin Robert thinks that a rabid fan of Hawthorne's blew up my propane tank."

"It's a possibility," he stated with a shrug.

I sighed. "I'm not sure what to think."

"It's an unusual situation," he said, and looked over at his men in the distance. "I'm going to join the troopers in case they find anything."

He headed for the woods on the side of the cabin, down past the concrete pad for the propane tank and the open pit where the forensics team had uncovered Rebecca's body.

I got down to the things that needed to be done. I put the washed sheets on the spare room bed, cleaned, and made sure I had whatever I needed for a visitor.

My alcohol supply comprised a half-empty bottle of vodka and a few bottles of wine. I noted I had not been drinking the way I used to, and this was good.

I liked Emily, and, more important I wanted to be with her. If I wanted this to work, I couldn't just coast along as I always had. I needed to change, to grow.

I had to confront my own flaws — the excessive drinking being one of them. But it was also just a symptom. In my marriage with Chandra, I shut down during tough discussions, let her run my life as I stayed blissfully unaware of what she was doing.

In the last few months leading up to the divorce, I had been angry and bitter.

Emily deserved more than half-hearted efforts and the excuses I'd used in the past. It scared me. The thought of truly committing and opening up to being vulnerable.

But I couldn't shake the feeling of what we could be together.

After an hour of neatening the place, I brewed a cup of coffee, and pulled out the bottom drawer of the desk and sat down with the manuscript.

I hoped it would tell me what I needed to know.

Twenty-Five

Lilliana

I planned on just glancing through the pages to get the gist of the story but I quickly became completely engrossed in the book.

To say the writing was good was an understatement. It was poetic, in the way Virginia Woolf could be. At other times, the narrative was stark and hard, like Ernest Hemingway. Yet Rebecca Hawthorne combined these styles with her own and, more importantly, embraced the character's emotions in her storyline.

The protagonist was thirty-year-old Adalynn Beecher, who was going on vacation away from her husband and daughter to a place of solitude to write a book.

Adalynn felt like a captured butterfly who was playing at a normal life, yet her true nature pulled at her. All she wanted to do was fly.

The scene where she tells her husband, Jack, she has to get away was magnificent. Two people spoke rationally, and yet I felt the heartbreak underneath. Adalynn deeply loved this man, yet if she didn't break free for a little while, her life would crush her. Meanwhile, Jack adored her and would do anything to please her, yet the thought of losing her, even for a little while, made him miserable.

It was as if Rebecca was writing to free herself of her own guilt, but telling the reader she understood the pain her self-imposed exile caused to a man she deeply loved.

The scene ended with Jack telling her to do what she needed to do, and that he didn't want to know. All he needed was for her to come back when she was ready.

Adalynn went on a train ride to vacation in what the book called 'the Pennsylvania Mountains,' to stay in a cabin.

The story was like Rebecca's own, yet different at the same time. Only one person met her at the train, and the description fit Robert well, perhaps exaggerating his own concepts of self-importance to make his character seem braggadocios.

Adalynn stayed at a cabin near a lake — once again familiar. She attended local parties and events, and there she met an earnest and troubled young man, who pursued her with abandon.

She shut down his advances, but finally, on a night she had too much wine, out of pity and desire, she bedded him.

The description of the act itself was once again poetic. I had read scenes like this in romance novels, but Rebecca took it to another level, and also expressed Adalynn's innate sexuality trying to bloom beyond her own limitations, and yet her fears kept her from fully expressing herself.

I was a third of the way through the book when Lilliana appeared.

To say she entered is far too simple. She appeared on the page, and all at once the book was about her, seen through Adalynn's eyes.

Lilliana embodied the exquisite tension between innocence and passion, a captivating paradox that drew the eyes and hearts of those around her.

Adalynn found herself utterly enchanted by Lilliana's ethereal charm; each glance, each whispered laugh resonated with a magnetic pull that tugged at her very soul.

The allure of Lilliana overshadowed everything, even the young man whose arms had once offered her solace. In pursuit of this new, intoxicating yearning, Adalynn stepped into uncharted territory, daring to explore the depths of her heart.

Adalynn referred to her as a girl — that was the term — girl, but Lilliana was well past eighteen. It was her lack of worldliness and experience that suggested an immaturity Adalynn long ago surrendered. Adalynn described her as a lanky girl with small breasts, blonde hair, and wide hips. She came across as awkward and loose-jointed, but these attributes added to her appeal.

Adalynn's once-quiet existence was suddenly ablaze with an awakening desire for Lilliana she couldn't fight. She makes love to the young man again, but her thoughts are only on Lilliana the entire time.

The situation comes to a head on a summer night, when the pair of them are talking at the dock of the nearby lake, alone. Adalynn suggests they swim, but as they have no swimsuits, they swim in the nude.

This leads to them swimming, giggling and laughing, the pair of them helping each other in and out of the water. Soon the touches on each other's bare flesh becomes too intoxicating and the women kiss.

Again, Rebecca wrote the scene with physical tension, but it definitely wasn't erotica. Like any superb romance novel, it was enticing without being vulgar, and I found it stirred my own desires. This scene awakens a passion within Adalynn she didn't know she held, and brings her to a state of exquisite euphoria, where waves of pleasure washed over her body and Lilliana's.

I looked out the window to see that the late afternoon was fading into twilight.

I put the manuscript back into its hidey-hole and replaced the drawer, my head spinning in the way you get when you're completely lost in the other world of a brilliant book, and you try to return to the real world.

Lesbian romance is an entire genre in the modern world, but twenty years ago Rebecca's book would have been a sensation.

But I still did not know who Lilliana was. Was she an amalgam of several people put together and imbued with all of Rebecca's desire? Hard to say, but no one person came to mind. The other problem for me was this didn't explain the rental car.

I made a quick meal of pasta with bottled sauce, sat down, and ate. I didn't want a drink. In fact, I only had the red wine the previous night.

I decided I would have a glass of wine once Ashley got here.

I didn't have long to wait. By the time I'd washed the dishes, I heard a car pull up, but this time there were no flashing red and blue lights behind it.

It seemed that my police detail was busy with something else.

I stepped out and waved at Ashley as she got out of the car. "Did you see any state police?"

"You have your own security?" she said.

"The police were staking out the place, but maybe that ended," I said. "They were searching the woods this afternoon."

"What for?" Ashley said as I led her inside.

"To figure out who shot at the house and from where."

"I didn't know you could set off a propane tank with a gun," Ashley said. She carried a small suitcase in with her. She gazed around the room. "Wow. You haven't changed the place at all."

"Just added my recliner," I said, pointing at my large leather chair in the middle of the room. "I didn't have much furniture after the divorce."

A strange look appeared in her eyes, and she walked past me to the desk with the typewriter on it. "Oh, my God. You found her typewriter."

I followed her over. "Yeah, it was next to the desk, in its case."

She picked up one sheet from the carbon pile and looked it over, frowning. "You're typing your new book?" She stared at it in disbelief. "And using carbon paper?"

"Trying a different technique," I said, taking the page from her fingers and returning it to its pile. "It's been going really well."

She spoke as if in a dream. "Just like she did…"

"You know how Rebecca wrote?"

This seemed to startle her, and she reacted like she was coming out of a dream. "I… stayed here with her the first week, remember? We bunked together in the spare room, in those two single beds."

"Oh, yeah," I said. "Mom and Dad used to push those beds together when we stayed here."

This made her smile. "And all of us were out here in sleeping bags."

"It's amazing we ever got any sleep at all."

She slid her hand to her hip. "So, where's this ghost of yours?"

"I can't conjure her like a magician. Why don't you take your things into the spare room, and I'll pour you a glass of wine?"

She headed to the room, overnight bag in hand. I pulled another bottle of wine and poured her and myself a glass.

She quickly returned to the main room, and I handed her one.

"What should we drink to?" she asked.

"To Liam's full recovery," I said and touched my glass to hers. We each took a sip. "So, how is he doing?"

"Better from what Bobby tells me," she said. "I had to go back to Clinton and Brew Haven."

"That's a lot of driving for you."

She shook her head. "Maybe if I weren't such a control freak, I would get out of the way and let my staff handle things."

"Is my entrepreneur cousin letting go a bit?"

She grinned. "Kate, my new manager is skilled, and she had everything under control. I just handled the financials and the things only I can do."

"Perhaps you can give her those duties as well."

"She has more than enough duties," Ashley said and lifted an eyebrow. "You see, Kate and I are actually more than just employer and manager. We... are lovers."

I tried to keep my poker face in place. "That's... great."

Her expression shifted. "You don't look pleased."

"I'm sorry, Ash. It's just that I didn't know you were gay."

She appeared surprised. "Really? I thought everyone knew." She stepped away, sipping her wine. "It's not like I made it a secret or anything."

She looked at the photos on the wall.

I followed her. "It's just that I haven't seen you with anyone who I thought was important to you."

"I find it hard to get close to people, so I was never looking for something permanent," she said, looking at the framed photos. "I can't believe you kept these photos up on the wall."

"It seemed a shame to take them down," I said. "There's one of all of us, see?"

I pointed to the group shot with the entire family, and my eye went to the young Ashley. The photo captured Ashley at around fourteen years old, standing tall with her blonde hair and her arms crossed.

—lanky—

I glanced over at her. Growing up, she was the middle child of the cousins and six years older than me, which always made me feel she was so mature.

"When did you have blonde hair?" I asked.

Her hand went to her chestnut brown, shoulder-length hair. "I was blond as a kid, then I dyed it blond into my early twenties." She shrugged. "After that, I just accepted myself the way I am."

I'd forgotten about her hair. But we were so young then.

We looked at the next set of photos, with my father helping me with the bow and arrow, and Uncle Rick teaching Ashley how to hold a rifle.

"What kind of rifle was that?" I asked, pointing at the photo.

"A Remington 700," she said. "Dad always liked it because it was lightweight and easy to handle."

I met her eyes. "I found the manuscript."

She looked at me, puzzled. "What?"

My heart pounded as I walked past her to the dining room table, putting distance between us.

"I found *Loving Lilliana*. Rebecca hid the carbon copy. I found it."

Ashley mustered a smile. "Oh wow, Joe, that's incredible! How did you come across it?"

"I read more than half of it."

"Good for you, what does—"

I shouted. "I know about Lilliana." The room fell silent. "It was you."

"What?" she said, but her eyes darted around the room.

"You were the model for Lilliana."

"I don't know what you're talking about," she said, but I saw her temper rising. The weight of my accusation lingered in the air.

"Ashley, how could you?"

"I don't know where you got this idea, but—"

"I want the truth, Ash," I said. My voice trembled with a mixture of anger and fear. My words hung in the air, amplified by some unseen force that made both of us gaze up at the ceiling.

Strange lights flickered in the room, casting an ethereal glow. The room grew colder, as if an arctic wind blew through it.

"What the hell is this?" Ashley demanded.

Amid this surreal spectacle, I saw Rebecca at the desk, sitting naked as I had seen her so many times before. Yet, this time, her image flickered in and out of existence, but she rotated in the chair, her piercing eyes fixed on Ashley.

Her voice came, echoing throughout the room in a twisted cacophony. "Is that all you want?"

Ashley took a step back, staring wide-eyed at the naked woman in the chair.

Rebecca grinned. "Sorry, dear, I'm working. I'm almost finished." She twisted back to the typewriter and typed again. "Tell you what, let me finish and we can celebrate."

"No," Ashley gasped. "It's not possible. This is a trick."

Rebecca stopped typing. "I told you, dear, you can read the thing yourself." She paused, listening. "Oh, you did read it? I hope you enjoyed it."

The wine glass fell from Ashley's hand, smashing as it hit the floor. The tiny amount of wine still in it spilled in a small puddle resembling blood.

"So you don't like the title, but it's just a title," Rebecca went on. "Yes, it's about you, and it's not about you."

Looking where Rebecca was facing, I saw another shape, faint and unreal, the figure of a woman.

Rebecca stood opposite the semi-translucent shape, talking to it. "Oh, don't be such a baby. I'll dedicate the book to that name, and no one will know it's you. Relax."

She headed for my bedroom, and then the shadow form went to her and grabbed her arm to turn her. I now saw features forming and a face.

It was Ashley. Ashley at twenty-six.

I'd always thought Ashley looked grown-up and mature as a child. She was older than I, and I adored her. But as a forty-year-old looking at a twenty-six-year-old, I thought she indeed could have been mistaken for a teenager.

The air became heavy, suffused with an odd weight. I glanced over to see Ashley's eyes wide in shock and disbelief as she witnessed the reenactment, and stared at her younger self.

Rebecca went on. "I told you all along I finished the dedication; now I just have to add the quotes, and then I'm going home, to my husband and my daughter. That's the plan; that was always the plan, and you damn well knew it. Now, you can be an asshole about it if you want, or we can have some fun before I go back to being Mommy."

Rebecca put her hands on her hips and faced the spectral Ashley, whose mouth was moving. In that weird, echoing way, I heard her say, "You don't understand. I love you."

Rebecca spoke as if picking up a cue. "Don't say that. You know nothing about love. Look, you were a good lay and great research, but that's all it ever was. I don't know what you're complaining about. You got your jollies as well."

Spectral Ashley raised her hand and slapped the solid-looking Rebecca hard in the face.

"That's it!" Rebecca said and headed back to the bedroom. "I'm locking the door. You can sleep by yourself."

I looked at the semitransparent figure of Ashley and saw anger twist her features. She spun Rebecca around, and her hands went to her throat.

"Wait — stop," Rebecca croaked, her face twisting in agony. She clawed at Ashley's hands, her gasps and wheezes echoing through the air, intensifying the nightmare unfolding before our eyes.

"No!" the real Ashley shouted. She had backed away several steps. Fear, anger, and perhaps a hint of madness flickered across her face as the reenactment of her actions unfolded before her.

Rebecca trembled and slammed herself against the wall, and like before, fell down to one knee.

"No!" Ashley yelled and ran into the kitchen and through the back door and out into the night.

"Ash!" I yelled and grabbed my cell phone off the table where I had left it.

I stopped in the doorway as I saw Ashley rushing down the hill. I quickly hit redial on my phone.

"Hello?" Emily answered, sleepily.

"Em, call the police. It was my cousin Ashley. She killed Rebecca."

"What are you talking about—"

"Em, there's no time. Call the police and maybe an ambulance; send them here. I think she's going to do something rash."

I broke off the call and set the phone aside. Hastily, I made my way down the hill, my heart racing as I hurried to catch up with Ashley.

The full moon cast an eerie glow over the forest, guiding Ashley's desperate flight as I ran after her. I still heard the echoes of Rebecca's words in my mind.

A full moon, like the night Rebecca and my cousins went skinny-dipping all those years ago. Was that the night Ashley first realized her attraction to Rebecca? Was that the inciting incident in their entire affair?

In the novel Rebecca wrote, she talked of the main character's love of Lilliana in epic and poetic ways. But Rebecca casually dismissed any feelings Ashley had and devolved the entire relationship to simple research.

I could see how that might push someone over the edge.

Ashley was getting closer to the lake and had a lengthy head start on me. As I carefully made my way down the hill in darkness, a chilling wind blew through the surrounding trees, sending shivers down my spine.

I saw Ashley stop and turn back momentarily, as if half-expecting to see Rebecca's ghostly figure chasing her. But all I saw were the dark shadows cast by the moonlight shining on the lake.

She spun and headed for the lake again. Not running, but with a purposeful stride, as if she had decided.

"No, no, no," I murmured, picking up my pace.

Ashley strode onto the dock, but in the moonlight she couldn't see that the wood had rotted, and her leg went through the wood and she fell to the dock, crying out in pain.

I hoped she would stay stuck until I could get there, but as I drew closer, she lifted herself and pulled free. With a glance back at me, she limped to the edge of the dock — our dock, the same one we played on as kids.

Her trembling hands clutched at her chest, as if the weight of her guilt was crushing her, suffocating her.

I was still too far away to stop her.

The soft lapping of water against the dock echoed in my ears. Ashley hesitated for a fleeting moment, as if torn between the pull of the water's darkness and the desire to run from her haunting actions.

But then, as if guided by an unseen force, Ashley stepped forward off the dock, and her body disappeared as she plunged into the abyss below.

I increased my pace, as I knew her clothes would weigh her down. Even though the summer heat warmed the lake, it was still cold, and her clothes would drag her to the bottom.

I sprinted towards the lake. As my feet hit the dock, I kicked off my shoes as I approached the water's edge. I paused, despite my adrenaline surge, and gazed at the dark water, the moon's light reflecting in ripples back to me.

I saw movement to my right, and without a second thought, I dove headfirst into the cold, murky depths, hoping to reach Ashley.

My body sliced through the water, my mind focused solely on the task at hand. My aim was true, and I ran right into Ashley. I fought to grab her and pull her upwards.

Ignoring my fear, I wrapped my arms around her. With all my might, I pulled her toward the surface, fighting against the water's strength, and the weight of Ashley and her sodden clothing.

As our heads emerged, gasping for air, I felt a mixture of relief and exhaustion. The long run and the sudden plunge into the water left me winded, and I sucked in air greedily. I held Ashley tight, her shivering body pressed against mine as we treaded water.

My muscles strained, and fatigue took its toll. Ashley's weight, coupled with the resistance of the water, sapped my strength. My strokes became slower. As I pushed forward, my breathing became labored, and sweat dripped down my forehead, mixing with the water.

I was determined to get her back to shore, and I was relieved when my hand touched the ladder on the side of the dock.

But how could I lift her up the ladder and onto the deck? I gripped the edge of the ladder. My ragged breathing echoed through the air as I attempted to heave us onto the wooden platform. Ashley wasn't helping, acting as a deadweight.

At that moment, I felt someone grab me under my armpits, though how they could do it from the dock at that angle I couldn't understand. Someone with immense strength pulled me and Ashley up the ladder, as if we weighed nothing. They didn't just pull us up; we all but flew.

The pair of us fell onto the dock, Ashley gasping for air and coughing up water. Confused and disoriented,

I looked around to see a glowing form near me.

It was Rebecca, naked and glowing in the moonlight. She was the one who pulled me and Ashley from the water, saving us both. She smiled down at me, and I could hear her in my head.

"Now, I am free. I can move on."

"Thank you, Rebecca," I whispered as Ashley coughed and moaned.

Rebecca smiled down at me. "That woman the other night. She is my daughter's friend?"

"Yes."

"You will be good for each other," she said, and looked up at the stars.

"Will I ever see you again?" I asked.

She smiled, nodded, and faded away, leaving only me and Ashley in the clear night.

Twenty-Six

Goodbyes

We lay on the dock, both of us too weary to get up, our clothes soaked.

"Ashley, are you all right?" I asked. "You won't try anything, will you?"

She coughed and gasped. "I won't fight you. I think I broke my leg."

I rolled on my side and looked at Ashley, who returned my gaze. She asked softly, "Why didn't you just let me die?"

"I couldn't do that, Ash," I said. "But tell me the truth. It was you who blew up the propane tank, wasn't it?"

Ashley's eyes glistened with tears as she watched my face, as if searching for understanding. "I didn't think you'd be home when I set it all up. I figured if I got rid of Whispering Pines, it would all just go away. All the goddamn memories."

"You loved Rebecca, didn't you?"

She coughed again. "Loved her? It was more than that. She was my addiction. She was like a drug, and I couldn't get enough. When we first got together, the night we first made love, it all seemed to become clear. I suddenly understood what was missing from my life."

"And you were the person in the rental car."

She nodded. "I'd rent a car and drive up here to spend the weekdays with her and then leave because Liam came up on the weekends."

"Did that bother you?" I asked.

"It killed me. I spent the weekends in despair, mad at Liam, mad at Rebecca, mad at the fact that I couldn't be with her. And then she let me read her book. My character was like a goddamn fairy tale. The characters parted at the end, but it was tragic, with both of them in agony. But in reality, Rebecca didn't give a shit about me at all. Lilliana was all make-believe. On weekdays, I was her research, and on weekends, she banged Liam. I meant nothing to her, nothing."

My heart jolted as a sudden flash of red and blue lights pierced through the darkness atop the hill, each strobe slicing through the night like a blade.

Shadows glided towards us urgently, dark silhouettes of men descending swiftly, their footsteps uneven and frantic. Between them, they carried a stretcher.

I watched the state trooper guiding them downward, his flashlight casting erratic sweeps across the tense, strained faces.

I went on. "So you strangled Rebecca. Then you hung her up, using the pulley in the bedroom, and burned the manuscript so that Liam would find her and think she despaired over the book."

"Yes, but I never found the carbon copy," Ashley said, barely above a whisper. "Joey, tell the police Liam isn't at fault for burying Rebecca. I told him to do it."

"What?" I said, surprised by this.

"He called me when he found her, in a panic, and not knowing what to do. I was the one who said that the police would think he killed her and he needed to bury her and her things." She lay back and looked at the night sky. "I wish I had told him to bury that damn typewriter as well."

By now, the men had reached us, I pushed up and got unsteadily to my feet.

"Mr. Riley?" said a state trooper, flashlight in hand, as he came down the hill.

"We need an ambulance and a stretcher," I said. "She broke her leg."

"EMTs are with me," the trooper explained. "A woman phoned us and said you needed them."

My lips curled into a hesitant smile, warmth swelling in my chest. Emily had thought ahead — she always did.

The EMTs carefully lifted Ashley onto a stretcher and secured her with soft straps. With steady determination, the two men began their ascent up the steep hill, focused on navigating the uneven terrain.

The trooper focused on me. "The lady who called the dispatcher said something about a murder?"

"Yes," I said as we started up the hill, following the stretcher. "Look, I'm going to have to ask you to contact Detective Sullivan. He'll be the one to straighten this all out."

An hour later, I sat in dry clothes as I told the entire story to Sullivan.

He listened intently, making notes as he went, and when I finished, he closed his notebook and nodded. Then he went outside and spoke on his cell phone for ten minutes as I waited.

He came back in and told me, "They've got Ms. Riley at the hospital and I've put an officer to watch her."

"That's good, I guess," I said.

"The doctors said that her leg is only a bad sprain, not broken. They're going to keep her overnight."

"What will happen to her?"

"We'll take her into custody. I don't know what charges the D.A. will pursue. She committed a crime, covered it up, and manipulated your cousin. Add to that the recent attempt to blow up the cabin. My men searched her car and found a rifle with ammunition that matches the shell casings we found in the woods, and she had one of those exploding targets — the chemicals were still in their separate packages."

There was a knock at the door, and Sullivan rose to answer it.

Emily stood there, her face a combination of anguish and relief, her eyes red. She rushed past Sullivan.

"Joe!" Emily exclaimed, wrapping her arms around me tightly. "Oh, thank goodness you're safe! I was so worried!"

"I'm alright, Em," I whispered, my voice hoarse. "It was close, but I saved Ashley."

"Since you have someone here to watch over you, Mr. Riley," Sullivan said. "I'll take my leave. But I may have more questions for you tomorrow."

"Thank you, Detective," I said.

He nodded at me and Emily, then headed out.

Emily looked at me, her eyes filled with concern. "Are you sure you're okay?" she asked, her voice tinged with worry. "You look exhausted."

She led me to the couch in the center of the cabin and urged me to sit down. She disappeared into the small kitchen area, returning with a steaming mug of tea.

I took it with trembling hands.

"Not as stable as you think?" Emily said.

I sipped the hot tea and felt its warmth spread through my body, easing my fatigue and tension. Emily sat beside me, and her fingers interlocked with mine, offering support.

"It's getting late," I said. "Don't you have to work tomorrow?"

"I've already called in sick. I'm not leaving you alone tonight."

I raised an eyebrow. "Not at all?"

She grinned. "Not at all."

She kissed me. I put the tea down and kissed her as well, and as we continued to kiss, hands roamed, touching and holding, caressing and moving. I noticed the room was not cold as we removed clothing. Finally, Emily took my hand and led me to the bedroom.

We made love, slowly, discovering each other as we went. It wasn't the frantic copulation as when Rebecca possessed us, or the needy coupling of the previous night.

It was gentle, loving, and satisfying for both of us.

During the night, there was no typing, no frigid air, and no sound except our quiet breathing.

In the morning, I pulled *Loving Lilliana* from its hiding place and Emily and I sat over coffee and toast, reading silently. I read the second half of Rebecca's manuscript and handed Emily the first half of the book.

She was wearing an old sweatshirt of mine. Is there anything sexier than a woman wearing your sweatshirt and nothing else? Not to me.

I was getting to the last scene, and it was as Ashley explained it. The protagonist, Adalynn, admits she must return to her husband and daughter, and Lilliana received the loss with tears and acceptance.

    Adalynn's lips brushed gently against Lilliana's forehead, a soft farewell woven with the ache of parting. She lingered in that fragile moment, tasting the bittersweet sorrow of what was and what could never be again.

    "My dearest Lilliana," she whispered, voice trembling like a fragile ribbon of hope, "I

will hold our memories close, cradled in the
depths of my heart. But now, I must summon the
courage to face the life I fled."

As Adalynn turned away, the stars
reflected in the rain-streaked windows,
marking the end of a time that flourished in
the shadows but could never escape the harsh
light of reality.

It was a fine ending to the tale, and it made sense for the story. I also knew it could not have happened in reality. Rebecca merely dismissed Ashley like a tool no longer needed once the work was done.

In a sense, it was Rebecca's cruelty that led to her own demise. Seducing Ashley simply to gain the experience of being able to write about her seemed callous. But I knew from my experience that Rebecca's sexuality was more about taking than giving.

I put down the pages and looked over at Emily. Her eyes were red, and I saw she was crying.

"What is it?" I asked.

"It's just so beautiful," she said, and wiped at her eyes. "The way she writes, the story, everything. I can't wait to tell Ellie. Do you think it will sell?"

I smiled. "Yes, and very well. I'm going to give it to someone who might be my new agent. I have to meet with her anyway."

She looked at the pages in her hands. "So, you'll need this?"

"I've scanned the pages into the computer. I think Rebecca would want Elora to have the physical copy."

"I'll phone her and let her know." She smiled and gazed around the cabin. "Do you think Rebecca is gone?"

I contemplated the surrounding room. "She rescued me and Ashley down at the dock. I didn't have the strength to pull us up the ladder, so she did. Now that we know the truth, she told me she was free and disappeared. She actually spoke to me, unlike the other times, when she only talked to us like we weren't there."

Emily nodded, very serious. "I have an answer for that. I did some research about ghosts in my occult books. It said that spirits get caught in the past. That's why she needed to communicate through conversations that had previously taken place."

"That makes sense," I said.

"Will you be able to finish your book without your collaborator?"

"Rebecca helped me get past my writer's block. I'll dedicate *Lost Soul* to her. I can finish the book on my own. I have only to write the ending. She got me to the climax."

Her grin became naughty. "From my one experience, Rebecca was good with climaxes."

Deciding that saying nothing was my best choice, I held up my hand. "Did you notice? The cabin isn't cold today."

"I was aware of that."

"I may have to invest in an air conditioner. Now, the cabin will get too hot during the summer."

She put the papers down and walked over to sit on my lap. "Then we'll just have to not wear anything at all."

She kissed me, and our kisses became more heated. Finally, she stood and pulled the sweatshirt off over her head. She took off her glasses, walked over to the desk and sat on the banker's chair, naked.

At that moment, I was stunned by how much she resembled Rebecca. Seeing her in the same place I'd seen Rebecca so many times was startling.

"Can you even see me?" I said, finding my throat was tight.

"You're a man-shaped blob."

"I have to say, seeing you there is extremely arousing."

In answer, her smile grew wider, looking incredibly voluptuous with her eyes half-closed, as if to conjure pleasures I could never know.

"Do I?"

All but overcome, I stood and walked to her, got on one knee and planted my lips on hers. She responded with a soft moan, then pulled back. "You're sure she's not watching us?"

"No, she's gone. But she told me we'd be good for each other."

"She might be right," Emily said and stood. "On second thought, it is chilly in here. Let's go into the bedroom and you can warm me up."

The next few months were a wild ride.

I finished Lost Soul and submitted it on time, ready for the publisher to review. I met with Meredith Thompson, who signed me and when I brought her the manuscript for Loving Lilliana, she claimed it would start a bidding war among the publishing houses.

Robert was true to his word about getting a prominent lawyer. The first thing he did was get a plea deal for Liam. He resolved the charges of filing a false police report and failure to dispose of a body properly. He served probation with the contingency that he find steady employment.

He was still trying to negotiate a deal for Ashley when I met Elora Hawthorne, Rebecca's daughter.

I had convinced Emily to move up to the cabin with me, no mean feat, as she liked her independence. But with her staying up at the cabin almost every night, or me staying at her place, she finally gave in, because it made sense.

Emily convinced her old friend to come up and stay for a few days, and Elora brought her husband and two children, a boy aged five and a girl, three.

When they arrived, Emily pulled her old friend into a hug, and there was laughter and a few tears. Watching them together, I could see why Rebecca had called them "the twins."

They looked enough alike, except for Emily's glasses. I also noted that Elora had her mother's eyes, bright green with a circle of brown around them.

Hazel.

"I'm sorry my father couldn't come," Elora said, and I noticed how her voice sounded in my ears the same way Rebecca's appeared in my head.

I had bought a box for the manuscript and we presented it to her, with Meredith Thompson's card in it. She took the manuscript, then walked over to the typewriter that was still out on my desk.

"It is hers!" Elora gushed, and looked at me. "Could I have it?"

"Of course, it's yours," I said. Though I had to admit, a part of me didn't want to let it go. It was like an old friend.

Elora and her husband slept in the spare room and pushed the single beds together like my parents used to do. The young daughter slept in the bed with them, but the boy insisted on sleeping on the floor of the main room in a sleeping bag, and I had to admit, it reminded me of my childhood.

They stayed the weekend, and Emily and I showed our guests the property and the places Rebecca had visited. We even showed her the place I found her mother's body, which I had long since filled back with dirt.

I had purchased a flat, black granite stone that was planted on top. It read:

In Memory of

Rebecca Hawthorne

Author, Mother, Wife

Fill your paper with the breathings of your heart.

Twenty-Seven

Two Years Later

I stood in the expansive foyer of Lehigh Valley Hospital in East Stroudsburg, the sterile scent of antiseptic mingling with the faint hum of distant voices and the soft clatter of nurse's shoes on the polished floor.

I glanced at my watch again — Liam was running a little late. Given the notoriously unpredictable traffic coming from New Jersey it was hardly surprising. My nerves tingled with anticipation as I watched the ebb and flow of visitors and medical staff.

At last, his slim frame came walking in the entrance. There was a determined purpose to his stride, moderate but brisk enough to show he was eager to get here.

Over the months, I had noticed with quiet relief how much healthier he looked—his face no longer drawn and gaunt, but fuller, the pallor gone. Ever since he'd quit smoking two years ago, the change had been remarkable. The habits he'd shed were nurturing a better version of himself, and it showed.

As he closed the distance, Liam opened his arms for a hug. "I came straight here as soon as I got off work," he whispered, breathless yet sincere.

"How's everything at Brew Haven?" I asked, grateful for the steady normalcy the cafe provided him.

"Most excellent," he grinned broadly. "Kate made me part-time manager. It's a relief for her, especially since she makes that weekly trek up to Frackville to visit Ashley."

My heart clenched when I heard Ashley's name. "How's Ash holding up?" I asked, my voice low with concern. My cousin's recent conviction weighed heavily on me.

"As well as can be expected," Liam said with a sigh. "Frackville State Prison is miles away, but Kate is steadfast. She goes every week without fail to see her."

I exhaled deeply, trying to steady the ache in my chest. "It's only three more years," I reminded us both, attempting optimism.

"Yeah, but remember, that was because you refused to let them press charges for the propane tank incident," Liam said, nodding with a wry smile.

I thought back to the tense days before the trial. The lawyer — who had successfully negotiated probation for Liam—had worked his magic again for Ashley. Her spotless record and a favorable plea deal had earned her four years in a women's facility for second-degree involuntary manslaughter, a bittersweet outcome considering the gravity of Rebecca's death.

I was grateful Kate stood by her, running the coffee shop with quiet determination, even taking Liam on so he could help. His deep desire to support Ashley fueled Liam's dedication to the coffee bar. And it helped him, giving him a place to go every day and a purpose.

"So, come on," Liam prompted, his face lighting up with excitement. "I didn't drive all this way just to see you."

"Okay," I smiled, "but we need to suit up first. It's the rules."

I pulled out the surgical gown I'd brought with me — identical to the one I wore — and handed it to Liam. He slipped it on without hesitation, the fabric slightly billowing around his slender frame.

"How's your book doing?" he asked.

"*Lost Soul* has earned enough to cover my advance — and I'm going to be getting more royalties," I replied, excitement creeping into my voice. "And the new character, Miranda, will be Soul Mason's partner in the next installment."

"That's fantastic!" Liam beamed. "I saw that *Loving Lilliana* is still on the best-seller lists."

I nodded, pleased. "Yes, and there's even talk of a movie deal."

Passing him a mask, I watched as he pulled it over his face. "Who would've thought a twenty-year-old manuscript could resonate so strongly?"

"Because it was quality writing," I said firmly, pulling my mask up. "Rebecca was truly gifted."

Together, we stepped into the private patient room. Emily lay there, fatigue etched into her delicate features but with a tender smile lighting her face. Cradled in her arms was the tiny bundle of warmth—the newborn wrapped tightly in a soft swaddling cloth.

"I just fed her, so she may be asleep," Emily said softly.

"How did the feeding go?" I asked gently.

Emily raised her eyebrows in honest appraisal. "Good enough, I think. She latched on okay, though it hurt a bit. I'll have to get used to that."

"You don't really have a choice for the next few months," Liam teased with an affectionate grin.

I reached out to take the baby, whose eyelids fluttered as she rested peacefully in my arms. Her soft, serene face was perfect in its innocence.

"Have you chosen a name yet?" Liam asked.

"Lilliana," Emily and I said almost simultaneously.

Liam's grin widened mischievously. "Are you sure that's the best choice?"

"It's beautiful," Emily said, her eyes glistening with pride. "For a beautiful little girl."

The baby yawned delicately and opened her eyes. Unlike most newborns whose eyes appeared a cloudy blue or grey, hers were startling — a vivid green ringed with a touch of brown around the iris.

Hazel.

I gently passed the baby back to Liam, who cradled her securely, smiling in awe and wonder.

"You'd better keep an eye on her," Liam said. "She'll probably be a handful."

The End

Also By Arjay Lewis

Doctor Wise Series
Fire In The Mind
Seduction In The Mind
Reunion In The Mind
Haunted In The Mind
Devotion In The Mind
Asylum In The Mind
Specter In The Mind
Vengeance In The Mind
Echoes In The Mind
Infection In The Mind
Justice In The Mind
Ritual In The Mind
Vanished In The Mind

Horror
The Muse
Kept In The Dark
The Vanishing
Digger
Ghost Writer

Romantic Suspense
(with Debra Snow)
A Study In Murder

NYPD Wizard Detective
The Wizards Of Central Park West
The Vampires Of Greenwich Village
The Werewolves Of Washington Square

Author's Note

Hail to you, follower of the Odd!

Many have inquired about the origins of my ideas, and this time, I can share a bit of the journey behind *Ghost Writer*. As with many tales, a convergence of inspirations led me to the creation of this book.

I had recently revisited a novella by my writing mentor, Parke Godwin, titled *The Fire When It Comes*. A female spirit narrates this remarkable ghost story, sharing an intriguing encounter with the male protagonist.

In addition, a fellow author requested my feedback on her book about ghostwriting, which I was more than happy to provide.

Around the same time, I revisited Stephen King's haunting masterpiece, *Bag of Bones,* a chilling tale that remains one of my all-time favorites. If you haven't read it, I highly recommend doing so.

With these influences swirling in my mind, the concept of a ghostwriter who was an actual ghost, took root.

I owe immense gratitude to my fantastic editor, Libby Broadbent, who meticulously reviewed my early drafts and illuminated my plot holes and errors with her keen eye. I also want to acknowledge Kathleen Shamp, a beta reader and valuable collaborator from my previous works, for her exceptional copyediting on this book.

And of course, I cannot forget my wonderful wife, Debra, who tirelessly hunts for mistakes and plot inconsistencies, providing invaluable support every day.

Each of these individuals has played a crucial role in bringing this book to life, and I hope you enjoy reading it as much as I enjoyed writing it.

About The Author

Known as the "Wizard Of Odd." Arjay Lewis is an actor, magician, and multi-award-winning author.

I write tales of the strange and the horrifying.

I have spent my life as an entertainer, amusing people as a street-performer in the 1970s; a Broadway and casino artist in the 1980s; a party performer in the 1990s and 2000s; a cruise ship performer in the 2010s.

Stories have always been in my mind, and I have been writing since the 1990s. My reason to write is simple: to entertain. I write the type of books that I like to read: murder mysteries, strange tales of unnatural gifts, odd happenings and horror.

Please visit my web site and sign up for my mailing list to be "in the know" for upcoming books. Visit me on Facebook, Twitter, or my Amazon Author page.

And thank you for reading. You are the reason I write.

www.arjaylewis.com

www.facebook.com/arjaylewis

www.twitter.com/arjaylewiswrite

www.amazon.com/Arjay-Lewis

FREE NOVELLA

VOWS

AND OTHER TALES OF THE MACABRE

For those who enjoy a good scare, here is a collection of stories designed to give you nightmares. These stories that have been published in *Weird Tales, H.P. Lovecraft Magazine Of Horror, The Ultimate Halloween,* and *Sherlock Holmes Mystery Magazine.* If you tried to get them from their original source they would cost over $20.00. But you get them for FREE by signing up for Arjay's Newsletter

VOWS: A story of devotion that extends beyond death itself.

SIREN: A Sci-Fi fantasy of a condemned prisoner lost in space.

THE DARK: A guard sees creatures in the night...are they really there?

DREAMCATCHER: A walk in the woods...but you are not alone.

THE TRAVELER: What do you do if your flight is delayed...forever?

INTO THE ABYSS: A makeup artist gets the dream job...at a price.

www.arjaylewis.com/free-stuff.html

www.ingramcontent.com/pod-product-compliance
Lightning Source LLC
Chambersburg PA
CBHW032341310726
48973CB00007B/1805